TOKYO MAYDAY

By

Maison Urwin

The power is in the East.

The Federal Republic of England & Wales is in crisis.

Western economic collapse has led to mass economic migration to China, Korea and especially Japan. Jordan May is offered a transfer with his Japanese employer and takes wife, Shaylie, and son, Alfie, to a new and bewildering life in the Orient.

They soon become embroiled in industrial politics, illegal unionisation and hostessing. Teenage love and the organisation of a mass demonstration take place against a backdrop of racial tension and the rise of the far right.

Could Shaylie's life be in danger? Is the mafia involved?

And to what extent are the Mays' new lives being manipulated by the mysterious, wiry Englishman who sits on Matsucorp's board?

To Stephanie, Jack & Mia,
with love

'By drowning their speaking
With shrieking and squeaking
In fifty different sharps and flats.'

The Pied Piper of Hamelin, Robert Browning

PART ONE
No Truffles on Bathside

Chapter One

"Mind out!"

Evie grabbed Alfie's forearm, rescuing him from a fall. The pavements were cracked and uneven, overgrown with weeds, long since abandoned as a priority. There had been far greater crises than highways and byways.

As Alfie steadied himself, Evie took his hand. They stepped over the crumbling kerb with care, picked their way around potholes where tarmac used to be and mounted the walkway on the other side. In his preoccupation, Alfie forgot to free himself from Evie's grasp. Content and concerned in equal measure, Evie wondered what was different about today.

A Thursday in early March, Alfie was taking the long walk home.

Children walked. It had become the norm across the Western post-tech wastelands. There was no more school run. That was a distant memory. A few cycled or scooted on battered metal frames, showing decades of neglect, but most walked.

Trickling out of the underused school, optimistic children, whose like-minded parents vainly aspired to some future employment opportunity, emerged onto a deserted Hall Lane. The few parents who managed to maintain a car worked long hours, five or six days a week for a derisory hourly rate, in order to afford that luxury. An occasional weekend trip made this luxury worthwhile, but only when fuel was available. Some made local trips by horse and cart, many never left the town, exhausted after long days working in the fields.

Today was like most days, no after-school activity, straight out at 3pm. Evie would often stay for the exam prep classes, Alfie not so often. Today he had the added pleasure of her company for some of his walk home. The spring day was warm and humid, the sky blue over the North Sea, but the descending sun was obscured behind them by rain clouds collecting over the estuary. The wind began to howl. Peninsular life was unpredictable.

"You OK?"

"Yeah."

"How's your day been?"

"OK."

"Got much homework?"

"A bit."

"So are we going to meet up later?"

He glanced sideways. There was a hint of a smile.

"Course."

The revived art of conversation did not come easily to Alfie. It had been the coping mechanism of his parents' generation when they lost the internet. Created for military intelligence, public use of the web had barely spanned two generations. Governments had fought terror by shutting down networks and now smart phones were carried by an elite, the licensing system making them rarer, in some countries, than guns.

Turning left, they strolled past the boating lake, greeting the swans who hoped to be fed. Today, just three of them dared venture out of the derelict sports centre, their shelter from human predators. No one gave a second glance to this 15-year-old couple as they meandered their way through the well-appointed but forgotten town of Harwich & Dovercourt Bay. Both dressed in T-shirt, jeans, trainers and the school hoody, they had walked this walk so many times together since they had become an item. Tall and slim, with his father's dark hair and aquiline features, Alfie was reserved and serious. His winning smile was cherished by those who loved him because of its rarity. He was popular at school, not because he was a jack-the-lad, but because he was a sporting talent. With the strength, physique and coordination to succeed at all sport, he was hoping to progress on to one of Colchester United's coveted football stipends once he graduated from middle school at the end of this year. He knew only too well how poor the prospects of employment were through the academic route for a boy of moderate ability and he was one of the few who had a chance of succeeding through a vocational sporting scholarship at a feeder club. Football could provide an alternative to working in the fields, but only the very best would find wealth via a transfer into the London bubble before being sold on to the Far East leagues.

Despite his popularity, Alfie did not have a wide circle of friends. He had inherited his father's social reticence and found idle small talk particularly awkward. He had a temperament like that of his mother, always compliant, and had inherited her ability at school, too, being a touch above average.

Friends had pushed Alfie and Evie together some months before as an obvious match and neither of them had resisted what the year 10 cupids had seen as inevitable. Alfie's parents found Evie adorable. Pretty and gregarious, confidence oozing from her petite and well-proportioned frame, Evie was academically able but modest and encouraging of others. The teacher's dream student. She was aware of the high unemployment figures for secondary school and university graduates but she was determined to achieve the best she could. She also knew that extending her education for another six years or more might allow more time for the economy and the job market to show some improvement. Neither she nor Alfie saw any need to become part of the crisis caused by migration to East Asia.

The drop in numbers at Harwich & Dovercourt Middle School, due to the exodus of recent years to escape the prospect of perpetual unemployment, meant that the issue of students that afternoon soon thinned into small pockets of children, returning to their homes spread across the isolated coastal town.

Below, to their right, the toxic sea lapped close to the tops of the cliffs. For two decades, pathways leading down to an ex-blue flag beach had been submerged. A mass of plastic was raised and lowered twice daily by chemical tides, the concentration of which no one was really sure. To their left, they passed the eerie vestiges of past seaside prosperity. The boarded-up cafés, the derelict amusement arcade and the disused outdoor roller-skating rink were now home to vagabonds. At this time of day, their chattering could be heard from their nests within the dilapidated buildings, whilst outside, here and there, a mischief of youths sat sorting through the fruits of their scavenging. Scavenging, petty crime and squatting were default. The removal of welfare support meant that homelessness could only ever be permanent.

They dragged one another up the hill, onto the cliff road above the submerged beaches, past the crumbling facades of the former hotels, the Continental and the Cliff, converted to flats which no one could afford. They turned left onto the Kingsway.

On the corner of Kingsway and Main Road, right in the centre of town, they passed the front of Pawn Stars, the pawnbroker's where Alfie's mother, Shaylie, worked a six-day week. They turned the corner and found themselves at the doorway of the climb to Evie's parents' rented flat, above Shaylie's place of work. It was getting dark. Alfie manoeuvred Evie into the ill-lit stairwell and placed a distracted kiss on her lips as he left her to ascend alone.

"Bandstand at seven?" she asked, as a precipitous mist rose over Dovercourt station from the estuary and descended on the gloomy town centre.

"Bandstand at seven."

The rain began to fall. Leaving the road which snaked through to the end of the peninsula, Alfie settled on the most direct route home. At the end of the Kingsway, he jumped from the platform of Dovercourt station and hurried along the abandoned rail tracks to Harwich Town, the next station stop. The Mayflower Line had continued to function for a while, a symbol of widespread renationalisation in the face of nationwide withdrawal of private investment, but national bankruptcy had put an end to that. Now the highest of tides would reach the tracks, but today it was just sodden, not flooded. Everyone knew the tide times, they had to, and Alfie knew that high tide had passed. Today the permanent way posed no greater risk than the crumbling roads and pavements as Alfie, careful and agile, picked his way along the sleepers.

To either side, artificial trees were intermingled with real ones, the latter dead and leafless, their leaves replaced by the tough, silken tents of the brown-moth caterpillar. The brown, hairy larvae resumed feeding earlier every year as the climate warmed. A careless larva would fall, its hair breaking off as barbs on contact with human skin. To avoid skin irritation, headaches and breathing difficulties, Alfie knew to minimise skin exposure.

The rain did little to ease the closeness of the air, so Alfie lifted his hoody over his head, leaving the sleeves over his arms. An awkward manoeuvre wiped his brow but there was little point in peeling his T-shirt from the small of his back.

It was a short walk through the old port from the Victorian buildings of Harwich Town station. He passed the half-finished replica of the Mayflower, the attempt to recreate the boat of the Pilgrim Fathers long since abandoned, and began to zigzag his way through the deserted streets. The dereliction removed little of the character of the narrow streets and alleyways, puddled at this time of the year as the spring tides brought the tidal bulge into the streets. Alfie often imagined smugglers mingling with women of ill repute in the smog-obscured cobbled lanes. He was oblivious to the boarded up windows on beautiful old buildings which had once housed thriving businesses, pubs, cafés, art galleries, restaurants and a healthy pre-crash tourist trade.

As he regained the terraced three-storey townhouse which he shared with his parents in Castlegate Street, the clock above the open fireplace hit 3:40pm. He had ninety minutes to spend alone, working on his exam subjects which would secure graduation but which were unlikely to serve any long-term purpose in a non-existent job market.

Chapter Two

"We had an agreement."

There was purpose in Yamada's statement which directed the focus and tension of the board meeting towards the head of the long, oak table.

Matsubara bridled. The direction of Japan's leading motor giant hung in the balance. The political and financial backers around the table had propelled Matsucorp to the forefront of the world's car and motorbike manufacturers over the past two decades, championing the global superiority of Japanese engineering and workmanship. Favourable running costs had led to the establishment of a number of assembly lines across the globe but there was a feeling that this measure had run its course. Western economies had collapsed.

Every morning, Shinji Matsubara was only too aware of his good fortune. He had created Matsucorp from the ashes of two of the previous giants of the Japanese automobile industry. He had had the courage to acquire facilities for knock-down prices and had been propelled to success by the Oriental boom.

That morning had been no different. Whilst the other executives were being driven between their daily engagements ahead of that evening's crucial board meeting, Matsubara had been on the overground suburban railway which took him from Hōya station into Ikebukuro, the hub of north-west Tokyo where he had built his company headquarters. He would never be chauffeur-driven. It was important for him to use public transport. Not only was it ecologically sound, like his hydrogen-fuelled cars, it also created a certain impression. People could see that he did not regard himself as superior, as above the common man who had worked hard to make Matsucorp a success. Matsubara was an astute and composed businessman. With an absolute belief in social equality, he valued his workers and the humane treatment of fellow humans.

And so he had looked around his train carriage and marvelled. He had marvelled at the magnificent Japanese feat of engineering which this train represented, providing a comfortable journey through vacuum tubes using magnetic levitation. He had marvelled at the affluence of his well-dressed compatriots, travelling to myriad jobs, some skilled and some unskilled, all sufficiently remunerated at a time of zero unemployment. He had marvelled, in the silence of the pristine carriage, at how lucky they all were to be living in this golden era.

Then, he had looked up to one of the TV screens distributed around the carriage to watch the rolling news. Older travelling companions did likewise, but the young had their own self-contained viewing experience. Many had headsets which resembled glasses, the sound conducted through the cheekbone. Matsubara found it harder to get used to those viewing through contact lenses. They were present but absent, staring zombie-like into nothing. Many revelled in the gloom from abroad, from outside of East Asia, but Matsubara could not appreciate the misfortune of others. There had been more trouble overnight in some of the holding camps at the ports around the Japanese coastline. European and African migrants, contained by barbed wire fences in insanitary conditions, had been fighting again, both amongst themselves and with the border police. Further afield, there was unrest in airports and seaports of former western powerhouses where desperate men, women and children battled for carriage without visa to Japan, China and India, for the privilege of being placed indefinitely in a tent, for the slightest chance that they may be offered a menial way into a burgeoning economy. Staring at the screen, Matsubara could barely imagine the grinding poverty and lack of hope which would make people tolerate the filth and malnutrition of a holding camp.

By the time the train landed in Ikebukuro station, he had watched a newsfeed of yet more stories of chaos outside of the Far East bubble, an atrocity here, a bombing there. Some of his compatriots found these events laughable, former world-leading countries leaving well-established, secular, Oriental nation states in the driving seat, but Matsubara was an *amateur* of history. What was the difference between one megalomaniac giving an explosive vest to a misguided young patriot and another giving a disposable fighter plane to a misguided young pilot? Matsubara had the two-minute walk to Matsucorp-Honsha to shed his melancholy and focus his mind on the job.

Now, at the end of another long day, the board of directors of Japan's leading industrial powerhouse was in conference. The all-male body of thirteen was still, after all these years, entirely representative of Eastern work culture. The men, twelve of them executive, generated a fusty atmosphere to combine with the custom-built sterility of the capacious boardroom on the thirteenth floor of Matsucorp-Honsha in Ikebukuro, Tokyo. It was the end of a long day for all and they had brought with them the sweat of sales pitches, pep talks and political battles to maintain their influence in a giant of the world economy. The damp smell of poorly aired clothes and the odour of deodorant-masked perspiration infused with the fresh, woody smell of expensive furniture. The air-conditioning laboured. All but one board member sat at the table's edge, leaning forward, illuminated by the three lights suspended directly over the table. It created a concentration for the group, the atmosphere redolent of a card school or a snooker hall. The thirteenth member sat back from the table, present but detached, non-executive and white-skinned, fiddling nonchalantly with an antique Zippo lighter which bore the logo of the long-since-defunct Mercedes-Benz automobile manufacturer.

Yamada continued.

"All those years ago, we agreed that foreign plants were a temporary measure. They enabled this corporation to corner the market. We did what we had to do when our competitors did not have the courage. But the intention was always to move into pole position and then withdraw all support for

Western economies. It is time to assert ourselves as one hundred percent Japanese. We have assembly lines throughout our country, using Japanese design, engineering and labour. We are selling high quality models in the booming economies of the East. It is our patriotic duty to keep all profit within Japan, to preserve our rightful place as GDP world leader and our reputation at the summit of the industrial world."

Halfway along the table to Matsubara's left, Kentarō Yamada had dark, taut skin and thick, black hair which betrayed his origins. He had short limbs, short, even for a diminutive man, with elfin hands and fingers. He was a small, compact individual who surprised his colleagues with the resonance of his fist as it crashed into the table.

"Japanese labour, Japanese profit, superiority for Japanese industry!"

Every man around the table had made his fortune by the success of Matsucorp's shares, but there was a greater interest for Yamada in his political rise. The Japan Social Democrats could expect to dominate for some years to come, following their success in foreseeing the collapse of liberal capitalism and the global free market. They had provided an alternative, a self-sufficient country which put its people first and ensured a good standard of living for all. They had risen on a democratic platform, the Japanese electorate had chosen them but, as the West had discovered, democracy was not a cure-all. Perhaps its usefulness had run its course. Matsubara knew better than anyone that, if Yamada could retain his influence and the support of the board of Matsucorp, he would be propelled into a significant role in the Ministry of Industry, where he would help to cement Japan's world domination for decades to come. National success would, in turn, enable the JSD to retain power for a very long time.

Respect for Matsubara could be faintly heard, detectable through the intakes of breath and *sotto voce* mumbling which followed Yamada's outburst. Old enough to be Yamada's father, Matsubara was short, stocky and grey. He had shrunk with age and his well-worn suits were half a size too big. His welcoming face, his measured, reasonable voice and the regularity of his smile belied his ruthlessness. A chain-smoker from the time of his youth in Tokyo, he had travelled west to complete two degrees in nuclear physics at the University of Osaka, before returning to the city of his birth to create his company from a motor industry which, despite its superior craftsmanship and technology, had become fragmented. Matsucorp quickly overtook its competitors through the success of a new model, the intellectual property of Shinji Matsubara. A communist voter in his youth, he had adapted his ideology to cultivate the success of a private business, later a public company, whilst considering the welfare of his employees. He wanted business success and national superiority as much as anyone, as much as Yamada, but he was troubled by a moral dilemma to which the likes of Yamada and the majority of the board were immune. Assembly line workers in distant corners of the globe were pawns, providing cheap labour to maximise Matsucorp's profits and influence. But to Matsubara they were still humans, after a fashion, and they were a small part of his empire. It was not their fault that they did not have Japanese blood. Did they not deserve his care? He was a shrewd businessman, he understood the necessity of compromise and of sacrifice. He also knew the value of a strong board, good advice, a variety of opinion and collaborative leadership.

"I am aware," he said slowly, at the end of an interminable silence, "that sacrifices need to be made and the price needs to be paid by the economies of less capable countries in order to further Japanese industry."

The next pause was weighty, as was the effect of his unfaltering eye contact with Yamada, held whilst he continued to address the board as a whole.

"I will never allow us to make poor business decisions. We will never make a decision which endangers our profit margin, nor the political influence of anyone around this table."

Yamada's gaze fell to the table, to the ever tighter intertwining of his fingers.

"However, I will always seek compromise which allows a human solution where possible. I appreciate your input,

18

Yamada-*san*, as I appreciate your passion. We all know that a reduction in our operations on foreign territory is part of our plan, but I do wish to know whether the great minds on this board have any idea how we can keep the welfare of our *gaijin* workers in mind, perhaps those who have performed particularly well for us."

Matsubara's use of the faintly derogatory '*gaijin*' – outsider – underlined to Yamada that he had not abandoned the concept of Japanese superiority at the centre of their business ideology. That would never do. But the migrant crisis currently being experienced by his great country was worthy of consideration. Matsubara did not feel that ignoring the hordes of Europeans, queuing up for a piece of the action, would be the honourable course of action.

This time the silence was broken from the shadows. Twelve Japanese heads turned in unison to the right of Matsubara and squinted at the tall, imposing figure leaning back on his chair which was placed, as always, a good metre back from the table. His angular features betrayed nothing as he finally held his lighter still and addressed the board in accented, semi-grammatical Japanese.

"We cannot look after everyone, but there is a better way to garner favourable PR."

The room mumbled interest, with slight embarrassment in the realisation that nobody else had thought to consider the PR impact of such major decisions.

"What did you have in mind, Stepson-*san*?" Matsubara shared the room's intrigue.

The figure on the edge of the meeting smiled, his pause deliberate, making no attempt to hide his enjoyment of the audience he now received.

"Shut down overseas operations as planned, make the inevitable redundancies, but offer jobs here to the very best skilled workers. Show that we are prepared to display compassion to our non-Japanese people, should they truly merit it."

Stepson Struthwin held the attention of the whole room. It was mostly reluctant, disapproving attention. He was the favoured *gaijin*. Accepted and favoured by Matsubara, the reason known only by the two men. They waited for more but, as always, he had been brief. As far as he was concerned, the Japs, his countrymen by assimilation, would sort out the detail and vote it though. The only non-executive member of the board was content to see an opportunity for mischief and then to sow the seed. On many previous occasions he had done just that, then sat back to watch it germinate. He was the outsider on the inside.

Chapter Three

On that Thursday in March, Jordan's world was to be turned on its head. For him, the fears of many working people were to be realised. At 2:57pm he was called to a general meeting for the 18 assembly line workers at Matsucorp's Bathside Bay factory.

Jordan May was now 44 years old. His parents came south to look for work when he was 11 and he had long since lost his Teeside accent. He never completely recovered from the move and felt an outsider throughout middle school. He graduated successfully at the age of 15, his son's current age, and then chose technical high school rather than the academic baccalaureate route. He was fortunate to fall into an engineering apprenticeship at the firm's futuristic factory, built on reclaimed land, following their multi-million pound acquisition of this wide but shallow wasteland at the edge of Harwich.

For many years, society in the Federal Republic of England and Wales, the FREW, had been falling apart. Rising unemployment had led to increased crime, house repossessions and homelessness. Industry had increasingly moved to other countries, to Asia in particular, and the need for skilled labour had plummeted. The influx of migrant workers had ceased. The NHS, in recovery from privatisation, lacked doctors as skilled health professionals could find better pay and working conditions elsewhere. Unskilled, undesirable jobs were now filled by indigenous workers to avoid defaulting on mortgage payments. An educated elite had gravitated to the London bubble, a walled, semi-independent enclave of prosperity. The excluded majority had found it more difficult to come to terms with the fact that life in the FREW no longer equated with that of the developed world.

Reflecting public opinion, the Mays had become increasingly angry with the widespread Asian abandonment of industry bases in the FREW, and this continued to be fuelled by the indignation of the FREW popular press which regularly pointed out all that Great Britain had done for the world. However, Jordan May had retained his *sang froid* and had been considering how his family was to survive the crippling of the FREW economy and its people. He had been dreading a summons such as this. He could not imagine a general meeting in the current economic climate providing positive news.

Jordan moved his spectacles from his Roman nose to the top of his dark, thinning head of hair as he entered the meeting room with Alex, best friend then colleague since the age of 11. Jordan was a tall, handsome man, his slim face only recently beginning to show the signs of life's stress and the lines of worry. He stood beside and above blond, chubby Alex as they stood at the back of the assembled group of skilled workers, dressed to a man in bright orange boiler suits, emblazoned on the back with the red company logo, complete with rising sun.

The workers, nine men and nine women, all lived locally. A workforce of eighteen well-qualified engineers could never have been sourced in Harwich alone, so Matsucorp had invested in relocation to maintain its worldwide model of a local community of workers, inspiring teamwork, loyalty and success. Who would not have jumped at the chance to avoid becoming a statistic of the speculative migratory exodus to East Asia? Every day, they rattled around in an enormous state-of-the-art factory, the robotic technology requiring minimal skilled human input to control the huge assembly line machinery. The clean, metallic smell of the factory floor was replaced in the meeting room by that of cheap, freeze-dried instant coffee. Air-conditioned mustiness was in every room. The provision of refreshments in a staff meeting was a further indication to Jordan and his colleagues of a blow which Matsucorp felt the need to soften.

The atmosphere was tense and the coffee remained largely untouched. An announcement was imminent and whoever had called the meeting three minutes ago had ensured that there was little time for speculation. They were faced by a life-sized hologram of Rob Garnett, manager of the three FREW factories. Squat and besuited, he hovered just above ground level, his unerring stare waiting for the clock to strike 3pm.

"What's this all about?"

"I doubt it's good news," replied Jordan to his friend, "but whatever it is, he couldn't be bothered to come to speak to us in person."

As if to respond directly to Jordan, Garnett began his address as the clock hit the hour.

"In case you were wondering, I am speaking to employees at all three FREW factories simultaneously, as requested by Mr Matsubara himself." Self-importance was, in Jordan's experience, always in evidence when Garnett addressed staff, whether one-to-one or *en masse*.

"I shall be brief. There is no point in prolonging what, I have to warn you, is bad news for you and for me. Mr Matsubara informs me that Matsucorp is being forced, by global economic pressures, to downscale its production of cars across Europe. This imminent downscaling is to include the closure of all three FREW factories one month from today. You are to take this announcement as one month's notice of the termination of your employment, which you will also receive in writing by intranet later today. You will each receive a redundancy payment of £10 000, to be paid on completion of your final month's work. On Mr Matsubara's behalf, I am instructed to thank you for all you have done to consolidate Matsucorp's place at the top of the world's motor industry."

As the hologram faded, 18 local people, skilled workers, were left abandoned in a meeting room. A meeting room full but at the same time empty. Emptied of morale and of comradeship. The silence was gradually broken by the soft sound of sobbing at the thought of defaulted mortgage payments, the cancellation of holiday-camp weekends, the surrender of the most basic of creature comforts. Grown men and grown women bereft as they began to grieve for the lives they had had. The lives which would be over in thirty-one days. Soon to be former colleagues and co-workers, ex-comrades, they knew what they had to do. The culture of loyalty and discipline would continue for the next thirty-one days. The rules had to be followed, there had to be order, they had to return to their posts. Dismissal would mean no redundancy payment, and deviation from procedure would not be tolerated. Under any circumstances. Not even the most difficult of circumstances.

Alex and Jordan returned to their posts in silence, the prospect of a miserable end to the day stretching far in front of them. 5pm was an age away. Colleagues around them forced themselves to regain their concentration. As Jordan reassumed his position at the control panel of the robotic chassis assembly, a pop-up message appeared on his screen. The message was brief.

>>Jordan May is to be present in the meeting room at 4pm. Come alone. Do not share this confidential communication.<<

At 3:55pm, Jordan logged a comfort break on his electronic timesheet and quietly vacated his post.

Chapter Four

That Thursday in March had seen a steady stream of customers visiting Pawn Stars. Some hoped for a temporary conversion of family treasures into cash, more accepted that they were bidding a permanent farewell to jewellery, ornaments and medals from twentieth century wars. Time had passed quickly for Shaylie. It was over an hour since her return from lunch at home when she saw Alfie accompany Evie past the shop front. She smiled to herself when she thought of how her son had settled into his new guise as a happy teenager, at ease with himself. The warmth of her feeling intensified when she reflected on how Alfie's teenage years were mirroring hers, how awkward she had felt until she had formed her first and only relationship with the man who was now her husband. Her smile soon faded as she considered the lack of prospects for her son's generation, many of whom would spend long days in the fields to cover rent and food.

Like her in-laws, Shaylie's parents had also come south for work. A former generation of ecomigrants. They had left Edinburgh when the UK was still intact. Soon after, it became the capital of an independent Scotland, precipitating the demise of the monarchy and of the union. Shaylie was born in Colchester General Hospital, five years almost to the day after Jordan's birth in Guisborough. She was an only child, quietly and cooperatively moving through the school years without a single year resit, achieving a standard baccalaureate pass, Humanities specialism, without distinction. Meanwhile her father was regretting his migration to the south, his rejection of the now-burgeoning oil industry, a hard taskmaster for the manual worker, even for the skilled engineer, and was trying to make ends meet with a postal round and the help of his wife's cleaning jobs. Shaylie had been getting on well as a legal clerk in Colchester until she had married Jordan at a young age. She had followed him to Harwich and, after some years of trying, fell pregnant. The travel to Colchester was no longer viable and Shaylie had spent her pregnancy making space in her cupboards, selling unwanted household items on an intermittent internet connection. Following a quick recovery from Alfie's birth, she had found herself six days a week as an assistant in a pawnbroker's shop. Now 39 years old, she was happy with her life, had friends and felt part of the community.

"Shaylie!" She was awoken from her reverie.

"Shaylie! Could you help this lady, please?" Misha, the shop manager, Shaylie's boss and friend, was trying to deal with two women who were keen to liquidate precious items. Thursday was Jade's day off but the two women could manage. Just. Misha could not serve two women at once.

"Sorry, Misha, I was in my own wee world," replied Shaylie after an awkward pause, her softened Edinburgh brogue at once charming customers and boss. Shaylie was an elegant woman, admired by all who encountered her. She was tall but not too tall, fair-haired and pale and conventionally pretty. Childhood gymnastics had bequeathed her a straight back and graceful movement which could not be diminished by the functional blue trouser suit which was the Pawn Stars uniform, 100% polyester, sticky in the armpits and the small of the back. Southern eyes were entranced by her Scottish lips as they negotiated beautiful, rounded vowel sounds. Nobody would ever guess the nature of this woman's single shameful secret.

"You'll need more focus tonight, love, if we're to have a chance of winnun." Misha was local, that much was clear to the listener. Misha was dark and plain, as tall as Shaylie but clunky and big-boned, and Misha was proud to be from the place she referred to as Harwich-for-the-Continent. She did this whenever she spoke within Jade's hearing. Jade came from Frinton-on-sea and knew that Harwich-for-the-Continent implied the punchline *Frinton-for-the-incontinent*. But Frinton had a sandier beach and Jade felt the superiority of the whole Frintonian community, or those that lived inside the gates, at least.

"Must be the games night, dears," said the older of the two ladies, as she rested forwards on her Zimmer frame and caught her breath.

"Yes," replied Shaylie, "we go every week. It's just a wee bit of fun, really."

The non-essential service industry had been hit hard by the economic storm. Not a single pub in Harwich had survived. Instead, the Park Pavilion community centre had become the only meeting place. It was busy most evenings with a varied clientele, providing entertainment and events for a beleaguered yet united community. Gone were the days of imported premium lagers, so popular half a century before, but the local people were happy to drink the beers of Harwich Town brewery, which they had transformed in a drunken haze from a one-time two-man craft beer operation into one of Harwich's larger employers. One of its only employers. Games night, with its whist, quizzes, and board games from the previous century, was one event which provided a structure to their lives beyond work. Jordan would sit quietly chatting to the men, whilst Shaylie was the life and soul, relishing the competition. Thursday evenings made Shaylie happy.

Once Shaylie had completed the paperwork for a loan on an elderly engagement ring for the ancient lady and accompanied another sad but satisfied customer to the door, the afternoon quietened down. She and Misha spent the rest of the working day rearranging stock and reliving the previous week's bingo and beetle drive. Thursdays provided plenty of opportunities to chat, the calm before the three busy weekend days to come, the cash service providing short-term relief in this hand-to-mouth time. A time which had seen the demise of many top-end businesses. Pawn Stars' clientele comprised the majority of local people, a populace which sought to maintain its pride in the face of economic adversity by restocking its larders, a superficial statement of the struggle to preserve a certain standard of living. The core market in the early days of the business had been the unskilled working classes, the unemployed and the ecomigrants, Britain's untouchables in the days of prosperity. But the days of the Czechs and the Poles had long since passed, as had the divide amongst the local working class people, the aspiration, pretension and one-upmanship replaced by humility and cohesion. Cohesion amongst those who had managed to remain, to hang on, to resist joining the ongoing evacuation of the republic.

At a minute past five, Shaylie followed Alfie's route along the tracks between Dovercourt and Harwich Town. She would more commonly walk the longer route along the roads to avoid the hideous caterpillar tents, especially in fair weather, but she was keen to jump in the shower and prepare for the quiz. That way, she would create a little more time to potter, drink tea and chat to her family about their day. On any other day, these banal but intimate conversations would have retraced very well worn pathways. On any day other than that Thursday in March.

Chapter Five

When Jordan regained the refuge of the terraced town house in Castlegate Street, an air of calm reigned. An awkward mix of sounds descended the steep stairs from the upper two floors. The soundtrack to Alfie's homework on the first floor was the usual technobeat, whilst early rock'n'roll, a century old, was faint evidence of Shaylie's presence in the shower on the top floor.

Jordan would often be home before Shaylie, the Bathside Bay factory towering a short distance from the old port, a ten-minute walk from his front door. Today, however, he had dragged his feet. The dead trees and their brown, hairy larvae had been afforded a wider berth than usual. He arrived still deep in thought, almost thirty minutes after shutdown. How was he going to tell them? What was he going to tell them? How would they react?

He was about to change their lives forever. In spite of the knowledge that he had only ever worked hard, had always conformed and played by the rules, guilt squeezed his skull. It forced itself through his throbbing brain, suffocating him, restricting his breathing and encumbering his slow passage through the lounge to the kitchen. He was slumped at the round wooden table across which gaiety had reigned every evening for as long as he could remember.

Jordan had been pleased to leave education, to marry Shaylie, to find work and to move on from his miserable teenage years into adulthood. They had had Alfie after years of trying and he had completed the life that they had wanted. Skilled work, mortgage, life-long supporters of Respect Labour, they had relative comfort and a son and heir. Alfie was barely out of nappies when Jordan had lost his mother, that strong woman who had held a strained family together at his father's funeral sixteen years ago. Since those two funerals, there was no longer a need, much less a desire for him to contact Ethan, his estranged brother. In front of his mother, Jordan had feigned a fond farewell, but after his mother's brief wake, Ethan's smug attempt at a fraternal handshake was met with a curt rebuttal from his older brother. Jordan did not expect to see Ethan again.

He had been able to settle into small-town life, with the occasional visit from Shaylie's family. He had lived a contented life with wife and child, almost oblivious to the haemorrhaging of the FREW economy, safe in his employ in a Japanese company. Almost safe. Whilst Shaylie and Alfie had lived each day, each week, each month, each year as content as the previous one, Jordan had always secretly feared this day, this inevitable Thursday in March.

She knew all was not as it should be as she entered the kitchen. They both did. Unsettled and cautious, Shaylie and Alfie greeted Jordan. The contentment, optimism and hope of the May family evaporated through the ceiling, the walls and the cold, beige, ceramic floor tiles. The kitchen was now smaller. There was an overbearing wariness in the atmosphere of the room, now small, chilly and forbidding.

"Tea?" Shaylie attempted to break the pervading dread.

"You'd better sit down. Both of you." Jordan's voice was small, humble, even pitiful. He pulled at his right earlobe with thumb and forefinger. He waited, but the right moment would never come. "They're shutting the factory."

A pained silence was broken by repetition, borne of shock.

"Shutting?" Shaylie spoke first.

"Matsucorp?" Alfie sought clarification.

Jordan explained briefly. "Not Matsucorp itself, just its entire FREW operation. Completely. Everyone redundant."

Shaylie took over the questioning. "How soon?"

"One month from today. We've all been served notice."

"But the house? The mortgage? Surely they have to pay you off?"

"There is a redundancy payment. £10,000 per person."

"But that's … that's …"

"About two months gross, tax free. I'd need to find something else by the end of June to keep up the mortgage payments."

"But won't the bank be sympathetic? Give us a wee payment holiday? You're a skilled worker."

"I can try but it's unlikely in this climate. They know as well as we do that there's little prospect of a job which pays just as well."

"So that's it. Finished." Shaylie's speech became more urgent as her mouth began to quiver and her eyes started to glisten.

"We'll live," countered Jordan unconvincingly, "but life will be very different, whichever direction we go in."

"There's only one direction we can go in." Shaylie's tears splashed onto the table, close to Alfie's elbows where he sat, his face veiled by his hands.

"There may be an alternative." It was time.

Shaylie's voice was raised in pitch. "What alternative could there possibly be?"

"Matsucorp have made me a confidential offer. To me and only to me. We have a massive decision to make. They've given me twenty-four hours."

Chapter Six

Wife and son sat agog as Jordan recounted his surreal experience between 4:00 and 4:05 that afternoon. This time he had been alone. Again there was a hologram but no Rob Garnett. Perhaps Garnett did not even know. It had felt furtive, and the feeling of disloyalty engendered by spinning a cover story to his colleagues to attend this surreptitious meeting was nothing compared to the betrayal he would be encouraged to commit.

This time the hologram had been beamed from Matsucorp Honsha, the company HQ in Tokyo. The company was known to have only Japanese executives, but Jordan was faced with the image of an awkward and wiry but imposing Westerner. A strange-looking man who did not feel the need to share his name with Jordan. There would be plenty of time for that. He spoke purposefully and with unerring clarity, his intonation clipped, his accent neutral English, perhaps slightly plummy. Jordan could recall their brief and one-sided conversation.

"Good afternoon." The address, coming from a dimly lit Tokyo office at midnight, was time-zone appropriate to the FREW. Japan was always eight hours ahead of the FREW since the UK's permanent adoption of BST during the latter days of the union. He continued without waiting for Jordan to reciprocate. "I will be brief. Matsucorp has no choice but to close down its FREW operations. However, it does wish to retain on the payroll its best and most skilled worker from each FREW factory. It wishes to reward you, Jordan May, with an opportunity to avoid redundancy."

Jordan did not dare interrupt.

"Rather than accept your £10,000 redundancy payment, you are invited to relocate to Tokyo and bring your not inconsiderable robotics skills to our local production line.

Your salary would enable you to live a similarly comfortable life to now. Matsucorp would take care of immigration procedures and your contract would be long-term. You would be able to start a new life in a more prosperous environment. Do you have any questions?"

"But … my family?"

"Matsucorp proposes to relocate your family, find you initial accommodation and a local school for your child. Matsubara-*san* desires a swift decision and equally swift implementation of your relocation, should you choose to accept. You will meet me here at the same time tomorrow with your answer. It is not possible to give you longer. Sayōnara."

The hologram faded, leaving one Japanese word as an inextinguishable earworm. Jordan was still hearing *sayōnara*, *sayooonara*, *sayooooonara*, the second vowel ever-lengthening, when he realised that Shaylie and Alfie were firing questions at him.

"What about my job? My friends?"

"What about school? My apprenticeship? My mates? Evie?"

And, in unison, "What about the language?"

Jordan heard himself tell his family that they had been invited to join the desertion of the FREW but under favourable conditions. Jordan waited for the right moment to interject. He had regained his composure and his voice was now calm but strong. He stopped his nervous pulling of his earlobe and leaned forward onto the elbows of crossed arms.

"There are lots of obstacles. We can avoid all of those obstacles by staying here and struggling. On the other hand, we can rent the house out and give it a go. We've been given a chance to survive."

"What are you saying, dad?"

"You … you think we should go, darling?"

"Sweetheart, Alfie darling," he addressed each in turn, "I don't think we really have a choice."

Chapter Seven

Shaylie knew that they had been handed an opportunity that many of their compatriots could only dream of. Citizens of the Federal Republic of England and Wales had been boarding planes in their droves, attempting to find a back door into the north-east Asian super-economies. Over there, the most menial of tasks was better remunerated than many jobs for working people in the ailing local industries. As a result, ports of entry into China, Korea and Japan were full of queuing Europeans, sleeping in arrivals lounges or held in immigrant camps, hoping to be needed by corporations in search of cheap labour. The Mays had an easy way in, a skilled job with guaranteed visas, accommodation and income. Their heads held high, they would arrange for the house to be rented and depart for a new life. A new life which would allow Shaylie to bury even more deeply that one terrible error of judgement. Two years, three, maybe even five years in an alien culture, until the local economy began to right itself.

For Alfie, it was a very different proposition. As his parents discussed details in the kitchen, their evening at the community centre long forgotten, he retired to his room, alone in his introspection, with doubts and insecurities which had not existed a couple of hours before. He now had to do what his dad had done at the kitchen table. Bite the bullet and break the news to Evie in the right way, whilst his own adolescent life was about to take a step into the unknown. He had a ten-minute walk in the dark, close Harwich evening, along the main road out of the old town and back towards Dovercourt, to collect his thoughts. He passed the community centre, where the townspeople assembled to play games without his parents. Just beyond, the bandstand in the park began to emerge from the dark, from amongst the trees. The first trees still a memorial, still covered in the photos of that boy, a boy his age who was killed there so long ago, so very many decades ago and still remembered, his life still commemorated by his friends who had completed their adolescence and lived their adult lives. Life was for living and Alfie was grateful to have opportunities that the boy had never had, but his young life would now be very different and he could not imagine the direction it would take. The near future was unknown, but at some point in the future he would return a young man, his education complete, to reignite his relationship with his one true love. He needed to know that Evie was committed, that she understood and was prepared to wait.

"Japan?" snivelled Evie, as they inclined against the railing at the edge of the bandstand. A light sea breeze cooled their damp clothes against their skin. "What are they doing that for? What's wrong with here? Here's fine!"

"You know how everyone's trying to get out, looking for a better life. You know we're not the first to go, don't you? Look at all the others who've disappeared over the past couple of years."

"But I don't care about *them*. I didn't love *them*! What about *us*, Alfie, *us*?"

"My dad's had a really good offer. I don't want to go any more than you want me to, but there is no choice. If we stay we'll lose our house. Things will be on the up in a few years and we'll come back. I'll come back. I can even come back on my own when I finish school. We'll be in touch when we can and, before you know it, we'll be back together."

The tears were flowing now, meeting the snot above Evie's lips. Lips to which Alfie had delivered many a reluctant kiss, but never really a proper kiss. Why not? Evie was a pretty girl who had never lacked interest from boys, but she could not read Alfie. He was kind and funny, but reserved and undemonstrative. They all admired his quiet nature; Alfie was *horizontal*, according to their friends. She wished she knew how he felt, how he *really* felt. He had even broken this earth-shattering news to her with the calm assuredness of an older man, his nerves given away only by a frequent, exaggerated blink, a tic increasing with heart rate.

Evie wiped her face with her school-issue hoody and a more intense, glistening stare searched for what she wanted to see behind Alfie's dark, inscrutable gaze. "But you might never come back. I'm not the only girl in the world. Why on earth would you put everything on hold for me when you will be surrounded by other girls, other opportunities?"

"I only want to be with you." Alfie's response was firm, as he rearranged Evie's dark bobbed hair behind her ears and placed his mouth onto hers. Alfie was far less sure of such opportunities in a strange land than Evie was. Would he have to move on to adult life now, missing out on the raw and prurient experience of teenage love?

For the first time, there was intent contained within his kiss. His left hand reached around the right side of her neck and pulled her face firmly against his. A modicum of resistance, borne of surprise, quickly subsided as Evie allowed their mouths to open together, their tongues to meet, passion to flow. They both relaxed into their longest kiss.

#

As Alfie walked home, only half an hour later, his lips sore and his pride hurt, he wondered whether he would ever see Evie again. She had told him where to go when he had offered to walk her home, but Harwich at night had become far too dangerous. The vagabonds came out at night. He had followed from a distance to make sure that she got home safely. Whatever he had done, he was determined to see her home, this time like every time. The last time?

It had all begun so well. He had wanted to show her his love and his commitment. He had wanted to feel hers in return. She had always complained about his reticence. When she demanded to hold hands, to kiss, surely more physical contact was what she had wanted. He should have thought it through but he didn't really know how it worked. She had initially tensed up but then gradually softened as he had plucked up the courage to caress her. It had seemed as if she was enjoying it, as if she were into him, as if she might have wanted more. He had listened to other lads talking about what girls liked, what they wanted. They were all at it. Or so they said. But how naïve of him to think Evie would want him to go *that* far. How naïve and stupid! And now he had ruined everything.

The next day, Jordan accepted Matsucorp's offer and was given a week to prepare for departure. Alfie's increasingly reserved behaviour was, quite reasonably, attributed to anxiety over a new life in the unknown. Simple shame prevented Alfie from knocking on the door of Evie's flat. He would leave for Japan uncertain of what awaited him and equally uncertain of what he had left behind.

Chapter Eight

"Did everything go according to plan, Stepson-*san*?"

The offices of Matsucorp-Honsha were deserted. Matsubara had dismissed his holographic PA with the push of a button. It was late on Thursday night and Matsubara addressed the board's two key players in Operation Gaijin across the desk of his office on the thirtieth floor.

As always, Stepson Struthwin replied in fluent if imprecise Japanese, skilfully communicating whilst displaying a practical disregard for *teineina nihongo*, the polite forms expected in business. "Their flight is on time, they will be on their way. All documentation was delivered by courier to all three households yesterday. It is all in hand."

Yamada did not care for Struthwin and was irked by his butchering of the Emperor's beautiful language, but Yamada knew that Struthwin was untouchable and that Matsubara would not tolerate criticism.

In Japan, pushed for space, a country 80% uninhabitable due to widespread mountainous areas, the Mainichi Shimbun had been conducting a '*Nihonjin no Nihon; Gaijin soto e!*' campaign, heavily supporting the nationalistic slant of Yamada's JSD party. 'Japan for the Japanese; Foreigners out!' said the newspaper's bullish slogan. Many people had been led to think that Japan's recently burgeoning population could cope with the demands of its economy and domestic production targets. More liberal thinkers saw the need for foreign labour, prepared to work in less desirable posts to obtain the strong yen, in order to maintain the ever-improving economy. The contentious issue in customer services was the education required to bring foreign labour up to Japanese standards, avoiding dilution. Yamada saw this as a problem beyond customer services. He saw employing foreigners as a risk to Matsucorp. Unlucky enough to be born without

Japanese blood, they had not been raised with the work ethic, the willingness to conform and the loyalty to the Emperor of the Japanese. He saw social justice as airy-fairy, hard-line isolationism as pragmatic. He was determined to keep a tight rein on Operation Gaijin.

"I have to be elsewhere shortly," said the politician, "but I want to be clear that these immigrant workers are not taking Japanese jobs. I also want to know that they have been vetted and will not cause any issues or voice dissent in the way that foreigners are wont to do."

Matsubara's response was cool, firm and confident. "We have been able to create jobs for them which fit their skill sets. Nagoya, Sendai and Tokyo have been briefed and await their arrival. A press release has gone to all national titles and we expect favourable coverage in the morning. Stepson-*san* has done the necessary research on these people, I believe. Do you foresee any issues?"

"Nagoya and Sendai will certainly be straightforward. The two women are single and travelling alone. They do not have any history of political activism and are not involved in any political body other than standard union membership. They. are both outgoing and well respected in their communities. They will make every effort to integrate."

Yamada was quick to interject. "So you are saying that the Tokyo appointment will not be straightforward? We cannot afford adverse publicity. The boat must not be rocked."

"No risks will be taken," responded Struthwin, "but it goes without saying that the relocation of an entire family brings with it extra complications. However, Jordan May is a reserved but skilled company man who has always cooperated. His wife and son will need help to ensure that the family settles, but they, too, are conformers. I will ensure that it is a smooth integration."

"What about political affiliations?" asked Yamada, now on his feet, trying to tear himself away to his next engagement.

"Standard membership of the union and on-off membership of Respect Labour, but no activism."

"Respect Labour? This is left-wing politics. The politics of challenge to the establishment."

Matsubara interjected. "Left-wing politics are inevitable in a changing world. Working class people all over Europe have returned to their traditional values since the collapse of free market capitalism. This is perfectly normal and simply a different political shade to your social democracy, Yamada-*san*. If you were to allow *gaijin* membership, perhaps Mr May would join your party."

As Yamada took his leave, Matsubara and Struthwin made no move to follow suit.

"You have done well, Stepson-*san*."

"I have only done what you pay me to do."

"So have you uncovered any possible flies in the ointment?

"There is very little which can make this operation difficult for us. Jordan May is loyal and he is a worker. He has a loyal family unit to support him. A couple of potentially unsettling mailings have been sent to Jordan and the boy since they boarded a couple of hours ago. We have managed to intercept them. Those messages will never arrive."

"Messages? I thought they lived in a prole outpost. No internet, no mobile phones and an unreliable postal system. Surely there is no prospect of contact?"

"It is unlikely, but I like to cover all bases. Their post does take ages but more than 50% of letters do arrive. International mail addressed to the May family, care of Matsucorp, Tokyo, Japan, however, is a different matter."

Matsubara lit up, poured a generous measure of Suntory whisky into a heavy crystal glass and slowly got to his feet, deep in thought. He turned his back to Struthwin and stood looking south into the distance, towards the Shinjuku government buildings which towered over the busy and well-lit city.

"Who sent these messages? And in what way were they potentially unsettling?"

"The boy has been sent a conciliatory letter from his girlfriend of several months. A girl called Evie. It would appear that they had some kind of falling out in the week preceding departure."

"And you feel, as I do, that we would affect a smoother relocation were romantic ties to be severed completely."

"That is certainly the case. We will continue to filter any such correspondence. The boy and the whole family will settle much better if he finds himself a local romantic interest."

"Remind me of the boy's name."

"Alfred. But they call him Alfie."

"Alfie? Yes, I have seen the photos in your case file. He is a good-looking boy for a Westerner. There will be much interest in him. He will be placed in Nerima High School, yes?"

"That is correct, Matsubara-*san*. He will be surrounded by the children of our employees and he will be observed closely. The family will be housed in our residence in Shakuji-kōen as soon as an apartment becomes available. Until then, I have found them a *gaijin* house nearby."

"Excellent."

Matsubara paused, inhaled deeply on his Mild Seven, then blew out a thick cloud of smoke which rose up the huge window and temporarily clouded the Tokyo skyline. The boy did not overly concern him. "So what could possibly unsettle Mr May, Stepson-*san*? What do I need to be aware of?"

"We intercepted a message from his younger brother."

"And what was the nature of this communication?" Matsubara emptied the cut glass in one large mouthful and turned back to face Struthwin.

"Ethan May appeared to be responding to a brief voicemail from his brother. They still have landlines although some lines are shared. Jordan was apprising him of his relocation to Tokyo. Having missed the call, Ethan wrote a short letter wishing him luck, telling him to be careful and asking him to stay in touch."

"I fail to see why this could be an unsettling communication, Stepson-*san*. It seems an entirely normal family nicety to me."

"Their relationship has been strained for years. For most of their lives, in fact. Ethan May is a troublemaker and Jordan May has kept him at arm's length for many years now. Indeed, he has been happy not to contact him at all. Ethan May has a chequered past and has form as a union activist. I wish to remove all potential negative influences."

"And you are right to do so, Stepson-*san*. You have been thorough, as always. Dōmo arigatō gozaimasu." The depth of Matsubara's bow reflected the genuine nature of his gratitude and Struthwin, still seated, inclined his head to reciprocate in that awkward *gaijin* manner.

Struthwin's privilege and well-remunerated position was maintained by clinical and effective job execution. Matsucorp would not tolerate the slightest dent to its domination and all means had to be used to ensure a steady ship. Struthwin may have uncovered more dirt on Ethan than he was prepared to share, but he would personally oversee a seamless integration of the May family into the Matsucorp community. The resulting PR would be relentless. Operation Gaijin could only strengthen their financial and political position.

Chapter Nine

The following Thursday, the Mays awoke on the hard floor of the departure lounge at Heathrow airport. They had arrived on the last Heathrow Express the previous night and bedded down on their luggage in a corner of Terminal 5 on the edge of the cacophony of many thousands of hopeful ecomigrants. The Mays were deafened.

The chaos inside the terminal was nothing compared to what had met them the previous evening. Police cordons surrounded entry points to every port of departure within the republic. The objective was to filter out every desperate soul without a ticket from harassing ground staff. The president had been told in no uncertain terms that English and Welsh travellers without the relevant paperwork would be repatriated immediately, to be returned to the overcrowded streets. The attitude of the great Eastern supereconomies had changed in recent months. The ingress of European migrants could no longer be tolerated. Japanese, Chinese and Korean corporations had access to all the cheap labour they could ever want from the airport arrivals lounges and the holding camps outside. Any further ingress would be treated without sympathy. Speculative ecomigrants would not get beyond passport control.

Wearily, the Mays joined the check-in queue for their Japan Airlines flight to Narita International, Terminal 2. Shaylie had their documentation organised, carrying a concertina file loaded with all papers of import, their passports and the package which had arrived by courier the day before. They had their flight tickets, their visas, a work permit and a letter confirming employment with Matsucorp which provided Jordan with exemption from the necessity of a bachelor's degree.

Finally, they approached the check-in screen to be confronted by an officious holographic clerk with a white badge, labelling her simply as 'Mori'. Shaylie had to squint to read the roman transliteration of her name beneath the bold Chinese character which resembled a triangular arrangement of three small trees.

"Documents!" she barked. Shaylie placed each in turn face down on the scanner in front of her. Jordan enquired after meal options on the flight. Ms Mori seemed not to hear as she viewed the scanned passports and took her time to vet all documentation with the utmost care.

When at last she was satisfied, Jordan received a curt response.

"Japan Airlines no longer offers a choice of meal on flights to and from Europe, other than in first class. All passengers will receive two Japanese meals, dinner this evening and breakfast before landing. Water and green tea are complimentary also, but you must purchase alcoholic drinks should you require them. Your checked-in luggage is within the weight limit. Gate 37 will open at twelve noon and close forty-five minutes later. Have a comfortable flight. Next!"

Once all three of them had been frisked and hand luggage emptied and repacked, the Mays found themselves airside and once more on the floor with time to kill. They were stunned by the stench of thousands of unwashed bodies, many of whom had begun their journey to Heathrow over 48 hours ago. It formed an overwhelming miasma as it came together with the grease emanating from restaurants patronised by the few who could still afford them. It was tough to choose between the cold ceramic tiles in the main lounge and the stained and worn carpet on which they found themselves at gate 37. They sat in a dazed silence and waited for the gate to open.

Shaylie found it hard to concentrate on her beginner's Japanese book, aware as she was of Alfie's increased diffidence. She thought she knew what, or who, he was thinking about but she did not understand what had happened, why he had not seen Evie in the week before they left. Jordan sat with his knees pulled into his chest, head resting on his knees, eyes closed. He took stock of his life, of how lucky he had been to meet Shaylie and of relationships and friendships which had been less successful. Jordan had found it difficult to meet girls, to get to know them. He had been content to connect with Shaylie when introduced by his best friend's girlfriend. Alex was one of very few friends. Now he had been left to take a hit alone, to take redundancy whilst Jordan had been favoured by their employer. He had slowly got to know Alex, sat at the same desk as him for four consecutive years of compulsory citizenship lessons. And now, following a strained and distant conversation over a farewell drink, Jordan felt guilt. More guilt. Guilt for uprooting his family and guilt for betraying his best friend.

Jordan's few friends had always been more important to him than wider family. It had been much easier to put 6000 miles between him and his closest living relative. Like Alex, Ethan was more outgoing than Jordan. Ethan was also arrogant. Alex and Ethan both had charisma and looked socially comfortable, though one did not need too long with Ethan to realise that this social fluency was superficial. It was an interminable source of angst to Jordan that his parents had not been able to see this. Ethan was the heart and soul. Ethan got on with everyone and got on in life. Ethan grew quickly in stature and was popular with the girls. Ethan lost his virginity long before his brother and Ethan rubbed Jordan's nose in it. Jordan would have been happy never to see Ethan again, but nonetheless he had left him a brief voicemail, on Shaylie's insistence, the day before they left.

Some old habits die hard amongst air travellers. Half of the bleary-eyed crowd rushed to form a queue when Ms Mori, now hovering at gate 37, called forward passengers with seats numbered 50 and above.

"Seats 53A, B and C," pointed out Alfie. "That's us!"

Jordan was at once amused and irritated by the rush. "Exactly, Alfie," he was quick to explain. "We have numbered seats. Whether we sit here and wait or stand in a long queue, our seats will still be there. I know which I'd prefer. We're going to be in those cramped seats for nearly 10 hours. There's no hurry, just chill out."

They waited until five minutes before the gate was due to close and then made their way onto the enormous aircraft, pausing briefly in wonder at how on earth it would make it off the ground. As they left the FREW, both Jordan and Alfie were oblivious to attempts to contact them, intercepted and gone for good.

The flight was uneventful, the atmosphere nervy. Minds were distracted from the cramped conditions of their standard class seats by a modest selection of subtitled Japanese films and two complimentary meals, both consisting of rice, vegetables and pickles with miso soup on the side. There were no Asian passengers in standard class these days and the service provided by staff, all female and all Japanese, was business-like and succinct but courteous.

As the internal clocks of the English passengers began to announce bedtime with heavy eyelids and yawns to accompany swollen throats, the aircraft began its descent into the rising sun of Friday morning.

Futile haste was again precipitated as the plane arrived at its gate. At the extinguishing of the seatbelt light, several hundred clicks of released catches filled the fuselage. It was a race to be reunited with hand luggage and to stand impatiently in an aisle topped and tailed with unopened doors.

Seated, the Mays observed their nameless and stinking travelling companions scrambling to be first in the race. The human race. Migrating here and there for centuries, back and forth, whilst objecting to the influx of others. Like migrating birds. Like herded sheep. Like teeming rats.

The English had resisted this human invasion for so long and now here they were, queuing up for the privilege of being regarded as an immigrant pestilence, inferior humans, fleeing their own environmental degradation. An invasive species seeking to feed on the prosperity of others.

PART TWO
Eastern Capital

Chapter Ten

The two large, black Matsucorp sedans whispered slowly to a standstill in a quiet road, bathed in spring sunshine. To the right, there was a row of modern, mansion-style houses and, to the left, Shakuji Park, resplendent with its multitude of cherry trees, beginning their seasonal display of blossom. Pensioners, decrepit in appearance but spritely in gait, made their way towards the shops scattered around Shakuji-kōen station. They were interspersed with young mothers with their charged baby buggies, all slaves to routine, all going about their daily business. Their eyes turned towards the foreign arrivals as they spilled out into their new lives.

The Mays found their feet on the pavement in a well-appointed neighbourhood. A short, smiling, besuited Japanese, wearing a Matsucorp lapel badge, emerged from the front car. He introduced himself simply as Kuni.

"Follow me," he said in heavily accented English, the smile never leaving his face. "Driver will bring your bag."

From between the two cars they crossed the street in silence, each one of them drinking in their new surroundings. Passers-by had now stopped in small groups and stood, staring and mumbling, as the new arrivals waded through an atmosphere of hushed disapproval which had descended upon the neighbourhood. Ominously, Kuni led them towards the unkempt mansion building which sat amongst a row of immaculate houses.

\#

The muted displeasure of the people of Shakuji-kōen paled into insignificance when compared to the opprobrium attracted by their arrival at Narita.

The papers from Matsucorp had guaranteed swift passage through the immigration section of passport control, where foreigners were funnelled away from Japanese passport holders. It had taken a matter of minutes for each May to be photographed, their iris scanned and their fingerprint taken, along with a DNA sample by means of a swab of the inner cheek. The 'company fast track' queue had galloped through the middle of the sterile hall, leaving in its wake the snail-like ranks of the desperate and the brave, attempting to enter Japan on a 90-day tourist visa in the hope of finding work. It was possible to distinguish some western European languages, blended in with the unfamiliar eastern European and African tongues which combined to make an almighty din.

Chaos had ensued at baggage reclaim. Sweaty body nudged sweaty body as the foreigners tried to catch sight of their suitcases. Armed officials restored order as frustration spilled over into pockets of aggression. Pushing and shoving was quickly brought to a halt by the proximity of a baton or a sub-machine gun, but where anger persisted, two officials unceremoniously dragged the aggressor across the tiled floor to a side-door, no doubt the door to deportation.

The Mays had fought for their cases and wheeled them to the customs queue. They could see before they arrived at the desk that thorough searching of luggage was neither selective nor random. One by one, they had stood and watched as their carefully packed suitcases and hand luggage were opened, neatly folded clothes unravelled, toiletry bags emptied and everything left in a pile for the owner to repack. As the two officials at each desk had systematically pulled apart the bags, not a word was exchanged, but both officials had repeated *hayaku* several times as the Mays tried to repack in a manner which would allow them to close their cases. There was no language barrier. The tone of the utterance and the severity of the facial expression both ordered the Mays to hurry.

They had been instructed to look for a man with a Matsucorp sign in the arrivals hall. As they emerged through the automatic doors, they quickly identified the laminated card bearing the company logo. Kuni was standing with two short-haired Western women. One was blond, tall, severe of countenance, the other dark and smiling, shorter than her companion but still taller than Kuni. They were briefly introduced as Elaine-*san* from Merthyr and Sophie-*san* from Middlesbrough. Shaylie marvelled at her own ability to decipher 'Middlesbrough' from Kuni's six-syllable attempt, but she was still wondering where 'Marsa' was as Kuni impelled them towards the exit, towards the shouting.

Outside on the concourse, they approached the pick-up zone. A large group of protesters stood behind a police cordon. Organised and vocal, their placards reflected the broken English of their shouts and chants. '*Nihon-jin no nihon; gaijin soto-e!*', 'Japan for Japanese person, foreigner outside!' Matsucorp's new and well-publicised imports got closer, so agitation and jostling increased. The police stood firm but, as the escorted partly quickened their march towards the cars, Alfie was struck on the cheek by a stone, thrown with force from amongst the throng. He cried out and the party increased their cadence once more, now almost running. The jeers were still ringing in their ears as they dived behind the smoked windows onto the cool, extravagant leather upholstery of the first of two black sedans.

All three of the Mays were shaking, none more so than Alfie who now bore, on his face, the first visible souvenir of his new life, a dark lump which extended the prominent bone of his left cheek. "What have we come to?" he whimpered. Shaylie tried to calm him and Jordan sat tugging at his right ear lobe.

"I'm sure that was the hardest part," she said, as the sedan accelerated onto the Shin Kūkō Expressway in the direction of Tokyo. Jordan gazed out of the window at the high expressway walls which hid the rice paddies, punctuated with small conurbations, below the elevated toll road. For the next hour, Shaylie speculated about the improved life they had come to, the land of opportunity where they would enjoy a better, secure life. The Mays had begun to enjoy a greater feeling of optimism by the time that they emerged from the expressway onto the Keiyō Road into Tokyo. Now they could begin to take in this enormous city through the car windows, bilingual road signs announcing exotic locales, such as Higashi-Ōjima, Akihabara and Shinjuku. A mess of dissimilar houses and odd-shaped residential neighbourhoods rushed by. Closer to the centre, these were replaced by towering office blocks and the neon excess of shopping districts. And now up onto another expressway which took them out of the centre, north-west past Ikebukuro, then west towards Nerima, Shakuji and Hōya. Jordan recognised Hōya as the location of the Matsucorp factory. They travelled beyond Nerima but, eyelids heavy with jet-lag, they stopped short of Hōya and came to a halt in front of their new home.

Chapter Eleven

Close-cropped head down, Kuni walked with purpose. He led them past the stairway in the entrance hall, down a corridor and straight into the communal kitchen of the gaijin house.

Shaylie had researched gaijin houses before their departure. She had discovered that it was an arrangement somewhat similar to that of the now-defunct student residences back home. They would be sharing kitchen, bath/shower and toilet with around twenty other foreigners, cleaning duties shared by a rota on the kitchen wall. Private rental involved key money and a deposit, equivalent to two months' rent in advance, plus the first month's rent, and this was prohibitive to anyone who did not have substantial spare cash. In addition, many landlords would not rent to foreigners. It could be a long time until a company flat became available. They would be here for a while.

The kitchen was not as clean as Shaylie would have liked. A thin coating of grease was evident on most surfaces. There was a worktop along the back wall and old-style electric hobs, causing Shaylie's nose to wrinkle. Then she spotted the absence of a baking essential. Ovens were superfluous to Japanese cuisine, and she did not feel that the microwave on top of the fridge was an adequate replacement. An MDF dining table and chairs dominated the middle of the kitchen. To their right, a door opened onto the house's one toilet, to their left a wet room, containing a short but deep bath with a shower above, attached to the wall.

"So where do we sleep?" asked Alfie, unimpressed with what he had seen thus far.

"So," Kuni announced, still avoiding eye contact, "you have biggest room in house, just here."

They all turned to where Kuni was pointing, to a pair of shōji sliding rice paper doors opposite the kitchen. Kuni slid one door across and they looked in onto a room with tatami flooring. There was a clothes rail, a low wooden coffee table and a fan.

Alfie did not understand.

"What? So where do we sleep?"

Always looking at the floor, Kuni removed his shoes and signalled to the Mays to do the same. "In normal Japanese house, you take off shoe at front door. In gaijin house, you take off shoe before enter bedroom. We Japanese never walk on tatami in shoe. Shoes breaks tatami."

He walked to one end of the room and slid open a large cupboard.

"Here are your futon. Three single futon, sheet and duvet and pillow. You make up bed on floor each evening and put away each morning, so you have space in daytime."

Kuni left the Mays standing in their empty room in silence, each of them trying to take in this different way of living. Jordan was first to snap out of the jet-lagged trance which had enveloped them all.

"Ok, this is not the end of the world. We can put up with this on a temporary basis and then we will have saved up for private accommodation. A nice little flat overlooking that beautiful park. This arrangement will allow us to meet people, other foreigners, get tips on how to get by here. We'll be fine. We'll support each other, work hard and eventually we'll go home. Don't worry, you two. Don't worry."

Kuni returned and handed Jordan an envelope, head bowed.

"Here. Please take. Inside, you will find helpful instruction. You start work and school on Monday. This explain to you how to go there, what time, what wearing. Also inside, you will find present from Matsucorp. Some yen for food and train ticket. This must last one month, until April payday. Good luck! Gambatte kudasai!"

Kuni bowed a deep bow in retreat, turned, stepped into his shoes and took his leave.

"I'm hungry, thirsty and tired," said Alfie, as he went to the cupboard to get out a futon.

"Wait!" said Shaylie. "I know you want to sleep. I know it's the middle of the night for us, but I've read about this. If we sleep now, we'll be awake through the night. We need to force our bodies to adjust as soon as we can. We will try very hard to stay awake until about 9pm, then sleep at night time."

"But, mum, I can't!"

"You said you were hungry and thirsty. Let's deal with that. We've got some money and it's a beautiful day. Let's find a shop, get some supplies, then go and eat in the park. We're on holiday until Monday."

"Your mum's right. Let's not make things more difficult than they have to be. Later this evening our housemates will get in from work. We can get to know them, get some tips on living here. But now we should explore. When we arrived, did you see how all the locals were walking in the same direction? I'll bet you if we turn left out of the front door and keep going, we'll come to the shops. And the station."

And so the decision had been made. A teenager new to Tokyo was not going to be allowed to sit and wallow. His parents were finding this new situation more than tough, but they both knew what they had to do. Shaylie had done the research. She had some practical ways to look after her son, to lift his morale. But, above all, it was Jordan who felt that he had to take charge and make a success of the situation. He had got them into this, he had made the decision. The three of them needed to enjoy Japanese life to have any chance of getting through this. Jordan would take charge. Jordan felt in control.

Chapter Twelve

Heads turned as they made their weary way alongside the park towards the square in front of Shakuji-kōen station. There had been a time when white faces had been relatively common. Some of the more mature locals remembered it well. There had been young British, North American and Antipodean graduates everywhere. They had been well remunerated in commercial language schools as English teachers to aspirational Japanese of all ages. English had dominated in popular culture as it had in business. Its demise had been swift.

In the west, the cult popularity of Japanese game shows at the turn of the millennium had paved the way for this cheap and manic programming style to dominate abroad. The English-speaking world bought such game shows and Samurai dramas also became popular as the bottom fell out of domestic TV production markets. The refusal of the FREW and the New World to compromise on the learning of other languages backfired in many commercial fields. Speakers of the world's other major languages raised the shutters. More and more areas of popular culture followed suit as J-pops conquered the world with the help of karaoke, although there was considerable resistance in western European countries which still, each of them, considered their music to be superior. What had been international suddenly became parochial. The Beatles and The X Factor became ancient history. Bollywood, Nollywood and Jollywood replaced Hollywood.

The Japanese people were no longer used to seeing Western faces coming and going as they pleased. The English schools had closed. Some other foreigners were welcomed. To a degree. They could identify the Chinese and Koreans through their fashion and the Indians through racial difference. But Asian immigrants did not turn heads. They were commonplace. Early on Friday afternoon at the beginning of spring in Shakuji, the Mays discovered that white faces were noticed. White faces caused some people to stop dead in the street. White faces attracted stares.

Stepping onto the square, they were surrounded. Old men stopped. Old women stared. Young mothers turned their baby buggies away, as if to protect their children from the Western menace. The Mays felt deeply uncomfortable. They could not stare back. They could not look at one another either. They looked at the ground. Alfie's exaggerated blink, his nervous tic, was working overtime.

"Let's go back," said Shaylie.

Jordan looked at Alfie, who had withdrawn into himself, then looked at his wife.

"That is the worst thing we could do," he said. "These people are just curious. We are an unusual sight. They will get used to us. We're not doing anything wrong."

Jordan knew that if they went back to the gaijin house now, he would struggle to get either of them out through the front door again.

The Roman alphabet was scarce in Shakuji square. There had been much more that they had been able to read on the huge neon signs in central Tokyo, but here almost everything was exclusively in Japanese. They began a tentative walk around the edge of the square. They could feel the humid air stick to them. Following one close call, they soon got used to side-stepping bicycles. The ring of a bell was the local substitute for braking. Every few minutes they stepped into a litter-free gutter, marvelling at the cleanliness of the streets.

But it was not uniquely the sights which were alien to them. They were bombarded by unknown sounds and smells. A wailing recitation, emanating from the loudspeaker of a nearby temple, floated through the air. An odd blend of odours wafted around them. The familiar smells of the bakery mingled with the aromas of the street food, served from market stalls by ageing merchants with thick white hair and tanned, weathered skin. The flavours were strong; the Mays could taste the air around them. The soy-barbecued chicken from the yakitori stall, served on a skewer, the sweet sauce covering the *dango* – dumplings of sweet *mochi* rice – served on a skewer, the stir-fried *yakisoba*, served in plant-gelatin glassware, and corn-on-the-cob, barbecued in soy sauce.

Human instinct took over. Hunger trumped discomfort and the Mays resolved to enter the bakery. In they marched. Alfie's long, elegant gait took him straight to the drinks fridge and his mother followed him. He soon chose a cold yellow can with the Romanised name *CC Lemon* on the side. Shaylie picked out two plastic bottles of what she was unable to identify as chilled barley tea. They joined Jordan at the glass counter, put the drinks on the top and then pointed at three baguette-style sandwiches, each containing a different kind of meat. It had been a long time since they had been able to afford meat. Shaylie then took a risk, pointed at a bun, glazed in appearance, and extended three fingers in the direction of the woman behind the counter, whose head bowed to avoid the unerring eye contact. She bagged up the sandwiches, the drinks and the three *anpan*, then handed Jordan a copious mixture of notes and coins in exchange for the ¥10 000 note he had proffered. Now her floorward stare was replaced with a curt bow as they retreated from the bakery.

They walked back past the unfamiliar shops and street food stalls, dodging bicycles and raising their heads high. For the first time, on the disused electricity lines above the train vacuum tubes, they noticed hundreds of ravens, biding their time, squawking and waiting for scraps. The Mays had begun to habituate themselves to scrutiny by locals as they arrived on the square. They made their way past the stares, through the gates of the park and alongside the boating lake.

They found a free bench and sat down to eat. Many of the benches were in the shadows of cherry trees but they found themselves exposed to the spring sun. It was a beautiful day, if hotter and stickier than at home, and they felt the warmth as they hungrily demolished the sandwiches, the pigeons oblivious to racial differences as they harvested the resulting crumbs.

Alfie and Shaylie greedily washed down the first course with the new, exotic drinks they had discovered, but Jordan struggled with the cold barley tea. They all shared his difficulty with the *anpan* as they bit through the sweet roll to discover the red adzuki bean paste filling. Sickly sweet, only the pigeons could ensure that nothing was wasted.

"We've had a meal and our first cultural lesson," said Shaylie. "I call that a success!"

They continued along the footpath and sought a side gate which led into their street. "Let's go back and read the info Kuni left us."

"But we haven't been to a supermarket, yet," said Alfie, "What are we going to cook tonight?"

Jordan had already made his mind up. "Have you seen all of the cash he gave us? We're eating out."

Chapter Thirteen

It was late afternoon when they returned to find two young women eating toast in the kitchen. Both tanned, both with long, dark hair, both attractive, they wore matching white towelling dressing gowns. Japanese pop music from a battered, battery-operated radio on the table provided the backdrop to a kitchen which was suddenly lived in. Toasted breadcrumbs were scattered liberally on and around the grill tray which they had left on top of the hobs.

"Hi!" they both said in chorus, "How are you doing?" their accent part mid-Atlantic, part Middle Eastern.

Shaylie greeted them, followed by the rest of the family. "Hello. How nice to be able to speak English," she added. "I'm Shaylie, this is Jordan, my husband, and my son, Alfie."

"Hey, guys, nice to meet you. Have you just got here?"

"We arrived around lunchtime. We've just been out to explore and find some food."

"Cool," said the chattier of the pair. "I'm Elisa and this is Aaliyah. We're not sisters, although everyone thinks we are."

"I can't think why," mumbled Jordan.

"Pardon?" Elisa asked.

"Nothing. Nice to meet you."

"Yeah. Hey, this is unusual. We don't get many *gaijin* families over here nowadays. Not ones that get beyond the camps, anyways."

"So there really are refugee camps?" asked Shaylie.

"Well, yeah, although the locals call them migrant camps. They make it sound as shameful as possible. The newspapers don't want the people to harbour any sympathy. The Daily Mainichi is run by nationalists. They are running a 'Japan for Japanese; Foreigners out' campaign. They set the agenda and we deal with the fallout. I guess you guys found it tough outside for the first time?"

"I can't say it was very pleasant. We've never been stared at like that before. Is it always like that?"

"It is until they get used to seeing you around. This is a small neighbourhood. They'll soon start to ignore you, and that's about all you can hope for. You must have had all that already on the trains to get here from Narita, right?"

"No, no, we were driven here by my husband's company, Matsucorp."

"Oh, right! So you have a proper visa and everything, right? That is so cool!"

"Yes, that's right. We couldn't have come otherwise. We *are* lucky, I suppose, although I don't think it is going to be easy. How about you, girls? Don't you have a proper visa?"

"Well, not exactly. We have the 90-day tourist visa which we have to renew outside of the country. Each 89th day, we have to fly to Seoul, get a new stamp and then come back."

"They don't stop you? Isn't that really expensive?"

"They don't stop us because they want us here, although that is not something they'd publicise. And we can do it because we are paid well. That's why we're here."

"Oh, that's good. So where are you from and what do you do?"

"We're from Israel and we have managed to work here for two years so far."

Elisa saw that Jordan and Alfie were barely following the conversation, that familiar jet-lagged look, eyes glazed over, dreaming of bed.

"Hey, I'm sorry, you guys, you must be so tired. You've skipped a night, right?" Jordan and Alfie looked up, both trying to smile. "You need to fight it, guys. You can't sleep yet. You need to wait till night time. Why don't you get showered and changed and we'll make you some tea. You're from the FREW, right? I can tell from your tea-drinking accents."

"Thank you so much," said Shaylie. "That would be lovely. There's so much to take in. And so many questions to ask. We still haven't bought any supplies."

"No worries, we can help you with that. We're going to get dressed now. See you back here in an hour?"

With that, the two Israeli girls, one quiet, one not, retired to their upstairs room to get dressed whilst the Mays retreated to their empty tatami room, empty but for a clothes rail, a fan and a low wooden coffee table.

As Shaylie closed the sliding shōji door behind them, she was about to compliment the friendliness of their new housemates, when Alfie offered the teen viewpoint.

"That was weird."

"In what way were those lovely girls weird?"

"Eating toast in their dressing gowns in a shared kitchen at four in the afternoon."

"So what? Maybe they feel at home."

"They are well-paid, but they spend the day at home?"

Jordan weighed in. "You have to admit, it's a bit strange, love."

"Nonsense! It could be their day off. Or they could work unsociable hours, whatever it is that they do."

"Isn't it a bit strange that you don't know what they do, love? Given that you asked them and that is the only question that they didn't answer?"

Chapter Fourteen

Shaylie had been exasperated at the attitude of the rest of her family to the first friendly people they'd met. She was making a big effort and she would not give in.

Whilst Jordan was first off to the shower, Shaylie decided to keep Alfie awake and engaged by going through with him the information that Kuni had left them in a bulging envelope. There was much to take in.

Nerima Private High School offers the exemplary delivery of the Imperial curriculum to the elite young people of the modern world. It prepares our young people for moral and economic success in the world's dominant nation state, promoting Japanese values and the knowledge necessary for our children to work to maintain Japan's position at the top of the social, economic and political world order.

Shaylie continued to read aloud: *Students will learn our language and those of other leading Asian powers, along with mathematics, science, Imperial history and citizenship, through the medium of the Emperor's Japanese.*

Lessons will commence at 8am, Monday to Friday, and finish at 5pm. All students will wear the school's navy blue uniform, white socks and black shoes, and will carry the standard issue satchel, containing note books and writing and mathematical equipment. Lunch will be served at 1pm in the classroom by the students, under the supervision of the class teacher.

Shaylie saw that Alfie had ceased to listen and so strayed from the prospectus to skim read the enclosed letter with specific instructions for Alfie. He was to catch the Seibu-Ikebukuro line train from Shakuji-kōen to Nerima and arrive by 7:30am on his first morning for his induction. The reality of the situation had begun to sink in. He blinked hard and blinked again.

"How am I going to manage in a school where all the lessons are in Japanese?"

Shaylie knew there was little she could say, but she continued, animated and warm.

"You'll get used to it and you'll learn quickly. They play football and other sports. You'll soon fit in, just like you did at home."

"I don't want this."

"I know, my darling, and life will be hard for me, too, at first, but this is for our family, to support your dad and to improve our lives."

Jordan had caught the end of the conversation. As always, his voice was quiet and measured.

"And I appreciate the efforts both of you will make. We'll get through this."

Still tearful, Alfie left the room to shower quickly before allowing his mother to do the same. When she returned to the room through the kitchen, Elisa was preparing tea as Aaliyah looked on, smoking a white-filtered cigarette.

As they sat around the kitchen table, the remaining residents of the gaijin house returned home, one-by-one introducing themselves briefly as they crossed the house's focal point to access the shower.

"Everyone is friendly here," said Elisa, "you'll get to know them later."

"They don't say much," observed Shaylie.

"Working life for a *gaijin* is pretty intense, you'll see. When you get home after an hour or more of standing on a packed train of sweating locals who are staring at you and talking about you, you need time to have a shower and unwind."

"You're not selling it to us. It sounds grim."

"Only to start with. It's sticks and stones. You're not in any danger and you get used to it. It just washes over you."

"So foreigners don't get attacked? They just get stared at?"

"Pretty much. Attacks are rare. Not everyone is against us. The older generations mostly are, but there are some younger people who are interested in life beyond Japan. And there are local people who appreciate that we do have our uses."

"So," Shaylie saw her opportunity, "what use do you two have? What is it that you do?"

Suddenly, Jordan and Alfie were alert. The conversation was becoming interesting.

"We're hostesses."

As Elisa pronounced their job title, this was the cue for Aaliyah to stand up and say to Elisa, with urgency, "we should be going."

"What does that involve?" asked Shaylie swiftly, as Elisa also began to follow her friend's lead.

"Basically," her tone suggesting a long story, summarised in a short sentence, "it's like bar work but you're not behind the bar. I'll tell you more another day, but we have to get round to Okachimachi by 7. Don't wait up!"

With that, the two girls departed, one in a dress, one in a short skirt and revealing top, both in high heels and heavily made up. Behind them, in the kitchen, they left the Mays with more questions than answers. The desire to ask about eating out was overshadowed by the mysteries of hostessing.

Chapter Fifteen

"*Irasshaimase!*" called all waiters and chefs in unison, as the Mays entered the *soba-ya*.

They had returned to the square in front of the station as the light began to fade and plumped for a small restaurant with sliding wooden doors. It had won them over with the window display of plastic models of each dish on the menu. The menu itself had photos of these models next to the name of the dish and the price. Jordan concluded that, in the absence of language skills, they would simply be able to point out their order.

The gestures and body language of the fifty-something waiter who greeted them helped to soften the ordeal. There was no welcoming smile, but at the very least their custom was accepted as they were shown to their table, no booking necessary.

The noodle shop was in the traditional Japanese style. Alfie was shocked to see that the table top was two feet from the floor, where cushions rather than chairs denoted each place. A cursory glance around the small room revealed local customers, legs folded uniformly beneath them, heads bowed into bowls of noodles. The Mays attempted the *seiza* position without success, Jordan and Shaylie, opposite one another, finally opting for legs folded beside them, whilst Alfie sat, legs extended into the empty place next to his father. Small Pyrex glasses of iced water and menus were deposited in front of them as the air, thick with umami smells and cigarette smoke, stirred the hunger within.

The leather-bound menus contained page after page of laminated images: bowls of noodles in broth, plates of stir-fried noodles, bamboo baskets of plain noodles with accompanying dipping sauce, thick white noodles, thin green and brown and grey noodles, myriad side dishes including deep fried tofu, tempura and even *furaido potato*, otherwise known as fries. For Alfie it was simple: stir-fried noodles with chips, his parents more adventurously opting for bowls of noodles in broth with an egg floating at the top, gradually poaching itself. Their waiter returned and, once they had pointed out their choices, he asked them, "*Biru wa?*"

Shaylie had got the hang of this already, nodding and raising two fingers in response to what she confidently supposed was an invitation to order beer. She then pointed at Alfie and said simply and slowly, "Coca Cola".

"*Kashikomarimashita,*" followed by a shallow bow and a retreat to the open kitchen confirmed that communication had been successful. Spirits were raised until the food and drink arrived.

"Where's the cutlery?" asked Alfie. Having worked out that the disposable chopsticks had to be broken into two at the base, the next half hour was a race, trying to shovel the noodles mouthwards before they went cold. There was no time for conversation, no break in their concentration and the chit-chat of their fellow diners was muffled by the sucking and slurping around the room. Alfie's cultural sensitivities were embarrassed. His parents gradually allowed their heads to dip closer to the noodles. They vacuumed them up from the bowl, periodically posing the chopsticks to lift the bowl to their lips. They succeeded in paying the bill and got up to leave, agreeing that the evening had been a positive step forwards in cultural integration.

They had perhaps spoken too soon. As they reached the door, they heard the word *gaijin* followed by some laughter behind them. The hard, wet globule of saliva and mucus which hit Alfie, first onto the square, in the face was a reminder of how little progress had been made. A group of men in their 20s, perhaps some in their 30s, stood in the road a few yards away. As Alfie stood in shock, they began to move towards the Mays, sneering, the word *gaijin* again evident in their loud and lairy speech. Jordan and Shaylie took one arm each, turned Alfie homewards and increased their cadence. Glances over Jordan's shoulder revealed that the danger was not over, but as the three of them broke into a run, sarcastic laughter revealed that this had simply been a successful exercise in intimidation.

As they regained the gaijin house, Alfie was a lost child in need of encouragement and understanding. He slumped, blinking, at the kitchen table, oblivious to the activity around him. His dad stood over him and his mother prepared tea. An unspeaking pair of Chinese housemates - or were they Korean? - cleared away the remains of their meal.

"We'll get through this," said Jordan.

"You didn't get spat at."

"It could have been any of us," said Shaylie.

"But it was me. This time and at the airport. Is this a better life?"

His parents attempted to assuage his fears, to repair the psychological damage and to limit the consequences of this setback.

Shaylie joined them at the table. "Here's some tea. This'll make you feel better."

Jordan felt Alfie tense at the trivial. "Come on, son. Settle down. We're in it together."

"I'm going to bed," said Alfie, jolting the table with his abrupt departure.

His parents were left to mop up spilt tea.

Chapter Sixteen

Shaylie had just got back from the station on their first Monday morning and was deep in thought. She had been considering the extent of the ordeals awaiting her loved ones today, when her mind took her back to how she had reached this point in her life.

A plethora of friends, both imaginary and real, had given Shaylie a happy childhood. As an only child, loved by her mother and adored by her father, she had conformed to her strict Scottish upbringing. Just like her son a generation later, she had failed to be a typical teenager, presenting her parents with few worries and passing her bacc.

In turn, she had felt close to her parents and her relationship with her mother was full of joy. The time spent with her father, however, had been tinged with melancholy. He had struggled on and off with depression, regretting his move south and the life that they might have had in an independent Scotland. She had tried so hard, she made him smile, he even laughed, but his eyes could never hide his desire for a different life.

He had carried his regrets into old age, into retirement. When she had married and moved to Harwich, the visits tailed off. They had called in now and then, had lunch and beach walks, played with Alfie. But his good health in old age had meant, to Shaylie, the prolongation of regret, her relationship with her beloved father dominated by the sadness in his eyes.

Her thoughts returned to Alfie's first day at school, when Elisa's lively *Ohayō gozaimasu* jolted her from her reverie. Most of the other housemates had left for work when Elisa and Aaliyah returned home from their shift in Okachimachi.

"Hi, hello, what did you say?" If Shaylie had the days to herself, she was determined to be of use. Becoming a Japanese speaker was at the top of her list.

"*Ohayō gozaimasu*," repeated Elisa, this time echoed by Aaliyah. Elisa explained. "It means *good morning*. You say it the first time you see someone each day. Bow your head when you say it."

Shaylie tried it out. "Do you want some breakfast?" she then asked, as she poured milk onto her bowl of cornflakes.

"No, thanks, they give us breakfast at the end of our shift," said Elisa, "but I'd love some of that tea."

Through her resting sad face, Aaliyah nodded in response to Shaylie's raised eyebrows and Shaylie placed Lipton's tea-bags into two more mugs.

"So you two work all night, then?"

"Sure, yeah, work all night, sleep most of the day. This is our bedtime cup of tea."

"Sounds tough."

"Naah, it's just a different rhythm of life. Everyone works hard here. We just work different hours to most people."

"I still don't quite understand what it is you do."

"It's complicated," said Aaliyah.

Elisa qualified this. "It's more easily misunderstood than complicated, I'd say."

Aaliyah scowled.

What could be misunderstood when foreign women worked as hostesses in a bar all night? Shaylie wanted to know in the way that people wanted to read the stories about sexual deviance in the local press.

"I'd love to hear about it," she said, without looking too curious.

"We'll tell you all about it this afternoon, once we've had a sleep."

"Won't you be getting ready to go out again?" asked Shaylie, hanging on to the company for as long as possible.

"Not tonight. Monday's our night off. The club is closed. What are you up to today?"

"I don't know where to start. I want to get used to being here, learn Japanese, fit in, but I don't know how. I need to get dinner for Jordan and Alfie later, but until then I'm at a loose end. What is there to do?"

"There is so much to do," said Elisa, "you should explore. Don't worry about the language. It'll begin to sink in and I can recommend you a local teacher. You could join a small class. But today, you should get out of Shakuji. It's like a goldfish bowl here. Get yourself on a train into Ikebukuro and see how the pace changes. You can be anonymous there, there are so many people. You get into a lift in the station and it takes you straight up into the Seibu department store. It's massive. Have a look around, get some lunch, then go down to the basement and do your food shopping for tonight's meal. You'll have a great day."

Aaliyah cracked a smile at last. "I love Ikebukuro. Go to Bic Camera. The gadgets are amazing."

"Thanks," said Shaylie, "I'll give it a wee go."

As Aaliyah and Elisa finished their tea and announced the arrival of bedtime, Shaylie sought reassurance.

"See you later?" she asked.

"We get up around 4 and hang out in the kitchen," said Elisa. "We'll come and watch you cook and tell you all about hostessing."

Curiosity about every aspect of life here was gnawing away inside of Shaylie, and hostessing really was an itch that needed scratching.

Chapter Seventeen

It had taken Alfie most of the weekend to recover from jetlag and to adjust his body clock. This morning, it had not been confused circadian rhythms, but rather first day nerves which had had him awake before first light. His mother had complimented him on his quiet acceptance of today's ordeal, although it had been guilt which had stopped him from complaining. His father was also suffering from first day nerves. He had said virtually nothing throughout a weekend with no further incident. His mother was acting as life coach to both.

By the time Alfie reached the eastbound platform at 7am on Monday morning, he was further accustomed to the stares which, this morning, were as much for his casual dress as for his white face. He was surrounded by suits. Dark suits, white shirts, black hair and shoes. He could not have stood out more. His mother had walked him to the station and helped him to buy a ticket. He now found himself on a packed platform, wondering how to react to the commuter crush before him. He had seen one train come into the station, already full, and an extraordinary number of queuing passengers crowbar themselves into the carriages. At each set of automatic doors, an official with white gloves pushed in briefcases and body parts which impeded the closing action.

Amongst the boarding disorder, Alfie could see that he needed to pick a queue at a designated spot on the platform. In the short time, perhaps two minutes, until the arrival of the next train, his queue became longer and longer. In order to contain the lengthening queue within the platform, Alfie's fellow travellers edged closer and closer together. His face centimetres from the pate of the man in front, he could feel breath on the nape of his neck. The train pulled in and the queue shuffled forwards. The queue shuffled forwards but the person at the front stood fast behind the yellow safety line. The train stopped and the queue, as one, moved to the opening doors. Alfie was squeezed and lifted towards the train.

Looking through the cropped hair of the suit in front of him, Alfie saw that there was no room on the train. Regardless, the queue continued to move. Alfie was carried into a packed carriage by the queuing commuters behind him. As he landed inside the carriage, those behind him pushed for access. Hands pushing against the doorframe, they levered themselves in. Briefcases and shoulders were pushed in by white gloves and the crush intensified. Bodies compressed one another to allow the doors to close, first the train doors, then the doors of the vacuum tubes. Despite the crush, Alfie shivered as he was hit by the contrast of the conditioned air against the humidity outside. It was hard to breathe.

The process was repeated through a handful of stops. Each time Alfie fought for greater comfort. 90° would get his head away from the armpit in which he found his nose. So many commuters held the grab handles on hanging straps above, so many armpits were exposed. As the train slowed into another station, he recognised the name *Nerima* over the tannoy. He fought his way to the opening doors and fell out onto the platform. Standing away from the crowds, he recovered his breath, pulled out the map from the information pack and made his way to the correct exit.

Reserved and level-headed, Alfie had been well-liked through primary and middle school, although he had never understood why. He appeared comfortable in his skin of reticence but he lacked confidence. Nobody would have guessed this as he strode with grace through the ticket barriers and followed the street plan.

The school was a few short minutes from the station and he followed early arrivals through the gates and into the main entrance. He stood on the concrete foyer as uniformed students, all of a similar age, all Japanese, kicked off their smart, black shoes. They stepped onto the elevated laminate wooden flooring, picked up their outdoor shoes and placed them in small wooden lockers, from which they retrieved their indoor slippers. Alfie was stuck. There was clearly a procedure to follow but he was not yet an insider. He needed help. This finally arrived in the form of a woman, roughly the age of his mother, who beckoned him to approach a locker. With stockinged feet and shoes in hand, he was able to take a pair of guest slippers. Beckoning again, she led him to a comfortable waiting room within the school's administration complex. There, Alfie was presented with a large cardboard box by his guide, who then bowed, reversed to the door and closed it behind her.

Conspicuous in his casual clothes, Alfie did not need encouragement to change into the uniform. It was an opportunity to begin to blend in. The material was thick and heavy. He buttoned the collarless white shirt right up to the neck, pulled on the navy blue trousers and, finally, closed the press-studs on the navy blue jacket, again collarless. The embroidered epaulettes made him feel like a sailor and attached to the front was almost certainly a name badge. The katakana script was square and functional and not at all like the decorative ideograms which he had come to recognise as Japanese. Even the writing systems were discriminatory. In the bottom of the box was a faux leather, navy blue, standard issue satchel, fully equipped. As he was slinging it over his shoulder, the door reopened.

It was to be the only time English was addressed to him in a civil manner until his return home later that afternoon.

"Hello, Alfie May-*san*, *konnichiwa*."

"Hello, sir," came the tentative reply, with an untidy attempt at a bow, following his mother's suggestion that morning.

"Sorry, my English. Japanese doesn't learn English now. At school, I learn English, long times ago. I am Kojima, *kyōto-sensei*, deputy head. Like you say *sir*, we say *sensei*. You can say *sensei* to all teacher."

Kojima's welcoming manner and willingness to communicate was a comfort to the nervous new entrant to Nerima High School. Alfie was the same age as other first year students and had arrived at the start of the new academic year, running from April to March. He would be the only one in his class, however, who had not moved directly from the neighbouring Nerima Junior High School. He would also be the only non-Japanese, the only *gaijin*, the only outsider.

"Headteacher Ishii-*kōchō-sensei* not speaking English so I help you," continued Kojima, his bespectacled, smiling, fifty-something face crowned by neatly combed grey hair, peppered with memories of his younger years. "It is difficult time for foreigner, but we want welcome you. Many fellow student are also member of Matsucorp family. You will be in *ichi-nen-sei-shī-kumi*, first year class C. First, here is your timetable."

Alfie took the A4 sheet and noted that Mr Kojima had diligently pencilled in English translations of the subjects. "All lesson are in Japanese. I think this is hard for you at first. *Gambatte kudasa*! Please try hard."

"*Arigatō*," Alfie began to try with a single word of thanks. "Do you have a map of the school?"

"I think you don't need map, Alfie May-*san*. In Japan, all lesson are in same room. Teacher move, student stay."

Whilst this would simplify Alfie's school life, he could already sense the claustrophobic school day with nowhere to run.

"Now we go to class C's room."

His induction over, Alfie followed Kojima out of the waiting room, the safe waiting room, and into the corridors of silent hostility.

Alfie had thought that the stares in public would prepare him for more of the same but, in an educational bubble where he was a minority of one, the *gaijin* experience intensified. He was rid of his conspicuous hoody and jeans, his trousers showed an inch of sock as did those of the other boys he passed, but the one item of uniform he lacked was the standard issue black hair. As 8am approached, the corridors and staircases were busy, students moving towards classrooms, immobile pockets of friends chatting. Most stared, some pointed, a few raised open hands in front of mouths in attempts to disguise whispered remarks. Soon the whole student population would be aware of the tall, white-skinned, brown-haired new boy.

A large '2' on the wall denoted their arrival on the first floor corridor. Kojima pointed out the toilets and led Alfie to the classroom of first year class C. Alfie's desk was designated by a label with identical script to that on his enamel badge. Once again, with a shallow bow, Kojima wished Alfie *"Gambatte kudasai"*, this time without the translation, and withdrew.

Now Alfie was alone in a well-populated classroom. The boys wore the same as him, the girls substituted trousers for heavy, pleated skirts to just below the knee. He was even more aware of the stares now, from within the room and without. The blinking intensified. The corridor wall consisted of windows, as did the wall opposite which looked onto the school yard. The teacher's desk was on a dais at the end of the room nearest the door. Forty individual desks were arranged in neat rows and, although the desks on either side were not yet occupied, from his central position he could see the pattern. He would be seated with a girl on either side.

A plain girl with bobbed hair took her seat next to Alfie with a brief k*onnichiwa*, as the maths teacher entered the room. Immediately all rose and waited for him to assume his position. The girl in the desk nearest the door projected her voice. *"Kiyōtsuke. Rei!"* With that, every student bowed deeply, asking the teacher in unison for the benefit of his wisdom, *"Yoroshiku onegaishimasu"*. Once seated, the student at the front of each row collected exercise and text books and distributed them. Alfie picked up that the teacher had introduced himself as Suzuki. He was relieved to be able to work through trigonometric problems, occasionally checking that he was doing the same as his neighbour. For the first hour the inevitable language barrier was avoided.

By the end of an incomprehensible hour of history he was pleased to have arrived at break. He took a deep breath, turned to his neighbour as she got up to leave and attempted an air of confidence.

"*Konnichiwa,*" he said. He then pointed at his chest and added "Alfie".

"Aruhi? Aruhi?" she replied, pointing to herself and saying "Noriko".

She could call him anything she liked. He had made contact, the first step in integration, in defeating solitude. In a shallow bow, she retreated into a giggling group of waiting friends as they followed the rest of the class into the corridor, towards toilets, staircase and school yard. Alfie suppressed his desire to urinate, more concerned with remaining on the fringe of the class group, and followed hundreds of students onto the shale playground. Respite from loneliness had been temporary as Alfie now contemplated a twenty-minute break standing in a group of one. He had come unequipped, the majority of his fellow students stood drinking water and eating rice cakes and *onigiri*. The smells of lunch in preparation, wafting over the yard, reminded him of his hunger.

Students stood in gender-divided groups which Alfie did not have the courage to approach. Not a single boy had shown any inclination to befriend him, so he wandered towards the shale football pitch. He was drawn towards a common language, one he was familiar with, one he loved, one which did not require words. The plan? Hang around on the touchline, wait to be invited. But the invitation did not come. They knew he was there. Some of them glanced at him. They knew what he hoped for, but they were not inclined to realise his hopes. He held back the tears. Hungry and ostracised, he glanced back towards the friendship groups nearer the school building. He noticed a group of boys, possibly older than him, looking his way. He felt that they were talking conspiratorially but could not be sure, their close-cropped hair adding a hint of menace. He turned his attention back to the football.

In years past, the youth of Japan would have rushed to invite a Westerner, a representative of the greatest leagues in the world, to join in. But much had changed. In recent decades, there had been a big influx of foreign footballers into the big Asian leagues. Talent had been tapped from the former powers in Europe and South America. The JPL accepted only the very best on huge salaries to play alongside their home-grown talent. The JFA was convinced that their 6 + 5 rule, keeping *gaijin* in the minority, was instrumental in their two consecutive World Cup wins in the 40s. Alfie did not doubt it.

He glanced at his watch. He needed to visit the toilets and be on time for the resumption of lessons. He made his way back across the yard. The intimidating group of boys had moved on, so he put his head down and walked back into the building, switching back to indoor shoes and retracing his steps to the first floor. Finished at the urinal in the deserted boys' toilets, he turned to the hand basins. His progress was blocked by a wall of older boys, the same boys he had noticed outside. He straightened his back, lifted his head and blinked again and again. He was a little taller than all of them, but he was outnumbered. Their faces were sneering; in unison they took a step towards him, then another step, forcing him closer to the urinals. Alfie was then subjected to what he could only assume was a stream of insults and abuse. He heard the word *gaijin* again and again. The gist was clear. It was five against one. The middle one took one final step forwards and shoved Alfie in the chest. As his lower back hit the urinal and his head bounced off the wall, he braced himself for more, but what came instead was the bell and an instantaneous evacuation of the toilets. He straightened his uniform and hurried back to the classroom. He was already sitting at his desk, shaking, when the rest of the class came in from the yard.

Chapter Eighteen

Half an hour before Alfie and Shaylie, Jordan had experienced the same overcrowding and curious stares on the opposite platform, battling to travel two stops west to Hōya. No map was necessary. He simply followed the uniformed Matsucorp workers on the five-minute walk to the domineering factory which had swallowed up farmland and rural houses.

The untidy yet uniform arrangement of houses and small businesses was indistinguishable from that outside any suburban station. Wood and corrugated iron screamed resistance to the modernisation of concrete render and brick. Past the 7-11, past the Family Mart, the stationer's and the tobacconist's, they poured along grey streets until it rose before them, benevolent, overbearing, imperious.

Through the gates and inside, it was clear to see that the Bathside factory had been modelled on this one, which was larger but almost identically organised. The difference was its shine, its glitter, its presence. Kuni's envelope had contained a pre-activated security pass which Jordan was able to swipe to clock on and to access the male locker room. The name label on his locker matched the katakana transliteration of his name on his security badge and on the enamel badge on his uniform, which he found in his locker. There were stares, but not of the intensity experienced by Alfie. It was obvious that Jordan was expected, if not welcomed.

Pulling on his boiler suit, Jordan considered how lucky he was to be part of the last generation to have decent employment opportunities. He was aware of his academic limitations, had favoured maths over English and had eased through middle school graduation in the middle of the pack. His next decision had been easy, eschewing the academic baccalaureate in favour of technical high school. His course had been centred on engineering and his imagination was caught by the robotics modules. He had excelled in this area and, at eighteen, had apprenticeship offers which would have taken him closer to the London bubble. However, Jordan was not only a homeboy but also a true devotee of robotic advancement. Matsucorp's offer would not only keep him close to home but would also give him the chance to use world-leading Japanese technology. His course was set.

Early arrival afforded him the luxury of a self-guided tour before the factory started production at 8am. He found his way around easily. It was a facility with greater production capacity, but operationally identical. He noted more workstations and a greater number of limited access areas which were not for the like of him, but it did not take long for him to find his post, again name-labelled. There was no plan for an induction. At 8, he would start work as if in Bathside, his colleagues had been briefed, it would be seamless.

Jordan also noted a busy cleaning and maintenance staff. A green Matsucorp uniform labelled each as unskilled. They were white and black immigrants, probably from Europe and Africa, and they stopped work in surprise at the sight before them. A non-Asian in an orange uniform.

Not one of them would have dared question Jordan but, oblivious to the extent of their shock, he was happy to engage them in conversation.

"Morning. I'm Jordan."

They looked at one another, wondering whether a response was acceptable.

Finally, after a lengthy pause, a tall, black man spoke in a FREW West Country accent.

"Hey, Jordan."

The other three men remained silent, hanging on to their buckets and mops.

"We're kind of surprised to see you in the same colour as the natives."

"I've been transferred from Bathside Bay."

"When they closed down FREW production, we weren't expecting transfers."

"I'm the only one here in Tokyo. There's one in Nagoya and one in Sendai. That's it."

"That's a new approach. I'm Gerald and these three guys are Pavel, Emilio and Jürgen. We all started together about a year ago. They speak a bit of English and we're all trying to pick up a bit of Japanese. I guess your Japanese must be pretty good."

"Not a word," replied Jordan. "I only knew I was coming ten days ago and I haven't had time to learn anything. How did you guys get this gig?"

"We got picked out from the camp at Yokohama. We're all boat refugees. We arrived within days of one another and we had all been over a year in the camp before Matsucorp took us on. Some tall, gangly fellow in a suit with a posh English accent showed up and picked us out. Very lucky. I guess he didn't pick us for our brains."

It was clear why they had been selected. They were all over six feet tall. Shoulders wide and muscular, they filled out their oversized, green boiler suits.

"No, I guess not," said Jordan. "You look like a strong bunch."

Gerald continued. "There is one other thing we've got in common. We all came alone. No families, no ties. The men with wives and children don't get a look in. I guess you're on your own, too."

"No," said Jordan, "I'm here with my wife and son."

"Well, you must have skills they really want."

"Maybe. Or maybe it makes them look good. They've told me to expect a press photo call at our gaijin house."

"So you're in a gaijin house, too."

"Yeah, bit basic, isn't it?"

"I can assure you, Jordan, that it is luxury. Don't knock it. You have obviously been nowhere near a holding camp."

"That bad, eh?"

"Worse. But they're not likely to broadcast it. It's on wasteland on the coast. Barbed wire fence, one gate in, one gate out. Watchtowers and armed guards. The guards outside the perimeter have dogs. People are crammed into tents, just a groundsheet to sleep on, no mattresses. Rice and tofu brought in daily, sometimes vegetables if you are lucky, not much to go around. But the worst thing of all? It's dirty. They were not prepared for us. No running water for the first few months and even now it's intermittent. Everyone stinks and loads get diseases. People are dying out there, but you will never see that in the newspapers. Oh, no. Gaijin houses are pure luxury."

Gerald's three colleagues nodded and mumbled their agreement at his description.

"So do they pay you OK?" Jordan was curious.

"Peanuts. But they feed us generously in our lunch break, seven days a week. Saturday and Sunday are half days but we eat before we leave. We can eat enough for the whole day. It's more nutrition than we've had in years."

"But there's no production at the weekend."

"That's when we clean. All morning. Uninterrupted. That's why it's sparkling."

Gerald's warm smile sparkled like the factory walls. He was glowing, basking in the rich hand his new life had dealt him, delighting in the opportunity to work his fingers to the bone seven days per week in return for food and shelter. Jordan was also revelling in this contact with other English speakers, fellow immigrants. Gerald's colleagues, however, had begun to fidget from one foot to the other, looking shiftily up and down the corridors.

"So what's up with them?" Jordan had noticed their concerned demeanour.

"We're supposed to be working. They don't tolerate chat here."

"I don't want to get you into trouble. Maybe we'll catch up at lunchtime."

"Our lunch is before yours. We're not allowed to eat with the oranges."

"It's like that, is it? That's a shame. Maybe after work?"

"Not unless you want to hang around for ages. We're here cleaning up long after you've gone home. That's just the way it is," said Gerald with a shrug, still smiling, "but I'm sure our paths will cross."

"It was good to chat," said Jordan, as the green boiler suits got back to work and he made his way to his post, wanting to be prepared and in position for the commencement of production at exactly 8am.

The extent of Jordan's armoury in his attempts to win over his new colleagues was "*Konnichiwa*", a nod and a smile. Two of the three were returned by nearby operatives, the smile would take longer, perhaps much longer, thought Jordan.

Matsucorp had been sure to remove barriers to Jordan's job. They had attached a standard QWERTY keyboard to his workstation, though the buttons on his control panel were labelled in Japanese. This was not a problem. The set-up was identical to back home and Jordan could do this in his sleep. His screen awoke as he touched his mouse and he was welcomed in both Japanese and English, before the operating system assumed standard workday mode purely in the only language which he could understand. Within minutes, Jordan was playing his part in automobile production as if he were still sitting in Bathside Bay. Time flew and his screen told him at 10:25am that tea would be served in the orange mess in five minutes.

Just as in Bathside, the system shut down across the factory at 10:30am for a fifteen minute break. He saw that men significantly outnumbered women, more than at home, as one hundred or more orange boiler suits converged on the capacious dining facility. Asian, African and European women in green served hot green tea and a variety of chilled teas, along with rice crackers and other strange-looking biscuit-type snacks. There were ten serving hatches and the toilets were equally numerous, allowing the mess to cater for the needs of all before a prompt resumption at 10:45am. There was just time for pockets of colleagues to gather around the circular, white melamine tables to exchange weekend tales.

Jordan sat at a vacant table with green tea and a cracker, watching the bustle of the speed break and observing that he was the only non-Asian skilled worker in the Tokyo factory.

Again he felt marginalised as he listened to enthusiastic conversation at this table and at that.

He was not a natural linguist but soon started to notice differences in tone to what he had become used to over the past few days. Was it conversational variation in subject matter or was he hearing different languages? He questioned whether he was hearing other Asian languages coming from a couple of tables in his vicinity. Visually there were no differences, to his eye at least, in the men and the women at these tables but, he thought, these people could as easily be Chinese or Korean as Japanese. And was he simply noticing linguistic patterns or could he detect relaxed chatter from some tables and discontented discussion from others?

The break was over almost as soon as it had begun and Jordan was pleased to be distracted from his uncertainties by the resumption of work. Another smooth, unproblematic session of robotic manipulation took him to lunchtime and a return to the orange mess. A full hour's break this time afforded Jordan the opportunity to try to begin his integration as a member of the work force.

A buffet had been set up along one wall of the dining hall and, having collected a chilled barley tea from one of the serving hatches, he took a tray and a sectioned plate and made his way past myriad food choices, none of them labelled. Strong umami aromas emanated from the rice, noodles, stir-fried vegetables, meats, curries and pickles on offer. Oblivious to cultural *faux pas*, he selected what was, even to him, an odd mixture of food stuffs and sat down at a table which was sparsely populated with a handful of more mature workers. He surmised that the younger colleagues, tending to sit in larger, more animated groups, had accessed a modified curriculum where European languages were a thing of the past. He hoped that older skilled workers may have had some previous experience of English lessons. Though language skills were limited, he was not entirely disappointed.

"*Konnichiwa*," a nod and a smile, Jordan once again tried his three-pronged way in.

As he began to struggle with his chopsticks, his persistence reaped some reward.

"I think you are Jordan May-*san* and you speak English, aren't you?"

"How did you know my name?" asked Jordan, picking up his tea to wash down the rice which had stuck to his teeth.

"We know on Friday, one Englishman come today from *Baasusaido* factory. All other worker are from north-east Asia. We can recognise you easily."

"I'm pleased to meet you. Your English is good."

"No. Not good. But older Japanese remembers some English from junior high school. Do you like Japan?"

"I've only been here for four days so I'm just getting used to it, but your country seems very nice. It was good of Matsucorp to give me a job here. What's your name?"

"I am Eguchi. Matsucorp give you job because you are best in *Baasusaido*. I know. Matsucorp only give job to foreigner who is best. Most job go to Japanese worker. This is Japanese company. You thank Matsucorp, it is good, you are lucky. Other foreigner should thank Matsucorp also, but many complain. It is not good."

After each set of staccato, heavily-accented utterances, Eguchi lowered his small, grey head into his plate and shovel-sucked in another mouthful of noodles whilst listening attentively to Jordan's response.

"I have no reason to complain, Eguchi-*san*. But what about the others? Where are they from?"

"Some worker are from China but most foreign worker come from Korea. Matsucorp take best worker from top Korean car manufacturer. For them it is not such big lifestyle change. Not like you, Jordan May-*san*."

"I guess not. But I told you, I am happy. I will adapt to a change in lifestyle and my family will, too. Why are they complaining? What is there to be unhappy about?" Now Jordan was curious.

"There is nothing to complain. Just small detail. Japanese company look after worker and worker's family. Nothing to complain. Complain is bad attitude. It is not Japanese way."

If Jordan were to find out more, he would have to ask elsewhere. For now, he would cultivate his new acquaintance and the other men in their fifties around the table. They had not found the confidence to try their English, too, but their concentration had been locked on this exchange, encouraging their compatriot and Jordan with serious nods and, occasionally, the faintest evidence of a smile.

"Well I am happy to be here and I am happy to speak to you. I am sorry I can't speak Japanese, but I will learn," said Jordan.

"Japanese is very difficult," said Eguchi, as he smiled ironically with his compatriots at the idea of a foreigner conquering their language.

They rose in unison and bowed.

"Now we smoke outside in smokers' area. You want smoke with us, Jordan May-*san*?"

Circumstances sometimes required sacrifices. The only Englishman was in a minority of non-smokers and instinct told Jordan to do what was necessary to continue to propagate his new acquaintances. Instinct and politeness. As Jordan rose, touching the empty breast pocket of his boiler suit, one of Eguchi's silent friends offered Jordan his packet of Mild Sevens. Jordan took a cigarette and followed the flow of colleagues through the fire doors onto a smokers' terrace, drenched in spring sunshine. The humidity hit as they left the sterile air-con behind. In the distance, beyond the perimeter fence, women young and old pushed baby buggies along the boulevard, lined with blossoming cherry trees.

Jordan attempted to appear at ease with his cigarette whilst limiting smoke inhalation, his comrades drawing greedily on their smokes, the lit end racing towards the white filter tip. Now they exchanged small talk, Jordan reciprocating questions about family and dropping polite compliments when asked about his meagre experiences of life in Japan.

Having felt inconspicuous thus far, he was not sure whether there was more staring now from the other end of the terrace. Was it that obvious that he didn't really know how to smoke? Or was there something else? Perhaps he was being oversensitive. His comrades certainly did not notice anything untoward, he thought.

He hoped that the unsmoked inch of cigarette had gone unnoticed, stubbing it out mid-conversation as many around him reached the end of their second chained smoke. He continued to glance around him as the workforce drifted back to post.

Chapter Nineteen

There followed two more hours of lessons, first science, then geography. Alfie could recognise the subject matter but lacked both the detailed knowledge and the communication skills to participate. He could not help but notice that Noriko had begun to glance at him with an air of concern which contrasted with her apparent indifference before break. He could only suppose that he was visibly as well as mentally shaken.

Lunch was a cultural revelation. At the bell the class rose as one, cleared their desks and moved them into groups. The students were going to eat together, as if in a restaurant, at large tables of eight students. Alfie attempted to decipher the system. Designated students made their way to the front of the room to collect essential items. One returned with a tablecloth, another with eight plates, a third with eight bowls and a fourth with eight sets of chopsticks. The group of eight nearest the door had wheeled two food trolleys in from the corridor and stood behind them at the front of the room. They donned aprons and chef hats and were armed with large serving spoons and ladles. Momentarily, Alfie had forgotten his misfortune as he marvelled at the orderly transformation of the classroom. Students were now lining up with plates and bowls as first year class C group 1 served lunch to their classmates.

Puppy-like, Alfie followed Noriko, successfully avoiding *faux pas* and returning to the table with a bowl of sticky rice and a plate of meat and vegetables, some of which he recognised. Pyrex glasses, a stainless steel jug of water and condiments were now in the middle of the table. Still struggling with chopsticks, Alfie worked quickly and with intense concentration to shovel the food into his mouth, his state of hunger barely allowing him to notice the tittering audience around the table.

Cocooned in a group of eight students, Alfie felt no menace and was as surprised as everyone when Noriko shrieked "*Yamere!*" and turned to the group directly behind them.

Quickfire chat around the table ensued as Noriko resumed her meal, wiping onto the tablecloth the small ball of sticky rice which she had picked out of her hair. Alfie was hit next and as Noriko saw him retrieve rice from his hair, she turned again to remonstrate loudly. A teacherly intervention from the front of the room achieved calm as they finished off their food, but there was soon uproar again as both he and his neighbour felt the water, flicked at the back of their heads. He felt helpless as Noriko again complained in her role as collateral damage in this undoubted attempt to provoke Alfie. He was soon following Noriko to the serving trolleys for dessert. Returning to his table with some kind of pudding and custard, he looked over to the offending table. Whilst the majority of the antagonist group had their heads in their bowls, one brazen boy, a mischievous look on his face, aimed a sly smile at Alfie, a barely distinguishable nod and the briefest wink. His proud look communicated as well as any words. Alfie ground his teeth.

They had nearly finished their dessert when a spoonful of custard found its mark. The shocked look around the table as Alfie wiped the thick, yellow sauce from his hair was accompanied by open mouths and gasps as he turned in rage and, for the first time in his life, landed a punch. The smirk had been replaced by a bloody lip. First to stand was the geography teacher. "*Oi de!*" he called, beckoning Alfie to the door and leading him away.

He would not need to struggle with citizenship or Japanese that afternoon. Within minutes he was seated back in the plush administration complex, on a chair outside the headteacher's study. He ran his hands through his hair again and again, the blinking more rapid than ever before. He was to meet Mr Ishii sooner than planned. Tears, shame and thoughts of deportation preoccupied the school's one and only migrant child.

Chapter Twenty

Alone again, Shaylie hopped onto a mid-morning train to Ikebukuro, the third busiest station in Japan and in the world. Crowd anonymity was guaranteed and the odd stare went unnoticed as Shaylie negotiated her way through the crowds. The busy Japanese brushed past her, navigating the enormous station, overtaking leisure-browsers such as Shaylie.

The uniformed lift attendant bowed a deep bow as Shaylie entered the capacious elevator which glided through the floors. Her high-pitched voice announced each floor and, Shaylie assumed, which departments were located at which level. Shaylie waited for the digital floor indicator to reach 12 and alighted at the very top of the Seibu department store. Over half an hour later, she had reached the other end of the top floor. No adjective could have enabled her to imagine how big this shop was. By the time she had browsed stationery, home computing, household goods, cosmetics and healthcare, she arrived on the 9th floor where she had no stomach for the books she couldn't read, nor the music shop, awash with the world renowned J-pops, derided by the English.

Descending to floor eight, Shaylie felt the need for lunch. Her problem was choice. Too much choice. She lost herself in a maze of restaurants and soon realised that she could either wander all day or be decisive. She was determined to integrate. It would be so easy to wander into a pizzeria, a trattoria, an Italian ristorante. But Shaylie wanted to master living, speaking and eating Japanese.

She strolled into a *soba-ya*. The noodles were her friends, but this time she would not choose a bowl of ramen in broth. No, she had noticed a dish on the menu last Friday which had intrigued her. She had seen other diners lifting plain brown noodles from a bamboo mat into a small bowl of dipping sauce, before shovelling them into their mouths. She pointed to the picture of *zaru-soba* on the menu, selected a bottle of Kirin beer and waited with her small Pyrex glass of iced water.

Service was quick, functional and courteous, but an unexpected item on her tray presented her with a dilemma. What part did the flat, metal implement and the curious root vegetable play in her consumption of this dish? For the first time since her arrival in Ikebukuro, she could feel other eyes upon her. This strange woman did not know how to eat. She examined the implement which looked, upon closer inspection, like a small grater. She turned the root around in her hand, its grey outside resembling ginger root but with a green middle, a green inside. The waitress came to her rescue. She took one object in each hand, held them over the small dipping bowl and mimed a rubbing action back and forth. Shaylie graciously inclined her head and, with a brief *thank you, arigatō*, took the two objects and grated the green root until a lumpy paste fell into the dipping sauce. The waitress smiled, pointed and said *wasabi*, which Shaylie soon understood to be a piquant root. Her mouth burned as she ate her buckwheat noodles. Kirin beer extinguished the fire.

Shaylie paid and decided it was time for some real shopping. Floors seven to one would be for another day. The lift took her into the basement where she found the food hall next to the station ticket machines. Again, the breadth and variety were mesmerising, but Shaylie walked past the counters and rows of prepared, packaged food until she came to the familiar supermarket fare of raw vegetables, fruit and synthesised meat, some of which she recognised.

Weighed down with the ingredients of a stir fry, a bag of rice and a few bottles of beer and soft drinks, Shaylie bought a train ticket, struggled through the barriers and onto a Shakuji-bound train. Elisa and Aaliyah were making toast in the kitchen when, exhausted, she let her shopping bags drop onto the kitchen table.

"So you went to Seibu," observed Elisa, noting the logo on the hessian bags.

"Wow," responded Shaylie, "just … wow!"

"Impressive, huh? Did you have a good time?"

"I'm glad I went. I'm tired."

"Overwhelming?"

"Just sooo big. Did you both sleep well?"

"Yeah, all set for Monday funday, now."

"Do you only ever eat toast?"

"We get well fed at work, plenty of nutritious Japanese food. We keep it simple when we're here."

"But you won't get fed tonight."

"No, but we'll have a few beers with some of the girls and then get a teriyaki-burger."

"That doesn't sound like much. Listen, I've bought plenty. Why don't you eat with us? I can make enough to go around. Perhaps you could show me how that rice cooker works."

"Sure thing, we'd love that, wouldn't we Aaliyah?" A nod and half a smile. "It looks like you're getting used to being a stay-at-home mum in Japan."

"I'm not sure I'll ever get used to that. I worked six days a week at home. I'm going to need to fill my time, learn some Japanese, find a part-time job."

Tired of talking about herself, Shaylie wanted to listen.

"So you were going to tell me about what you do."

The conversational ball was back in Elisa's court as Shaylie set about unpacking the shopping and preparatory chopping. She glanced at her two companions.

"There's not much to tell which you don't already know." What reason did Aaliyah have to want to abridge this part of the exchange of information?

"It's no big deal," said Elisa. "She wants to know."

Now turning to Shaylie, "We're bar hostesses. In a hostess bar. A members' club."

Shaylie waited for more. Elisa took a deep breath.

"We're paid for our company. We're paid to chat to businessmen, to socialise, to light their cigarettes and to encourage them to drink more from the bar."

"Go on," Shaylie's interest was piqued. Her chopping paused. She opened a bottle of beer and came to the table with three small glasses.

"There are ten of us," began Elisa, "and we sit at the bar when it opens. It's a trendy place with the bar to one side and it's dominated by comfy leather sofas, set around low coffee tables. The businessmen drift in from the offices around Okachimachi and they are allocated a booth. A few preferred clients get to choose who they want to drink with, but mostly it's the club manager who sends them one or two girls from the bar, foreign girls, mostly Asian. We ask them what they want to drink and then they have their drinks brought to their table. Sometimes they order snacking platters, too. We sit with them and chat to them, flatter them, share their food and drink, lean over them in our skimpy tops to light their cigarettes. After an hour, we rotate. You get the picture. We are hostesses. We look after the needs of our guests."

"And that's it? You get well paid to socialise?"

"The basic pay is OK and the tips can be very generous. You make sure they are having a really good time."

"And they have a good night and then they go home?"

"You know we are out all night. Many of them don't make it home. They are out all night, or they stagger off in the early hours and find themselves a capsule."

Shaylie had read about capsule hotels. Minimalist accommodation.

"There must be some who want more than a few drinks and a chat."

"Well, we try to be entertaining. We're a modern version of the geisha."

"But didn't geisha girls often give a lot more than company?"

"Not in most cases, but there were some, yeah."

"So there must be some of these businessmen who want to go beyond socialising."

"It's not prostitution, you know," interjected Aaliyah. But that is what it sounded like to Shaylie. At the very least it was a dodgy and dangerous gig.

Elisa continued. "Of course, there are some who want more, but very few get it."

"Very few, but not none at all, then?"

"The security men are very good. They enforce the number one rule, which is no touching. Well, minimal touching."

"But some girls take it further. How is that possible when there are security guards?"

"Some girls are favoured by certain rich clients and get invited to meet outside the club, go for meals, even go on trips away."

"And so you may be expected to have a relationship with a client?"

"Expected, no. But yes, you are right, some do accept invitations in the hope of lavish lifestyles and more money. But this is something we don't do. It's too risky. Very occasionally a girl will accept an invitation and never be seen again."

"They disappear?" Shaylie was horrified.

"They may disappear to a better life. They may find love. Who knows?"

Shaylie was visibly shocked but, nonetheless, hungry for more information.

"It must be hard to say *no*. Doesn't it piss off the clients?"

"*No* is the expectation. We have said *no* and heard nothing more about it. Security is excellent. We are well paid and well protected. Most hostesses last less than six months. We've been there for over a year. They are very happy with us."

"We do a good job." Aaliyah protested once more.

"I'm sure you do," said Shaylie. "It's fascinating," she added, draining her glass and returning to her cooking.

Elisa took a trip to the toilet, leaving the other two to their mutual awkwardness.

On her return, she stood in the doorway with her back to the kitchen and sparked up another cigarette. She drew a deep toke and, still turned away, said "So, Shaylie, how do you fancy a piece of the action?"

Aaliyah broke the stunned silence, as Shaylie turned from her chopping board to face them.

"Her?"

"Yes. Shaylie. Why not? She could do that. She wants to work. We could get her a trial." Turning to face them at last, Elisa suddenly wanted Shaylie on board.

"But … but … she's …"

"Old? I'm older than you, but I'm not old. I can get dolled up and flatter middle-aged men. And I bet there aren't many European hostesses. I'd be a novelty. I'm marketable."

Shaylie was twice horrified. Horrified by the thought that she might be interested in this kind of work, then horrified again that Aaliyah, with her face like a smacked arse, might think that she wasn't up to it.

"Aaliyah doesn't mean to be rude. But I'm glad you're interested. I didn't realise you'd be so up for it!"

"I'm not! That is not the kind of job I need to be doing."

"So you're not too old to be a hostess, but you are above the kind of work that we do." Aaliyah was not impressed.

"No, Aaliyah, that's not what I meant, but I am here with my husband and my son. There are meals to cook, evenings to spend together. I wouldn't manage night work."

Elisa had her answer ready. "You'd cope and so would they. They wouldn't need to know the job description. You can't spend your days browsing Japanese life when there is excitement to be had and money to be earned. You could work fewer shifts than us. You could be part-time."

"Well, I suppose it's not impossible," said Shaylie, turning back to her vegetables.

For the time being she would tell Elisa what she wanted to hear. She had no intention to titillate, part-time or otherwise.

Elisa was pleased. "There's no harm in asking. I'll talk to our boss."

Aaliyah struggled to hide her misgivings. Elisa turned to her. "It'll be fine. Shaylie's a babe. Tsubasa will like her. There's no harm in asking," she repeated.

Shaylie smiled as the large knife sliced through the flesh of the smallest aubergine she had ever seen.

As the conversation approached a close, Elisa had a curious afterthought, her smile no longer natural.

"This is our little secret, yeah? Best not tell your husband and son."

All traces of a smile disappeared as Shaylie turned to face them again.

"Given that it is highly unlikely that I will become a hostess, there is no need to say anything. But I don't keep secrets from my family."

Her response was a sober nod from each of the tipsy Israeli girls. Elisa crossed the kitchen floor, holding eye contact, and raised her eyebrows.

"Now," she said, "let's show you how to work this rice cooker."

Chapter Twenty-one

It had taken just half of the first day for them to break Alfie. Rage had given way to disappointment and shame as he worked his way through the box of tissues which had been placed on the chair next to him by a sympathetic office lady. The headteacher was making him wait.

"Alfie May-san?"

He looked up to see a small, well-presented woman of secretarial demeanour looking out from what he believed to be the head's office. Alfie stood and stepped from the ubiquitous laminate floor onto the first carpet he had seen since his arrival in Japan.

He was ushered, by the head's PA, through a compact but plush ante-room, past her desk on the right-hand side, to another door straight ahead of him. Another door labelled with a Japanese enamel sign. As the PA signalled for Alfie to enter, he took a deep breath and resolved to remember his cultural niceties.

The large, comfortable office was L-shaped and appeared empty; a grand desk with lamp, laptop and a multitude of papers was unattended at the far wall. As Alfie stepped inside, the office stretched out to the left to reveal a handful of formal, cushioned chairs around a conference table.

The headteacher rose. He was not alone. Alfie bowed as deeply as he felt able and, first clearing his throat, managed a shaky *Konnichiwa*. Ishii reciprocated the greeting with the shallowest of bows and gestured towards a chair next to his at the head of the table. He made no attempt to introduce the girl sitting opposite Alfie. Another student. Alfie was puzzled.

Nobody spoke. Alfie did not know where to look until the silence was broken by a knock at the door.

"*Hairinasai!*" shouted Ishii. Kojima, the deputy head who Alfie had met earlier, entered and circled the table, finally coming to rest next to the girl.

As Ishii began proceedings, Kojima explained that he was there to interpret. Each time Ishii paused, Kojima addressed Alfie.

"Ishii-*kōchō-sensei* say he think your first day is not smooth. It is shame."

Alfie avoided eye contact, his head bowed towards the solid wood table.

"I know. I'm very sorry, sir."

"He think you are sorry. He understand other student have maybe not be nice. Situation is difficult for you. He understand."

There was a pause. A pre-but pause.

"But violence is not happening in Japanese school. This is not our way. This is already last chance for you, Alfie May-*san*. If this happen again, even Matsucorp not save you."

Alfie nodded contritely throughout. He knew there was nothing he could reasonably argue with.

"Ishii-*kōchō-sensei* say look at him."

Alfie raised his head, blinking, and turned to his right. He felt Ishii stare through his pupils and into his head.

"Wakarimashita ka?"

Alfie was already nodding solemnly as Kojima translated *Do you understand?*

"*Sore de ...*" he continued, and the attention of the conversation and of the two senior teachers now turned towards the girl who sat, arms crossed and serious, regarding Alfie.

"This is Tomoko-*san*," translated Kojima. "She is one of prefect team. From time to time, we use buddy system to help new student. Ishii-*kōchō-sensei* think you need help from prefect. Tomoko-*san* is rare in her generation because she speak a little English. She will have regular meeting with you and help you avoid trouble. She is like student boss for you. You must do what she say."

They all looked at Tomoko. Her accent was American as well as Japanese. And she spoke more than a little English.

"Hey. If you cooperate, I'll help you. I hope we can work together. I have to report to Ishii-*kōchō-sensei* on your progress, so let's make sure you avoid any more trouble."

There was still no smile. The two men nodded as she spoke.

Bobbed hair, a pretty face and an immaculate uniform, Tomoko came across as confident and authoritative. Alfie was pleased that the first two characters on her name badge were familiar to him. Some of the script was beginning to sink in. She wore another badge which he assumed denoted her prefect status. Ishii spoke to her and she began to address Alfie again.

"You are being sent home early today. You will start over tomorrow with a clean slate. You will report to me in the school yard at break every day this week and we will also meet at the school gates after lessons to check how your day has been. Then, on Sunday at noon, you will meet me at Harajuku station on the Yamanote line. We will have lunch, discuss your progress and plan for next week. I am expected to make you settle in successfully. It is my responsibility. Please do not let me down."

It was quite a speech. Very forthright from a student only a couple of years older than Alfie. The slightest hint of a softening in her manner, as she spoke of a Sunday meeting, did not make her any less formidable, intimidating even. As Alfie left for his early bath, letting Tomoko down did not strike him as an option.

Chapter Twenty-two

Jordan knew the drill as they all reconvened for the final, quarter-hour break of the day at 4pm. The extra hour in the working day in Japan meant that 105 minutes of his first day's work remained. He thought back to Alex in Bathside as he drifted towards the canteen.

Alex and Jordan had gone to Matsucorp together. They were a mutual admiration society. Both capable engineers, Alex was happy to concede that his best friend had greater flair. Outside of work, Jordan shrank in stature as Alex chatted and charmed in the pub and at gatherings. Jordan was glad. He preferred to listen rather than to throw himself into conversation. Alex had a quick wit and Jordan would sit at his side and smile and nod and grin and nod and laugh. Jordan liked girls, but not enough to risk humiliation. He was comfortable with Alex because Alex did not try to thrust him forwards. They both knew that one day it would happen and, when it did, Alex knew it before Jordan.

He felt it in an instant. They had been celebrating the successful end to their apprenticeship and full-time contracts. Chatting to a group of high-school girls in a dance hall in Colchester, a bright-eyed blonde girl said "hi, how're you doing?" to the group of Matsucorp graduates. The eye contact and the soft Scottish accent turned all of their heads and Jordan responded most quickly. It was so out of character. Alex felt the electricity and offered Shaylie a drink. It was Jordan's round and, as he went to the bar, Alex suggested to Shaylie that Jordan could do with a hand. Jordan never looked back.

And now, having abandoned Alex, he found himself at the back of one of the serving hatch queues, but on the other side of the world. The two men in front of him, speaking in a language less familiar to him than Japanese, turned to face him.

"Hi," said one in confident English with a hint of America. "I'm Kim."

"I'm Jordan."

"Yes, we know. Everyone knows. We are *gaijin*, too. You understand *gaijin*?"

"Yes, I've already heard that word many times."

"When we use that word, it means *foreigner* without prejudice. We come from the outside. That's simply what it means. But when the Japanese use it, it is often negative. Disrespectful."

"I did get that impression."

"And so we have *gaijin* contracts. These, too, are disrespectful. Do you have a *gaijin* contract, Jordan-*san*?"

"I don't know, I..."

Jordan was unsure how to respond. These were surely the complainants that Eguchi-*san* had been bemoaning. If Eguchi was a barometer for the local workforce, Jordan was now being drawn into a conversation which would be seen as disrespectful. Anxiety abridged his responses as he wished himself to the front of the queue.

"¥10 000 000 basic annual salary, no bonuses, three weeks' holiday? These are our conditions of employment and they are inferior to those of Japanese skilled workers doing the same job. Is this fair? Is it right?"

"Well, no, I guess…"

"It is unjust, of course. I can see you were unaware. Please consider this, Jordan-*san*. There is no union representation in the Japanese automobile industry. Not yet, anyway."

The Korean pair turned as they reached the front of the queue and Jordan watched them take tea and turn away, leaving him to breathe out, to release the tension in his shoulders, to drink his tea and to return, unnoticed, to his post.

He tried to push the unsettling encounter to the back of his mind during the final session of the working day and his mind was firmly back on the job when a message appeared on his console screen.

>>Jordan May to meeting room A at 6pm. Confidential.<<

It brought back memories of less than two weeks ago in Bathside, the curiosity and anxiety preceding a meeting which had changed the course of his life. He battled to retain focus to the end of the day.

As colleagues made their way to the locker room at 6pm, Jordan slipped quietly to the row of meeting rooms nearby, as they had been in Bathside Bay. No sooner had he closed the door behind him, the hologram appeared.

It was the same man, the awkward, wiry Englishman, seated behind a desk, leaning forward onto crossed arms, concentrating on Jordan.

"Hello, Jordan. How are you?"

"Hello, yes, fine, I think, fine, thank you."

"The past few days must have been very difficult for you and your family."

Conscious that he was pulling on his right earlobe, Jordan wanted to paint a positive picture.

"Yes, but I think we are settling in and getting used to life here."

"Good, gooood." Struthwin hesitated. "And how have you got on during your first day at work?"

Jordan wanted Matsucorp to see gratitude, only gratitude.

"Well, it's very similar to what it was in Bathside Bay. And they have given me an English keyboard. And I've been able to do my job just as efficiently as before, I think."

"Good, gooood. And I am sure you have appreciated our excellent dining facilities. Have you managed to integrate socially? There are very few operatives who can communicate in English."

Concentrate on lunchtime, Jordan, you did have a positive social interaction at lunchtime.

"Yes, well, I tried my best. I was lucky to find someone at lunchtime who could speak some English. He was friendly, but I know I need to make the effort to learn Japanese if I want to integrate with more of my colleagues. It's very important to me."

"Yes, gooood, very important. Try to get on with your Japanese colleagues, Jordan. They will reward you with loyalty and friendship. It is good that you have had a positive experience. Try to have more positive experiences. Positive. Always positive. You will find that there are negative people, too. Avoid the negative and stick with the positive people. Always positive, Jordan."

It was as if he knew. He couldn't know. Jordan had to be careful.

"Well, Jordan, I just wanted to check in with you. Make sure everything was OK. There is nothing I can help you with?"

"No. No, thank you. All is well."

"In that case, Jordan, you should go home and spend the evening with your lovely family."

"Yes, I will, thank you."

"Good bye, Jordan."

The hologram faded before Jordan could reciprocate. He hurried to the locker room and changed back into civvies, then joined the tail end of the mass of his colleagues, walking to Hōya station. The light was beginning to fade above the cherry trees, the smell of blossom was interspersed with that of burning tobacco and the occasional street food stall, and Stepson Struthwin was in Jordan May's head. The image was taking an age to fade, as were the words. The slowly enunciated words, key words repeated. Positive, always positive.

Jordan had had a positive first day at work, but he had now been told that there were negative people to be avoided. Even now he felt as if he were being watched. In the mass of workers, amongst the smoke, he sought anonymity. But he was Jordan May-*san*, the only European skilled worker; he stood out and could be approached by anyone able to speak his language. He wanted to integrate, but he needed to be careful.

Avoid the negative, Jordan, avoid the negative.

#

"O medetō gozaimasu, Jeremiah-san!"

Father said the congratulations, along with the gifts, just kept coming when I was born. He had been posted to Tokyo just two months earlier. It was his first full ambassadorship so, despite Mother's delicate physical situation, the opportunity had to be taken. Twas ever thus, as no one really ever says, in the diplomatic world. Several decades behind reality, in the West at least, the FCO still favoured promoting married men, especially those with socially adept wives of a certain milieu.

So Mother took the hit for Father's career. Again. Her first and only child born in a strange hospital on the other side of the world. Imagine that. Still, at least she provided a son. That totally helped. And it was back in the days when they were still teaching English. The doctors could communicate in medical jargon, even if there was no accompanying small talk.

Father was not a natural father. It was lucky for him, less so for Mother. Mother said when I emerged I was handed to her, but when she offered me to Father, the nurses vetoed.

"Dame! Kitanai!" *No! Dirty!*

Father or not, he had come in from the outside world and brought germs with him. He was, however, allowed to view me through the observation window for the next ten days. Newborns all together in one room, fathers side by side in the gallery, mothers allowed in to breast feed only, then leave. Consider that. At the time, the prevailing wisdom in the West was in favour of immediate post-natal physical and emotional bonding. But Japan had the lowest infant mortality rate in the world. Still does. So who could argue?

I often wonder if this initial separation was the harbinger of the ever-increasing distance between us through my childhood. Although this was not a separation they chose, unlike the more definitive one which came later.

#

Chapter Twenty-three

On Tuesday, Alfie completed his first full day at Nerima High School. He was determined to integrate. Failure was not an option for any of the May family. He had been on time for all lessons, the majority of which had been incomprehensible to him, and met Tomoko when required. He was still wary of her as he found her at the gates at the end of school, but she was somehow less severe, less officious off site, different to how he had found her at break.

"So, I guess nothing bad happened today. You're here at the end of school, huh?"

"Yes," replied Alfie, "today was better, thanks."

"So, how did lunch go this time? No provocation? No throwing food at you?"

"No, nothing. I mean, it was quiet. I think the class was nervous that something would happen, but they were polite to me. Still not that friendly, though."

"Friendly will take time. The time it takes you to learn a bit of Japanese. Yesterday morning they were wary of you because you are a foreigner, today they are scared because they know you decked Tsubasa-*kun*."

"He wasn't in today."

"I know. They are all talking about it. He is ashamed and so are his parents. He won't be back until his split lip has healed."

They stood on the same platform together at Nerima station. Alfie had warmed to Tomoko a little and became increasingly curious.

"How far do *you* go?"

Tomoko smiled for the first time and Alfie blushed.

"You mean on this line? I go as far as Hōya – two stops further than you, right?"

"Hōya? That's where my dad works. He works for …"

"Matsucorp. I know."

"How? How did you know? And how do you know where I live?"

"Everyone knows. Your family are like local celebrities. Word soon gets around."

"I suppose."

Alfie found it bewildering, but he was pleased to be able to have a conversation, make a friend. Had he made a friend? Was friend the right word? In a way, she was his probation officer. But there was potential here. She was helpful, she was pretty and she spoke English.

"So, how come you speak such good English?" Alfie wanted to know.

"I'll tell you another time. This is your stop, Alfie May-*san*. *Ashita ne*. See you tomorrow."

Stepping onto the platform, Alfie reciprocated Tomoko's smile, a smile which broadened as the train pulled away, a smile which was to be erased as quickly on his arrival at the gaijin house.

Shaylie had been waiting for Alfie to come home. Their first item of mail had not been the letter of her dreams. She had been at home, alone but for the sleeping nightworkers, when she had heard the postman's moped stop outside. For the second afternoon in a row, she had collected the post from the mailbox outside and sorted it into the room-numbered shelves by the front door. The same address was on each envelope, either in Japanese script or Roman alphabet, the names and room numbers distinguishing between them. *Shaylie May*, handwritten on a small brown envelope was a surprise, but she pocketed this for later as the formal look of the smart white envelope to *MAY Jordan & Shaylie SAMA* hit her between the eyes.

Nervously sitting at the kitchen table, she ripped open the envelope and read the succinct letter in perfect English.

Dear Mr & Mrs May

I regret having to write to you so soon to issue a warning regarding your son's behaviour at Nerima High School.

During lunch today, Alfie punched a classmate in the face and caused his lip to bleed. We believe that he may have been provoked; nevertheless this is not behaviour which we will accept. We treat all instances of violence very seriously. This is why I sent Alfie home at lunchtime yesterday.

I have decided that Alfie would benefit from the support of a senior student and so I have assigned an English-speaking prefect to this end. Alfie is required to meet regularly with her, whenever she deems it necessary, in order to review his progress. It is a condition of Alfie's continuation with us that he cooperates fully with his mentor. Further instances of violence will result in the withdrawal of Alfie's place at Nerima High School. A copy of this letter has been sent to Matsucorp.

Please do not hesitate to contact me should you wish to discuss this matter further.

Yours sincerely

Ishii Headteacher

Shaylie had expected difficulties, but perhaps not quite so soon. Jordan had enough to deal with. She would deal with this herself.

When Alfie got home, more upbeat than yesterday, Shaylie was preparing food. Elisa and Aaliyah were eating toast in preparation for departure but today, Shaylie was unable to focus on their conversation. She greeted her son, handed him a cup of tea and took him into their room.

"What's up, mum?" Alfie asked. He was buoyant and her concerned demeanour had not yet registered.

"Is everything OK?" She had not expected such a positive mood and at once became guarded. She needed to confront him but did not want to crush his cheer.

"Fine, thanks. Today's been OK."

"Better than yesterday?"

"Err, yeah." She knows. "Why do you ask?"

He tried to give nothing away. Yesterday he had wandered, ensuring that he did not arrive home early.

"Your headteacher has written to your father and me to tell us about the lunchtime incident and the prefect who's supporting you."

Alfie's head and shoulders fell, eye contact lost, his secrecy defeated.

"Does dad know?"

"You father has enough to contend with. We can keep this to ourselves for now. We knew it wouldn't be easy. Just tell me what happened."

Shaylie's sympathy grew as Alfie recounted his first day at school. Of their individual ordeals, she felt that starting at a Japanese language school with no friends was the toughest. She was far angrier with the provocation endured by her son than she was with his reaction. So why had he become so much more positive just one day later?

"I know I have to get through this. I know my place is sponsored by dad's company. So I kept my head down today and actually, I think Tomoko-*san* really wants to help me."

"The prefect?"

"Yeah. She speaks good English. I have to do what she says, meet her when she says, but that's fine. On Sunday I've got to meet her to discuss my first week."

Shaylie beamed. "I'm so pleased you want to do well."

"I need to, don't I? But yesterday I felt so alone. Now they've given me a reason to cooperate. Maybe she can help me to meet people."

"It sounds like Mr Ishii knows what he is doing."

"Whether it's him, I'm not sure, but somebody has recognised what I need and given me a chance."

Thankful for the mysterious Tomoko, Shaylie hid the letter amongst their documents and returned to the kitchen.

Chapter Twenty-four

"I am told that there have been some teething troubles, Stepson-*san*."

Matsubara spoke through an ever-thickening atmosphere in his office, smoke emerging from nostrils and mouth. He stood behind his desk and gestured for Struthwin to sit. Struthwin was cool, relaxed and did not have the air of failure about him.

"All is well, Matsubara-*san*."

"No trouble at all, then?"

"One minor incident. They have all been here nearly a week. I would say that that is rather successful."

There was the slightest hint of a smile as Matsubara settled back into his chair with his Mild Seven and his glass of whisky.

"So let me have your update, then."

"My operatives in Nagoya and Sendai are extremely positive. Absolutely everything has gone to plan there. The women have settled into their gaijin houses and into their roles at work. They had both made an effort to learn some basic Japanese before they came and they have both arranged classes to continue their study. As a result, they have been largely accepted by their new colleagues."

"What about the people they left behind? Have they had any unsettling contact with the FREW?"

"No. These were always going to go smoothly. Neither was in a relationship, they both have supportive families and they are both very independent women. No problems to report."

"But this is not the case here in Tokyo." It was a statement rather than a question.

"Relocating a family, an entire family, was always going to be more difficult, but also better for PR. The Mays have actually settled in very well. Jordan is an excellent operative and he has transferred his high rates of productivity to our Hōya plant. He has an excellent attitude and is desperate to integrate. I am sure that he will start to pick up enough Japanese to converse with his colleagues. Some of the older guys speak a bit of English. I had a word with Eguchi and he intercepted Jordan over lunch and fed him some positive thoughts." Struthwin laughed. "He is so desperate to integrate that he went outside for a smoke with his new colleagues. He hates smoking!"

"But, Stepson-*san*, if he is desperate for integration and social contact he will gravitate towards others with English-speaking skills. Often bad influences."

"This is why I am pushing our older Japanese workers to cultivate his friendship. He has had a harmless chat with some cleaners and he was approached by a couple of dissatisfied Koreans, but I am keeping a close eye on this. I had a videolink chat with him at the end of play yesterday. I will keep him away from talk of inequality and unionisation."

"This is very important. Now, what about the wife?"

"Very positive. She keeps them together, boosts their morale and she's made great strides in integration. Shopping trips to Ikebukuro, getting to know housemates. It is all going very well for her."

"Getting to know housemates in a gaijin house could present problems."

"I picked this house carefully. I profiled all residents. I believe that this is a good environment for the May family. She has been chatting to a couple of Israeli hostesses. What is the worst that can happen?"

"That she becomes a hostess?"

"At her age it is unlikely, but it would not be the end of the world. I will monitor her situation, of course."

"See that you do, Stepson-*san*. Now tell me about the child. I am concerned by this violent incident."

"Matsubara-*san*, I understand your concern, but a provoked incident involving the only *gaijin* student in the entire school was always a strong possibility. I had planned for it and it actually puts us in a stronger position."

"How so?"

"Because it has enabled me to persuade Ishii-*kōchō-sensei* to assign a pretty, young prefect to the boy. Now he cannot move without her say-so and, even better, he is happy about it."

"I think this is a good move, Stepson-*san*, but this family does still worry me. There is so much potential for disaster. The wife and son are complications in Jordan May-*san*'s assimilation, as are past union affiliations. His situation does not have the stability of the two females from the FREW. My fears are tempered only by your supreme confidence."

"And, I hope, your confidence in my confidence, Matsubara-*san*."

Matsubara smiled, nodded and stood.

"Thank you, Stepson-*san*. That will be all. Please keep me informed."

Struthwin retreated into an untidy *gaijin* bow, turned and exited the office. He pulled out his phone as he got into the lift.

"Yes … he's happy … no reason why he shouldn't be … it's all going as smoothly as we can expect."

Now there was a longer pause. Struthwin concentrated as he stepped out onto the pavement. Finally he responded.

"No further action is not a standpoint I generally agree with. I am paid to foresee problems and get solutions in place, whatever they cost. So you sort out the paperwork and get him over here as soon as possible. Got it?"

Struthwin terminated the call. He could not guarantee to Matsubara that difficulties would not arise, but manipulation would go a long way to ensuring that the Mays' daily existence would not attract any negative publicity to Matsucorp. Not for the moment.

#

We lived in the grounds of the Embassy in Hanzōmon and I went to the British School, first in Shibuya, then in Setagaya. Mother accompanied me on the nine-minute metro journey to Shibuya, but from year four I was expected to do the thirteen minutes' train plus ten-minute walk alone. Eight-year-old kids travelling alone through a big city. Only in Japan. Then and now.

But it was fine. Comfortable. Unthreatening. Off the train at Sangenjaya, bumping into friends all the way. Perhaps friends is a bit strong. I don't think I've ever had friends. Not in the way that others understand it. I floated between cliques in an international school. At that time, there were students of all colours, shapes and sizes. The shape and size variants still exist. The return of fascism to Western Europe did for internationalism.

Father was forever at work and Mother did what she did. Kept house, prepared to entertain, entertained. I ploughed a lone furrow. Winter is short in Japan and any memory is of playing outside and alone for most of the year. The warmth of spring, a short rainy season, then the searing humidity of the summer, followed by a warm and deep red autumn. I would trot out of the gates, turn left and walk down to the banks of the moat which separated the embassy from the grounds of the Imperial Palace. Groups of teenagers would leave me be, heads in their mobile phones, back when everyone was able to have one. Decadent days.

I lived in my own world, colliding with that of others, including Mother, on an occasional and amiable basis, and even more rarely with that of Father. The life of a child in Japan has a distinct lack of faction with its accompanying threat and trauma. And the British School took students through to the age of eighteen. I could have stayed. There was no upheaval necessary, no ordeal, no separation.

But Father insisted. How could I hope to access the old school network if he hadn't had the courage and the foresight to send me back? At least, for him it was sending me back. To me, it was being sent away to a foreign land.

#

Chapter Twenty-five

By Wednesday, Shaylie had settled into a routine. A little over a week ago, she had been a retail assistant, a working mum, the secondary breadwinner. Suddenly, she was a housewife. An unspectacular role in an exotic culture remained unspectacular. Cooking and cleaning, self-taught Japanese lessons, trips to Ikebukuro to fill her time, she could not continue like this long term. Housewife was never her goal, not now and not way back then.

She never could have imagined this life in her high school days, studying hard during the week and letting her hair down at the dance hall on a Friday night. Her group of friends was young but it was all innocent fun. Very few had had boyfriends and all they thought of was chatting and drinking lemonade and dancing the evening away. They were used to the young men flirting with them but the atmosphere was friendly rather than predatory.

It was quite usual for an outgoing girl like Shaylie to lock eyes with one lad or another, smile and inquire "Hi, how're you doing?" The evening she met Jordan differed only by the electricity between them as he smiled back. She barely noticed his friend's offer of a drink, until Alex followed up with the suggestion that she give Jordan a hand at the bar. They chatted all evening and, before she knew it, they were dating, engaged, married. It all happened in a flash, but pregnancy took a little longer.

It had taken endurance, persistence and miscarriages before that moment when she had had to squeeze Jordan's hand to bring him back from the brink, back into the room before the final push which brought Alfie into the world. Their lives were complete, their future in Harwich mapped out.

Sixteen years later, in Tokyo, it was time to prepare dinner. She decided to change into more comfortable clothes and picked up a pair of jeans she had left on the floor next to the bed. Pulling them over her hips, she felt the unopened envelope she had filed for later. She sat on the futon and tore it open. She felt the blood fill her cheeks as she took in the crude scrawl.

>>Be a hostess and Jordan will never know.<<

Below the message was a heart shape. Inside the heart shape, it read *SM 4 EM*.

#

"Hey, Shaylie!"

Unspeaking, Aaliyah followed the effusive Elisa into the kitchen, where Shaylie was preparing vegetables.

"Hi! You want tea?"

Shaylie sounded off colour, but the Israeli girls never refused tea. Elisa asked after Shaylie's day and received a brief and dismissive account of the quotidian train-train. Then, steeling herself, she quickly shifted the topic to last night's stint at the hostess bar.

"Nothing unusual to report," said Elisa. "Tuesdays are never that busy."

"So did you manage to talk to your boss?"

Aaliyah rolled her eyes, still unconvinced.

"Yes, I did. Why? Have you changed your mind? He is happy to meet you, maybe give you a trial."

Shaylie turned to face them, desperation masquerading as enthusiasm.

"When?"

"He told us to bring you tomorrow night. Thursday. Are you sure you want to do this?"

"Yeah, sure. I thought about it today. I'm so bored. It'll be something to do. What do I have to wear?"

"Why don't you get yourself to Ikebukuro tomorrow morning and buy yourself a new dress? Dignified and maybe just a little revealing. You might need to get tomorrow night's meal ready early so there's time for us to help you with your hair and make-up."

"You don't mind doing that?"

Elisa's enthusiastic nod trumped Aaliyah's scowl.

"Be prepared to stay up all night, though. You might want to find time for a nap during the day tomorrow."

"Oh, I will, don't worry!"

At Shaylie's behest, while she threw her ingredients together in the pan, Elisa regaled her with hostessing anecdotes. Shaylie needed to be prepared. Her tenseness and Elisa's excitement were tangible when Alfie and then Jordan returned home. As the May family congregated in the kitchen to eat, Elisa and Aaliyah went upstairs to finish preparing for the night's work.

"What's going on?" asked Jordan, immediately curious.

"I might have found a job!" Best get it out in the open. Shaylie had had enough of secrets.

"What? A job? What kind of a job?"

Shaylie hesitated.

"Bar work," she decided on the spot.

"Not in that dodgy bar with those girls?"

"It's not dodgy. Elisa's been telling me all about it. It sounds like fun. It'll give us some extra money. It's just what I need."

"Why do you need a job, Shaylie? I earn a reasonable salary."

"I know you do, darling, but a bit more would be helpful. Anyway, it's not about the money. I'm used to working. Being at home all day is only going to get boring."

"But how will you cope with working at night?"

"I'll be home in the morning to have breakfast with the pair of you, sleep 'til early afternoon, do a wee bit of food shopping, cook and get ready. Then I'll eat with you both before I leave."

"You've worked it all out, I see." Jordan was visibly unimpressed.

"I've thought about it a lot and I think it's manageable. I'm going tomorrow night for a trial. If they take me on, I'll give it a go and, if I don't cope, I'll stop, OK?"

No response from Jordan who could see that Shaylie's mind was made up. He did not object to Shaylie working, she knew that, but he had serious misgivings about that particular working environment. Not wishing to dampen the mood any further, Jordan manoeuvred the conversation towards Alfie's day at school. Fortunes across the family were looking up, with Alfie progressing beyond one-word answers and showing more enthusiasm every day. They chatted away, Shaylie remaining on the periphery of the conversation, distracted by a terrifying new venture and premature first-night nerves.

Chapter Twenty-six

"Oh yes! Very nice," said Elisa. Even Aaliyah could not hide her surprise.

"You scrub up pretty well. That's a classy dress. Tsubasa will be impressed."

Shaylie wore a red dress with an open back which finished just above the knee, a gold necklace which hung above her neckline, nude tights and black heels. She had had a sleep and food was ready. She had accepted that she had no choice but to be a hostess and adrenaline was pumping. Elisa had brought her make-up bag and curling tongs to the kitchen and, by the time Jordan and Alfie got home, the transformation was complete. The men were speechless, but a rare public display of affection from Jordan told her all she needed to know.

Half an hour later dinner was done and they were on their way. First, the Seibu Ikebukuro line to Ikebukuro. Early evening into town was moderately busy but the three women found themselves standing, chatting in one corner of the carriage. They elicited stares and some raised eyebrows from people in suits, but nothing more intrusive than that. These conventional, local people were satisfied to be able to confirm their prejudiced views of *gaijin* women. They had heard what kind of work suited such women. Shaylie knew what they were thinking. Perhaps because Shaylie was thinking it, too.

Elisa suspected that Shaylie was yet to experience a rammed commuter train and Shaylie confirmed that she had only heard the tales from Alfie, who travelled townwards at the busiest of times. Early evening, she told Shaylie, the Yamanote Line would be very crowded. Although it was not crowding of the level requiring the infamous white-gloved staff, it was uncomfortable nonetheless. The green Yamanote Line was central Tokyo's overground circle line and, arriving on the platform at Ikebukuro station, Shaylie was led to a specific point and a specific queue. A female-only queue.

"Is this really necessary?" she asked. "It's a bit worrying that you feel the need to be in a women-only carriage."

"Take it from me, once you've had your nose in a sweaty salaryman's armpit and the same bloke has put his hand up your skirt and reached for the holy grail, you will be eternally grateful."

Shaylie's shocked look told a story. These carriages were not a precaution, they were a necessity to reduce surreptitious sexual assault which, judging by the number of women seeking the same refuge, was substantial.

A little less than twenty minutes on the clockwise Yamanote Line and they had alighted in Okachimachi. Shaylie soon put the thought of dirty, old men out of her mind, but she was about to realise that they were to be the focus of her new job. As the light faded on a mild spring evening, they descended the main strip in Okachimachi, the air thick with aromas from street stalls selling noodle soup, and found themselves in an old lift which took them with the occasional clunk to the top floor of a ten-storey building, busy on each level with office workers eating and drinking in *izakayas* and singing in karaoke booths.

The lift opened into the foyer of Aphrodite's Hostess Bar and Shaylie stepped forwards into another new world, another exotic culture. The expansive open-plan room was dimly lit, the music soft, a fusion of blues and jazz, the furniture a cheap, synthetic imitation of what it aspired to be. Left and centre were dominated by chat booths, soft seating arranged around Formica tables at knee height. To the right was a long bar, girls behind it preparing cocktail shakers and polishing glasses, girls milling around in front, preparing for a night of lucrative socialising. As far as Shaylie could see, the staff was 100% female. From what she had been told, it was also 100% foreign, although many of the girls were East Asian in appearance and could quite easily have been Japanese.

They approached the bar and said *hi* to some of the other girls, then Elisa led Shaylie to the end of the bar, around behind it and knocked on a wooden door. "*Hai?*" came the male voice and Elisa led them into a small, bright office. A single, unshaded light bulb hung over an untidy wood effect desk, behind which sat a man of unconventional appearance. Shaylie had been used to seeing Japanese males in uniform: boys dressed for school, men in suits, perhaps the odd university student in T-shirt and jeans, always of sober colour. Tsubasa existed in a different world and Shaylie had entered that world. His hair was orange, the result of peroxide on jet black hair, and his eyes were drawn out by subtly applied eyeliner and mascara. His lips were glossed. His floral shirt was open to the base of his sternum, revealing a hairless, perhaps waxed chest, decorated with a gold pendant on matching chain. As he rose to greet them, his powder blue tie-dyed trousers led Shaylie to imagine equally extravagant footwear beneath the desk.

The appearance and the demeanour did not match. He leant forward into a formal Western greeting, a brief smile and a limp handshake. He signalled for Shaylie to sit and, following a brief Japanese exchange with Elisa, suddenly she was on her own.

"So," he said in heavily accented English, "you want work for me, *deshō?*"

She had to get this job. Shaylie was now ready to sell her enthusiasm. Her sparkling eyes locked in contact with his.

"I'd like a trial. I really would like to work."

"Elisa told me about you. She likes you, *ne.* She told me you have family, *deshō.* Can you manage work at night? Do you know what is hostessing?"

"Elisa has told me all about it. I think I can do it. I'd like to try. But my Japanese is not very good yet."

"Your Japanese is not great concern to me. Like me, many of my clients is, let's say, mature. We went to school when English was taught, *deshō.* We enjoy to practise, *ne.* Do you know what we expect of you?"

"Flatter and flirt, serve drinks and light cigarettes, chat and entertain, that's what Elisa told me. I can do that."

"And sometimes sing karaoke, *ne*. Karaoke is important part of Japanese culture, *deshō*. It not matter if you can't sing, it is what we all like."

"Well, I can do that, too."

"You are enthusiastic and you are very well dressed, *deshō*. I am happy to give you trial. I not usually pair my girls, but tonight you will work with Elisa. You learn from her, *ne*." He stood. "Come with me."

Shaylie watched his thick-soled, purple brothel creepers emerge from behind the desk. She did not notice his knowing smile as he watched her eyes drawn to his shoes like so many before her. They retraced her steps from five minutes before and found Elisa amongst the other girls at the bar, mirrors out, checking make-up and hair.

"Elisa, please stay with Shaylie tonight." He spoke in English, perhaps for Shaylie's benefit, perhaps to show off. "Make sure she know what to do, *ne*."

Elisa gave Shaylie a broad smile and squeezed her hand.

"No problem. It'll be fun."

Business was slow to begin with, so Elisa ran through how it all worked. A few regular clients were rich and influential enough to choose their hostesses, but on the whole it was the club which allocated the girls. Clients had to be signed in as members or guests of members and the tuxedoed hosts now positioned by the lifts vetted each arrival. The first guests were beginning to arrive, individually or in small groups, all besuited, all considerably older than the company they sought. They would be taken to a table with their allocated girl, who would then return to the bar with a drinks order. Girls were expected to stick mostly to non-alcoholic cocktails in order to manage their guests effectively and to last the shift. Besides, the mark-up on these elaborate juice drinks was even greater than that on the spirits favoured by the salarymen, rich salarymen to whom the price of drinks was immaterial, and the girls shared the profit on each drink equally with the bar. In addition to this, the best girls were paid a handsome hourly rate. Despite Elisa's claims to the contrary, it was hard to believe that such a generous remuneration did not include danger money.

As Shaylie pushed for more detail, it became clear that she could expect some unwanted physical contact. A hand on the thigh was part of the job. It was a sign that the client was happy, would order more drinks and would reap more profit. It was also a price Shaylie had to pay. If the hand moved too high, a delicate brush-off accompanied by a coy smile would not offend. Sooner or later, invitations to meet outside the club would certainly be forthcoming if you were popular and successful. You could say no, but alternatively you could enjoy an evening as a very well-paid escort.

Shaylie had to ask, "And are you telling me that girls who agree to private meetings are not expected to have sex with these men?"

"This can certainly happen. Girls can make huge money if they go all the way. But the men know that they can't expect it."

"I bet some of them are pretty insistent."

There was no time for Elisa to answer. They had been summoned to Shaylie's first gig as a *kyabajō*. Operating as a pair, they had been allocated to a larger group of salarymen, six in total, waiting on sofas arranged around one of the larger tables.

"Stick with me and keep smiling," said Elisa, bringing Shaylie alongside her with her hand in the small of her back.

They sat amongst the rowdy party of six, the two women opposite one another in the middle of the two sofas. They had a man on each side and the two remaining salarymen sat on soft chairs between the ends of the sofas. The party was already half cut and Elisa took their order of a bottle of Scotch and six glasses, ordering two juice cocktails at the bar for Shaylie and her. As the men all took out cigarettes, Shaylie followed Elisa's instructions. Leaning over the men, she steadied one hand with the other and brought a flame to their fags, white all the way to the filter tips.

For the next hour, stilted conversation ensued. The men tried very hard to impress with their schoolboy English. Elisa helped the conversation along in Japanese, but the focus was on Shaylie. She was the only hostess of Western European appearance, an exotic rarity. The lecherous faces leant in from all angles, stale whisky breath and, periodically, a stray hand to the knees, the thigh. They tried to pry, though it was a struggle, the level of their English restricting them to small talk. Each was similarly effusive, save for the man directly to Shaylie's right, quiet, reserved, smiling politely when she lit his cigarette. He was less drunk, less lecherous, and Shaylie wondered whether he truly was more attractive than the others or whether this was simply the impression given by a less inebriated demeanour.

It was the club's policy to rotate the girls every hour. The time came and the two women found themselves moving on, still all smiles, as they were replaced. They spent time with smaller and less rowdy groups for a couple of hours, before a lull and the chance to collect their thoughts at the bar. Tsubasa came to compliment them on their efforts. He had been watching them and they had dealt well with the first group which was big and boisterous.

"This group is regular, *deshō*. They usually drunk before they arrive. They are rich and powerful men, so it is important to me that you gave them good time, *ne*. Thank you."

Tsubasa bowed deeply and the women turned away from the bar to see that very group stagger past them on the way to the lift. The quiet man, the only one who could walk straight, separated from the group to speak to Tsubasa. There was a respectful exchange, more bowing and a polite nod to Elisa. He then took Shaylie's hand, kissed it gently, smiled and spoke directly to her in English for the first time that evening.

"My name is Ken. I enjoy meeting you. I hope see you here again."

His unerring eye contact was unusual for the Japanese. Shaylie was unnerved by this attention which was very deliberate and not at all drunken. He cannot have been much older than her, he was immaculately turned out, even at this stage of the evening, and his small hands were soft and childlike as they touched hers.

Tsubasa and Elisa watched Shaylie's curious expression when the man turned to the lift. They wondered if she had spotted the unnaturally short little finger on his left hand. Shaylie was wondering if only she had spotted this and asked herself why a minor deformity had momentarily bothered her.

But there was no time to ponder. There was more flirting to be done. It was time to work.

Chapter Twenty-seven

Life in Japan had soon dispensed with Jordan's concept of the family weekend. Gone were Sunday lunches, often with Evie present, gone were board games around the kitchen table, gone were the opportunities to stand with Shaylie, watching Alfie play football. Gone, too, was the struggle against poverty, and Jordan knew not to complain.

He would have time to himself over the weekend. He was relaxed and satisfied to have completed his first week at work. He still had misgivings over Shaylie's new line of work, but she was happier, reinvigorated even, and he would learn to endure her new schedule as she once again readjusted her body clock. There were advantages. Shaylie came to bed between 6 and 7am with a cup of tea for Jordan, and on Saturday this had not been a signal for him to get up. Slumbering whilst Shaylie fell into a deep sleep, he had eventually risen, breakfasted, showered and pottered. He had braved the walk to the station square, the stares diminishing but still present. He had returned to the gaijin house with take-away sushi to find Alfie finally awake.

Alfie was far more settled and chatted to Jordan about his school whilst they demolished *futomaki, tekkamaki, kappamaki, oshinkomaki* and *nigiri,* all dipped into a bowl of soy sauce and wasabi paste. Still chopstick inept, they profited from the relative privacy of the kitchen to use their fingers. Both had, within a week, learned to appreciate the quality of institutional food in Japan, which was way above school dinners in the FREW.

"It's not beans on toast, but it's pretty good," said Alfie.

Jordan agreed. "I'm getting pretty used to the local food now. The canteen at work is very good." A pause. "So…"

"So what, dad?"

"You up to much this afternoon?"

"I've got nothing planned. Thought I might go for a look around the shops."

"In Ikebukuro?"

"Maybe. But Tomoko was telling me about a place called Electric City on the Yamanote Line, near where mum works. Do you want to have a look? It's where they sell all the latest electronic gadgets."

Jordan did not need persuading. He knew that he would be spending Sunday alone, so an afternoon out with his son was what he needed.

Sitting in quiet contemplation next to his son on the train, Jordan rewound sixteen years.

He choked back the tears. Minutes earlier he had been seconds from crashing to the delivery room floor. It was the sight of Alfie's head and the splattering of Shaylie's waters which had nearly done for him. He had been sweating and sweating and could feel his pulse in his neck. He could hear it in his head. His vision had blurred and, for a fraction of a second, he had lost his equilibrium.

Mid-push, Shaylie had retrieved the situation. She had squeezed his hand and cried his name as she pushed Alfie's head from her body. She was forever in charge. She had done what was necessary and Jordan was back in the room.

And now he made his futile effort to hide his emotion. He was a dad. He knew after a difficult pregnancy that this would be their one and only chance. Boy or girl, he didn't mind. They had a healthy child and he was a dad.

He had always thought that this day would come easily and that there would be more of them. From the moment he met Shaylie, he had their future mapped out. It was a future which Shaylie bought into. They had a church wedding in Colchester, a white wedding. It was a dying tradition but Jordan had a romanticised view of his life with Shaylie. A white wedding, a nice house in Harwich, a mortgage, a job, membership of Respect for Labour and a place in the community.

And now a kid. The tears continued to flow as he sat on the edge of the bed, his smiling wife cradling their new-born son. A happy family life lay ahead, a life which could never deviate from perfect. A settled life in Harwich.

An hour later they emerged from Akihabara station onto the main strip of Electric City. Towering on both sides for as far as they could see were what must have been a hundred retailers of everything from kitchen appliances to audio-visual equipment. Over the past decades it had taken longer and longer for the latest technologies from Japan and Korea to make it to shelves in the FREW. Now so few people could afford such luxuries that they could only be seen in a few specialist shops in London.

Jordan and Alfie spent a couple of hours browsing and did not get beyond two shops, each with ten floors to explore, each floor specialising in a different area of domestic electronics. Smart phones had once been widespread, but since the restrictions on communication technology across the world, consumers contented themselves with smart versions of everything else. Artificial intelligence controlled by touch, by voice, by iris recognition and by remote control. They saw smart fridge/freezers, smart microwaves, smart cameras, smart speakers and smart vacuum cleaners. By the time they arrived on the games floor of Bic Camera, Jordan was craving a rest. Japanese men and women played the latest games using technology never before seen by Jordan or Alfie. Adrenaline was tangible across the room as people interacted, not only with 3D images on screens but also with realistic holograms of sportsmen, wrestlers, and samurai warriors. Rowdy groups in their teens and twenties goaded and encouraged their friends, as Jordan and Alfie navigated their way back to the steep and narrow stairwell.

They arrived at the top of the stairs at the same time as three young men who politely stepped aside to allow the foreigners to go first. The act of courtesy took father and son off guard. They managed one step before both received a shove in the back, falling over one another until they reached the next floor down, heavily bruised. Their assailants were nowhere to be seen. Concerned shoppers and staff watched them slowly regain their feet, not getting too close to the *gaijin*, not knowing what to say. Alfie was first to his feet. He dusted himself down and ran his fingers through his hair, discovering a lump on the back of his head. He turned to Jordan and helped him back to his feet. Bones intact, they limped down one more floor into the street and sought the closest café.

"Are you OK, dad?" Alfie asked with grave concern on his face as they sat at a table for two in a café twenty metres further on. "You've got a bruise on your face."

"I've got plenty more elsewhere, but I'll live. How are you?"

"More shocked than anything. Just a couple of bruises. I was enjoying today."

"Me too, son, me too. Racist bastards. You've just got past all that nonsense at school and now you're getting it in the street."

"We'll get over it, dad. Things have got better this week. Let's forget it."

Approached by a waitress, they noticed the costumes for the first time. The waiting staff was all female and dressed as French maids. As they lifted their heads, their gaze shifted from the thick platform of elaborate, black suede boots, to the tops of black-and-white horizontally-striped socks which terminated above the knee. Past the flared pink-and-white petticoat, showing beneath the black velvet dress, the white lace pinafore and the ends of the long pigtails, their gaze came to rest on a pretty, smiling face, topped with a white lace hat. Smiling and nodding as the French maid reeled off her patter, Jordan and Alfie ordered coffee and pastries by pointing at pictures on the laminated menu.

Alone again, it was Alfie who was able to explain their new surroundings to his father. He now recalled what Tomoko had said that Akihabara was also famous for.

"Apparently they have all sorts of costume cafés where the customer can live in a fantasy world. Lots of them have waiters and waitresses dressed up as characters from video games, but I think we've walked into a maid café. That long speech she gave us, I think she was calling us 'Master' and saying that she was here to serve us and give us whatever we want."

Jordan smiled. "Well, that is weird all round. Weird that they have maid cafés and weird that you have such a good knowledge of the local culture already."

"I'm getting to know these things," Alfie smiled. "You'd be surprised at some of the weird stuff they have here. There are butler cafés for women to fantasise about men serving them and there are also school-themed cafés where you sit at school desks and the waitresses are dressed as schoolgirls."

"That is perverted," said Jordan, suddenly concerned with the decadent side of Japanese culture, hidden behind the formal facade to which he had thus far been confined.

"Yeah, it is a bit. And so are the little sister cafés, the shrine girl cafés, the railway cafés and the cross-dressing cafés." Alfie was now revelling in the shocked expression on his father's face.

Jordan paused to think. "Nice coffee, though."

They had become used to holding on to the positive but their chatter on the way home was cooled. Each laugh made them wince as they felt their bruised ribs. By the time they were back at the gaijin house, the racist assault had been mentally archived. Archived by day, only to return in their dreams.

Chapter Twenty-eight

What a difference a week made! His dad had settled in at work, his mum had got a job and even school was not such a trial for Alfie. Lessons were still incomprehensible, but in his class at least his presence had been accepted, and he now looked forward to meeting Tomoko twice daily.

Yesterday's incident had been unfortunate, but Alfie still remembered it as a pleasant day spent with his father. Sore and bruised, he had scaled staircase after staircase, negotiating his way for the first time beyond the Seibu-Ikebukuro line. He had found his way onto the anticlockwise Yamanote line which would take him from Ikebukuro, through Shinjuku, the world's busiest station, to Harajuku. He had no idea why it was necessary for him to meet Tomoko on Sunday lunchtime at a destination which was nowhere near their homes, but he was not about to question her.

He wore his standard uniform of T-shirt, jeans, hoody and trainers. Comfort always trumped style. His scent was supermarket brand, faintly floral, and his complexion was smooth.

He exited the station onto a street which teemed with young people. There was a vitality and a variety of styles which could not have provided a greater contrast to the homogeneity he had experienced so far. But he could not see Tomoko anywhere.

He stood in front of the station and waited, the frequency of his blink increasing. Sunday in and around Shakuji Park was pedestrian and reserved, a little like Harwich only with a more bourgeois feel, but the scene now in front of him made him dizzy. Both retro and ultra-modern, the youth of Tokyo displayed every colour and style imaginable, from the music-inspired Western modes of a century before to the latest Asian daring, and from the historical elaboration of the geisha to the head-to-toe black of Gothic vogue. Individuals, groups of friends and couples of diverse sexuality spilled into Harajuku, liberated from weekly convention, not a suit in sight, transforming the neighbourhood into a weekly carnival.

His reverie was broken by a tap on the shoulder. He found himself facing a beautiful smile, fashioned in purple lipstick, and inquiring eyes, intensified by deftly applied mascara and thick eyeliner, topped with blue, glittery eye shadow. He looked up to the hair, blue streaks running through the jet black plumes which defied gravity at assorted angles. Neither of them had spoken as Alfie now allowed his open-mouthed gaze to fall to this girl's clothes. The jeans were not outrageous, but they were tight and stylish, accentuating a stunning figure and leading down to black, leather boots with built up soles, without which, Alfie thought, she would be significantly shorter. Her powder blue T-shirt bore the head-and-shoulder silhouette of a freedom fighter from the previous century, an icon who had never gone out of fashion.

Alfie regained his composure enough to close his mouth, but the quizzical expression remained, as did the girl's smile. The silence had now lasted close to a minute and Alfie was still confused as to why he had been singled out by her. In response, the girl tipped her head to one side and raised her eyebrows, challenging him to articulate his question. As Alfie opened his mouth once more, her quirky smile broke into a broad grin, revealing a familiar set of teeth, clean and sparkling but overcrowded. She laughed as she watched the penny drop.

"Tomoko?"

"Didn't you recognise me? Come on, let's go."

She led him towards a large group of youths with a similar array of avant-garde, if not outrageous styles. So it was not a head-to-head meeting to discuss his progress, as such. Perhaps that would come later but, for the moment, Alfie was part of a band of teenagers out for Sunday afternoon shopping. For the first time, he did not feel racially conspicuous, though the sobriety of his clothes did attract some attention.

He was learning why Tomoko was highly rated by the school and had been assigned to him. She was clearly a popular student but had the confidence not to feel the need to be the centre of attention. She was sensitive to the situation, sensitive to Alfie's struggle on the periphery of this new culture, this new life. She walked with him at the rear of the group, one step of his long and elegant gait equivalent to two of hers. They advanced under an archway and entered a narrow pedestrian street which could have been compared to Carnaby Street, London, seventy or eighty years earlier.

Every Sunday, Takeshita Dōri was Tokyo's hub for fashion-conscious teenagers. Weaving in and out of large groups of high school students, Alfie tried to take in the array of boutiques, cafés and fast-food restaurants which passed quickly by on both sides. The speed at which they bypassed fascinating shops and side-streets suggested that shopping was not the priority.

Since his arrival in Japan, Alfie had not seen such colour. The familiar oriental food smells were present but intermingled with burger grease. Shop windows reflected the colour of the street fashion, selling outlandish tops, trousers, jewellery and posters, much of which was inspired by the alternative Japanese music scene. Music shops sold sounds in all formats, the latest technology vying for its place with the retrospective popularity of vinyl.

The purposeful march ended towards the bottom of Takeshita Dōri as Tomoko and Alfie followed their companions into a café-bar. He was grateful for her company and felt relaxed, insulated against the frenetic activity around him. They had been chatting about the popularity of Harajuku and Alfie had had little time to think about why she had brought him here.

It took a while for each of them to be served but they were all eventually sat at tables upstairs where it became evident that their group had grown. Hush fell as first one then another impassioned young man or woman rose to address them, applause punctuating the speeches. No explanation was forthcoming from Tomoko, Alfie remained in the dark.

132

Nevertheless he joined in with the applause, further confused as the fervent clapping was at times accompanied by glances in his direction. Surely this was paranoia.

As time passed, some began to look at their watches. Then it fell to Tomoko to contribute. What sounded like a rousing address met with unanimous approval. Tomoko was effusive in tone and enthusiastic in gesture. Her shoulders raised in question, her left palm resting on her chest in compassion, her arms spread out inclusively. She pointed to the heavens, she pointed to her comrades; was she also, at times, pointing towards Alfie? Little over a week into his new life, he found himself in the thick of a protest group of some description. A protest group to which his presence had some kind of significance.

Tomoko had made the closing speech. Another girl, not dissimilar in appearance to Tomoko, had issued an instruction, "*Ikimashō*," and they vacated the café-bar to resume their march to the bottom of Takeshita Dōri. They turned right at the bottom, the pace of their advance not yet affording Alfie the time to ask questions, and they soon found themselves joining a mass demonstration in the middle of a grand boulevard by the name of Omotesandō. Thousands of young Japanese with a smattering of visibly foreign youths marched, some with banners, back in the direction of Harajuku station.

Despite the singing and the chanting, Alfie could contain his curiosity no longer.

"What's going on?" he asked Tomoko, shouting to be heard.

"We are protesting against the JSD."

"The what?"

"The Japan Social Democrats, the right-wing government."

"Social Democrats aren't right wing, are they?"

"Their name is misleading." Tomoko shouted as the march increased its volume. "This country is controlled by a right-wing government. They are isolating us economically because they do not what to share what we now have. It is such a short-term view. What happens when the wealth shifts elsewhere? They are trying to freeze out the rest of the world and they are trying to make stricter and stricter laws against immigration. They do not want to help people who need help, like migrants from Europe and Africa where there are no jobs. You know about the camps? They don't want us to help any of these people. If they had their way, you would not have been allowed in."

Alfie could not argue with the cause. The plight of foreigners, such as the May family, was being protested by young local people with comfortable lives in a prosperous country. He wondered whether it was churlish of him to question Tomoko's motives in inviting him. Was he there as a token *gaijin*?

Advancing up Omotesandō, Alfie took in the scene. The colour and the noise were overwhelming. At once he felt a part of something big, whilst also remaining an outsider. He was all too aware of his conspicuous foreign appearance as he began to notice the armed police presence on the pavements, flanking the demonstration. Occasionally he would lock eyes with an unfamiliar comrade, garnering an encouraging smile as they raised placards skywards and continued their chants.

Some kind of speaker system, perhaps a megaphone, brought a speech through the air to them, closer and closer as they marched. Alfie was unable to identify how this speech was different in quality to what he had heard in the café-bar. Again it was in Japanese, again he did not understand a single word. That was almost true, but as they approached, he did realise that there was one word, often repeated, which he could pick out. *Gaijin*, once, then again and again. This speech struck a consistent monotone in contrast with those he had heard earlier, and it struck Alfie that, for the first time today, he was listening to a more mature voice, not the voice of youthful protest, but aged political diatribe.

The projected voice became louder until the march came to a halt, hopeful chanting suddenly changing in tone to shouts of mocking disdain. They found themselves face-to-face with a *gaisensha*. The converted minibus was painted black and decorated with the Imperial seal, the Japanese military flag and the world-famous Hinomaru, red disk on white. Topped with speakers, a middle-aged man of angry disposition continued his harsh staccato pronouncements into a microphone as he leaned out of a side window. One policeman stood either side, as if to protect him, as he attempted to broadcast his message beyond the small grey audience in traditional dress. Provocation alone could explain the choice of location. The JSD had brought repressive politics to the flamboyant enclave of Tokyo's progressive youth. The objective could only be a reaction.

Tension was tangible, progressive energy stagnating in the dead end at the top of Omotesandō. It was an opportunity for Tomoko to spell out the significance of what Alfie was witnessing.

"It used to be just minority nationalist parties who travelled around shouting horrible right-wing views from a *gaisensha*. But this is a new thing. The JSD are the majority party in our parliament. They are using the economic collapse in the West and the migrant crisis to put nationalism at the centre of our government. They have massive support in all age groups above 30 and they are hoping for such a big majority in the next election that they can do what they want and rule for many years. It is in the interests of the big corporations and their workers, so it is hard to see them fail."

"So why do they need to bother with speeches in Harajuku to young people. Are they trying to convert you?"

"They know they will never convert us. They want to provoke us. A violent reaction will discredit our message and could even lead to a police crackdown. They would love that."

"Would anyone react violently when all these police are armed?"

"It's unlikely, so the police presence helps in that respect. Anyway, they know that we won't get the media coverage we want."

Their conversation was broken by a surge forwards, followed by a sharp recoil as the police between the march and the *gaisensha* brandished their weapons. Protestors ran into one another, pressed flesh against flesh in the style of a packed commuter train, and the JSD vehicle sped away, the political tirade now replaced by the Kimigayo, the national anthem.

The danger of confrontation now passed, the crowd dispersed, away from the smart boutiques of Omotesandō, some back into Takeshita Dōri, some towards Harajuku station. Tomoko's friends regrouped in an orderly circle outside the station entrance to thank one another for their combined efforts. They uniformly bowed to a unified cry of "*Otsukaresama deshita*". On the platform they allowed three packed trains to leave before being able to squeeze into a carriage which was an infinitely more colourful version of what would be seen across Tokyo the next morning. Alfie, pressed closely against Tomoko, found pleasure in the discomfort. Evie had never felt further away.

Changing at Ikebukuro, the two of them finally found a seat. The Seibu line was less busy. They were now completely separated from their companions.

Alfie was still curious. "That was a pretty cool demo," he said. "Why did you say it wouldn't get media coverage?"

"Did you see any reporters?" Tomoko responded with her own question.

Alfie was deep in thought.

"I thought not," she continued. "This is how strong the JSD is, how much influence they have. They can keep the press away. Then, if there is a reaction by us, they take their own photos and basically write the report themselves. The newspapers support them and will print what they're told to print."

"But that's terrible," was all that Alfie could muster. It was all so far-fetched. "So who were all those people we were with?"

"There is a growing movement of people in Japan, mostly young people, who want to fight for social justice. A kind of humanitarian youth movement. We know how our fellow human beings are struggling outside of East Asia. We do not want to gloat at how the Western version of capitalism has collapsed, how society has broken down, how people now find themselves on the breadline, how tribalism and civil war is emerging. We want our government to use our wealth and influence to help other human beings across the world. They have the power to do this, but instead they want to paint us as silly idealists. We are able to meet and organise events like today, but the problem is that we can't get media coverage. Not unless we organise something much bigger, something which involves other parts of society."

"I don't suppose there's much chance of that."

"Well, not necessarily. Some groups of workers in the corporations, especially unskilled workers, are secretly organising unofficial union meetings."

"Why is it secret? Why don't the unions do something officially?"

"The unions? There are no unions. We have a no-union culture in this country. The government say that workers are well looked after, so unions are not needed."

"I've never heard of that before. My dad has always been in a union."

"I'm sure he has, but that's not how it works here. So, we are trying to get workers involved by creating underground unions first."

"Wow! You are an activist! Even though you have a comfortable life. Kids are not like that in the FREW, even though they have more reason to be."

Tomoko didn't reply. She was enjoying Alfie's compliments and allowed them to sink in.

"Can I ask you something?" he continued as they left Nerima.

"Sure." Her American r no longer bothered him.

"Why did you ask me along? I thought we were meeting to discuss my progress."

"That was an excuse. I'm sorry. I hope you're not angry with me. I thought you might like to be involved in the cause."

"Only if it won't get me into trouble. And really, what I'm wondering is, did you get me there because I'm a foreigner and I helped make the demo more relevant?"

Alfie lost eye contact as he asked the question. He didn't want to offend, but the question had to be asked.

"Sorry," he added.

"This is your stop," Tomoko said. "Come on, let's get off. I'll walk you to the barrier."

Relieved that there was time to finish the conversation, Alfie sauntered alongside Tomoko towards the ticket barrier.

"I don't blame you for asking me. I know it looks like that and I have an idea what it's like for you to be here. I bet you get stared at a lot in Shakuji. It's so conservative around here."

"Well, yeah, it is really."

"I really believe in social justice and I really want to help foreigners. We are not going to let it rest, you know. We are planning something big, something the media will have to report. I want you to be part of it if you want to. Not because you are a foreigner, but because I hope you believe in it, too. Don't you?"

"Of course I do."

"Well then. That's what I thought. You don't come across as selfish. I invited you because I thought you would be interested. I knew you were a good person. I haven't known you long, but you're nice, Alfie, I like you."

They were standing close together. She took one step closer, tilted onto tiptoes, kissed him softly on the lips, then took one step back. She smiled.

Alfie recovered from the shock to return a bemused smile, softly saying "Thank you".

"You don't have to thank me, you mushroom," she beamed. "See you tomorrow."

She turned back towards the platform.

Floating home by the park in the fading light, Evie did not even cross his mind.

Chapter Twenty-nine

The beginning of a new week offered Jordan new opportunities to cement his place amongst the skilled workers. He went about his job quietly and professionally, as he had always done, and spent breaks in the canteen, cultivating the comradeship of Eguchi and his companions, some of whom were beginning to try out snippets of clichéd English. Jordan was avoiding the Koreans who had approached him the previous week; in fact, he was avoiding all of the large and loud tables of non-Japanese workers.

At the beginning of the week, Jordan wondered whether he was becoming over-sensitive to the negative elements he had been told to avoid. He could not be sure, but he thought that the voices of dissent from the other end of the canteen were becoming stronger, more unruly. By the middle of the week, Eguchi and friends had become less proficient at hiding their irritation. Patience had been eroded and occasional dirty looks in the direction of the Koreans and the Chinese gave away the subject of the hushed and angry conversations for which no English explanation was offered. Jordan was pretty sure, however, that the word *gaijin* was not being used as a casual racist insult. Kim had told him that there was a race-based contractual gripe. Eguchi had explained the importance of gratitude to Matsucorp, especially where the company had been generous enough to employ foreigners. It was as hard to see a simple resolution as it was for Jordan to envisage perpetual avoidance of his fellow foreign workers.

By Thursday lunchtime, tensions had increased amongst the workforce. Following hushed discussions at Jordan's table during morning break, he had resolved to ask Eguchi and friends some questions. There was no need, as Eguchi broke the ice. Flanked by his companions, a panel of magistrates, they watched Jordan intently for his reaction to Eguchi's interrogation.

"Jordan May-*san*, have you notice bad atmosphere this week?"

"Yes, it does seem a bit different to me."

"Do you know why, Jordan May-*san*?"

Jordan tried to feign complete ignorance of the contractual issue, "It seems to me that the foreign workers are unhappy for some reason, but I don't know why."

"Not all foreign worker, Jordan May-*san*. Oh no. You are happy. You try very hard to integrate with Japanese worker. You are grateful to Matsucorp. You are just like Japanese worker."

Jordan nodded acceptance of glowing praise. The Japanese considered themselves superior in the humblest way. To be compared to them was a compliment which was difficult to surpass.

"Some foreign worker complain about money. I think you are happy with contract, Jordan May-*san*. Japanese worker are unhappy because foreign worker talk about union. We do not need union in Japan. We have good job with good company. Union is not Japanese way. Korean worker and Chinese worker talk about union to unskilled worker, maintenance worker and cleaner. And protest. And strike. This is not respect!"

This was the first time that Jordan had seen passion on the faces of Eguchi and friends. They were affronted by the ingratitude of immigrant employees. As the only foreigner in orange, Jordan needed to tread ever more carefully. It was clear to him that in the short time he had been at Matsucorp Tokyo, a divide had opened. A racial divide of which Jordan did not want to become a symbol.

Jordan remained deep in thought for the remainder of the day. In the restroom that afternoon he was oblivious to the comings and goings around him. Standing at the end urinal, one man swiftly replaced another to his left. He thought he heard a muffled greeting but dismissed this as preposterous.

His observation of Japanese urinating habits suggested that such chat was taboo. This time, Kim leaned towards him.

"Hi," he said, going beyond his previous whisper, his voice urgent and purposeful. "Have you thought any more about what I said to you?"

"Well, not really, I've…"

"There's not much time," interrupted Kim, his voice staccato as he delivered verbal jabs to the injustices of the Japanese automobile industry. "I saw that the old Japanese men have taken you aside to keep you away from the other *gaijin*. Because you are the only European, you are symbolic, I think. They want you to be an example to the rest of us. The model foreigner who accepts his inferior contract with gratitude."

Jordan spoke quickly. "I've been here one week and my life is vastly improved. It is hard to be ungrateful. And I want to integrate. I approached those old boys because I had no one to talk to. They didn't come to me."

Jordan had an acute sense of justice for the working man, but he resented the suggestion that he was being toyed with, that he had been annexed like a small country by Japanese colleagues.

"More new workers have arrived today, both skilled and unskilled. They are increasing production by bringing in more Chinese and Koreans. There are also more Europeans from the camps to do unskilled jobs. All new staff is *gaijin*, all on inferior contracts. You must see that this is not right, Jordan May-*san*."

"Of course I see that, but…"

"Now that our numbers are greater, we can do something about this. We are going to form a union. We're going to meet next week and we all need to be united. You will come on Monday night after work, won't you?"

Jordan felt like a pawn, pulled between Japanese colleagues and other Asian workers, led by Kim.

"I'll have to consider my position," was his parting shot, as he packed himself away and moved to the hand basins.

Kim followed him. "It's important." His voice was now desperate.

"I understand," said Jordan, leaving the washroom without drying his hands. He believed in the cause, of course he did, but the words of Stepson Struthwin rang in his ears as he finished the final shift of the day. Union involvement would not be looked upon favourably. It was only Thursday. Tomorrow he would gain the benefit of advice and wisdom from colleagues on both sides again and again throughout the day.

At this point Jordan, happy at work for nearly two weeks, had no idea how to proceed.

Chapter Thirty

Shaylie was the new sensation at Aphrodite's Hostess Bar, although she had done nothing special. She had settled into the job no better or worse than anyone else. Despite her misgivings, she was enjoying the feeling of power over the guests as well as the financial reward. Tsubasa could not deny, however, that business was booming, guest numbers were up and requests for the blond Westerner far exceeded all others. Shaylie's presence had inspired a retro chic, a desire to revisit the hostess experience of the fathers and grandfathers of today's salarymen.

Tsubasa recognised this as a situation which required careful management. Very few requests were granted. That was a necessary policy which prevented unmanageable evenings and also protected his girls from obsessives, from stalkers. But Tsubasa also needed to retain his richest, most powerful regulars. For this reason Shaylie was spending time in some very illustrious company. Where the size of the client group merited two hostesses, Shaylie was paired with a different girl each time. That way, Tsubasa managed to avoid resentment.

A week had passed and the three housemates had eased themselves into the Thursday night shift once more. Business built gradually. Shaylie had spent an hour with a pair of harmless, bespectacled, toothy men, perhaps similar in age to her, when she noticed the arrival of a rowdy group of six men. The same rowdy group with whom she had had her first hostessing experience the previous week. They were Thursday night regulars. Eyes locked and Shaylie discreetly returned the gracious nod of the man who had introduced himself as Ken.

The treatment of this group was different. Tsubasa emerged from his office for the first time that evening and bowed a deep bow at the group's regular table in one of the larger booths. Following a brief conversation, Shaylie and Aaliyah were summoned. Again, Shaylie found herself between Ken and one of his associates. Aaliyah, on the opposite sofa, was more animated than Shaylie had ever seen her before. Her habitual reticence was not borne of a lack of social skills as she courted the more drunken men, smiling, lighting cigarettes and fending off stray hands. They communicated in a mixture of Japanese and English, the women giving short answers to a range of personal questions. They gave nothing away.

"Where you come from?"

"How old are you?"

"Why you come to Japan?"

"You like Japan?"

"What are your hobby?"

Shaylie knew the score. Give a short answer, then ask *them* and feign deep interest in their answers.

"You play golf? Wow! That's fantastic! I bet you're really good! Can I top up your glass?"

Within a week Shaylie had already become bored with the standard questions, which gradually became more intimate.

"Do you have boyfriend?"

"No," was technically true in Shaylie's case. "But I am hoping to find one just like you. Do you have a wife?"

The reciprocated question leading to uproarious laughter, those sporting wedding bands making no attempt to hide them.

"Your dress is very gorgeous. What colour are your pants?"

The underwear question was the cue for coy mode. Head bowed, eyelashes fluttering, Aaliyah and Shaylie achieved the desired level of modesty.

"*Sōyū shitsumon yamerō!*" snapped Ken, speaking for the first time, objecting to the inane and bawdy direction the conversation had taken.

Shaylie was quickest to react to the momentary awkward silence, leaving Aaliyah to work the benign, drunken group whilst she isolated Ken in a more sober exchange.

"Your friends are silly but harmless, I think."

"Silly, yes, silly," Ken accepted, struggling twice with the lateral *l* sound.

"I can see that you are more sensible, more mature."

"Mature?"

"Yes, I think you are the leader of this group. The boss."

"Yes, the boss. Like you, Shay-ree-*san*."

Shaylie let slip a coquettish laugh. "Me? The boss? No, I am new here."

"New, yes, but different. You are not girl. You are woman. I prefer speak with you."

"Thank you, Ken, you are very kind. So, tell me about yourself."

"I am not so interesting. I am businessman. Most woman are not interesting in this thing. You are more interesting. Western woman living in Japan, working as hostess and," he paused, "a little older than most hostess." Another pause. "Sorry," he added.

"You don't need to be sorry. It's true. I am older than the others."

"And more beautiful."

"You're very kind."

"No, not kind. Truthful."

This time Shaylie blushed for real.

"So," she said, once again redirecting the conversation, "do you have a wife at home?"

"No wife," he replied, Shaylie's gaze resting only momentarily on the indentation at the base of his ring finger. It was unclear to Ken whether her eyes were drawn to the evidence of his lie or the adjacent clue to the nature of his business interests. "And you?" he quickly added, again preventing the subject of the conversation from resting upon him.

"Also no wife," responded Shaylie with a giggle which turned swiftly to embarrassment at Ken's confused look. "I'm joking. I mean, I am not married." Shaylie made a better attempt at concealing the finger from which she had removed her ring on arrival at work. The humour explained, Ken gave a weak laugh.

A week into her new job, Ken was a very different proposition to the drunken salarymen Shaylie had entertained thus far. Whilst a sober and thoughtful conversation was a pleasant change, this was harder work, both parties skirting around requests for personal details. Following the hostesses' code, she gave brief answers to his questions. She painted him an alternative picture, protecting her real life, then reflected the focus back onto the client. He was, however, skilled with his broken English at providing the scantest of information, before rebuffing her intrusions and turning the spotlight back onto her.

The initial hour came and went, time for hostesses to circulate. Aaliyah was replaced, the bawdy chat restarting from scratch, but Shaylie was not moved. It was clear that Ken had pull and that Tsubasa was anxious to please. They moved on to personal interests and life in Japan, Shaylie pushing hard to find what was below the surface of this mysterious and somewhat intimidating exterior, but Ken worked harder to maintain his facade and to break Shaylie's.

As the atmosphere around them became restless and the bottles were close to empty, Ken sought greater intimacy once more.

"Shay-ree-*san*, I have enjoy this evening, but I think we leave soon."

"I have enjoyed it too, Ken. Thank you."

"No, Thank *you*. I come back soon to see you. I am not interesting in other hostess. Only you."

"You are very kind."

"I enjoy talk with you. Maybe one day we eat in restaurant together. I think you enjoy sushi banquet. And Japanese *sake*."

Shaylie was wary. "You are very kind," she repeated. "But I am not sure if we can do that."

"Yes, we can," his reply was almost too quick, too bullish. He rediscovered his composure. "It is allowed. I think Tsubasa-*san* likes *dōhan* for his hostess." His insistence, accompanied by a measured smile, made Shaylie question

146

whether this was an invitation or an expectation, an instruction. This soft-spoken self-assurance, from the first client who had not attempted to establish physical contact with her, hinted at his position of power.

As he rose to depart, Shaylie could only manage to thank him again, once she had accompanied a coy bow with a dubious promise to consider his proposition.

Chapter Thirty-one

Arriving at the factory on Friday morning, unrest was evident on the outside for the first time. Heated conversations took place as new workers began an unofficial induction by groups of Koreans and Chinese. Before they had even arrived at the gates, newcomers were taken to one side and briefed on inequalities and the necessity of their presence at Monday's meeting.

Temporarily the heat was off for Jordan who had not slept well. He could not trouble Shaylie for her opinion as he would have done in the past. She was busy, was out of the house within an hour of his arrival and got home only shortly before his departure. So Jordan had tossed and turned alone on their double futon, his mind racing between Struthwin, Eguchi and Kim.

It was still playing on his mind as he entered the factory and took up his post, nodding curt greetings to colleagues of all nationalities. Sitting at his screen, tugging at his ear lobe, the vest beneath his boiler suit soaked up the sweat in the small of his back. His vest stuck to him like a second skin. He raised the back of his hand to his brow and wiped away a feverishness unrelated to physical exertion. He was burning up with the stress of indecision, in the knowledge that all roads were fraught with danger.

On the short trip to the canteen and back during morning break, Jordan noticed a proliferation of green boiler suits. The rumours had been true: more unskilled workers. Europeans, Africans, perhaps some from the Americas, all of solid build. The factory was shining, bleach with a hint of citrus, walls and floors gleaming, automatic glass doors transparent, porcelain bowls and basins brilliant, unsullied, sparkling. The working environment sterilised. Sterile. Conditions beyond dispute.

Throughout the rest of the morning, Jordan's focus was on his screen, on production. The quality of his work was beyond reproach, equal to that of his local colleagues, regardless of terms of employment. He had maintained the quality of his performance for so many years and was able to filter out distractions, which today took the form of green boiler suits in his peripheral vision. His focal point remained the production line, on the outskirts, increased activity, rubbing and scrubbing, cleaning and maintaining. He could not blot it out. He felt an attachment, a solidarity with those men. They were economic refugees, like him, at sea in a foreign culture, like him, settling in, trying to adapt, but without the skills which afforded them a privileged position in front of a screen.

Lunch time came and Jordan visited the rest room *en route* to the canteen. He now had time to devote to his recently acquired obsession. He felt a need to convey empathy, appreciation, fraternity. He sought eye contact, now and then locking momentary stares with men who wished to impress, to appear essential to the operation. Rare were those prepared to return his nodded greeting, even a half smile. He wondered whether orange guilt originated his awkwardness around the increased green presence.

One or two green boiler suits in the canteen had become five or six today. All spillages on clean tables and floors were removed, neither a drop of green tea nor a stray noodle allowed to rest for more than a few seconds. They were stationed around the room, burly operatives, armed with cloths, buckets and mops, awkward bows dissolving below the radars of their superiors.

Equipped with a glass of barley tea, Jordan approached the buffet tables, stepping carefully with his tray around a kneeling green boiler suit, who was removing a spillage of Japanese curry from the easy-wipe flooring. A brown head of hair suggested a white man, perhaps a fellow European. Jordan again hesitated, imagining himself in this man's position. The man was of smaller build than the rest and, as he rose, Jordan stepped back to protect his tray. He struggled not to drop it as he came face to face with his brother.

The awkward silence, a second or two, was interminable. Ethan recovered first, whispering a brief greeting to his open-mouthed brother. As Jordan moved along, his appetite gone, Ethan risked one further utterance.

"Toilets in twenty minutes."

One third of an hour. Twelve hundred seconds. An eternity. Jordan ate little, said little to Eguchi and friends, smoked half of his daily social cigarette and attempted a facade of composure.

"I've only got a minute," said Ethan as they stood side-by-side at the hand basins, regarding one another in the mirrors.

"Go on," replied Jordan, still in shock but now consumed with curiosity.

"I had a phone call from Matsucorp. Out of the blue. Offering me a job. Saying they looked after their workers and it was policy to keep family together. A chance to start again. Decent money and a contract. A couple of nights in one of those festering migrant camps for appearance's sake. Now I'm in a gaijin house with loads of other blokes just around the corner."

"Why? Why you?" was all that he could muster.

"Because I'm family, I said."

"You don't really believe that, do you?" said Jordan. "We've barely spoken in years."

"That's what he told me."

"Who?"

"The bloke who called."

"Didn't he give a name?"

"No name, no." Ethan was drying his hands. "Well-spoken, short and to the point, with a strange turn of phrase."

The description was sinking in as Jordan saw his departing brother's reflected wink from over his shoulder.

Chapter Thirty-two

"What do you have for me, Stepson-*san*? Is our migrant programme running smoothly?"

The smoke hung thick around Matsubara's head as he awaited another late-night update in his office. This arrangement was strictly one-to-one, man-to-man, scheduled late enough for the executive floor to be empty of the prying eyes of Matsubara's significant admin team. Relaxing, whisky in hand, the boss was still confident in the abilities of his top advisor. Troubles would always be shot by Stepson Struthwin.

"There have been very few problems. We should be pleased. Not only have we been sympathetic to our best workers from the closed FREW operations, we have achieved additional positive PR by taking pity on some of the men in the camps. As a result we have bigger cleaning and general maintenance teams who, for little remuneration, provide us with the cleanest, smoothest-running factories in the world."

"I don't doubt it, Stepson-*san*, not for a minute. These are, for the most part, grateful migrants who have come to us without the complication of family ties. I would like reassurance, however, where there are complications. In the case of the May family, for example."

"They continue to settle in well. The wife is now busy. Friends from the gaijin house have got her a job hostessing in Okachimachi."

"Such jobs are not without risk, Stepson-*san*, as I am sure you are aware."

"This does not worry me. She is at one of the more reputable establishments, she is happy and she has the opportunity to learn Japanese whilst earning money. Initial reports from the owner, whom I know personally, suggest that she is popular and strong guidance will allow her to be successful whilst remaining in control."

A pause. Matsubara was considering Alfie and his initial difficulties at school.

"Can I assume that the boy is also receiving strong guidance?"

"Of course. The headteacher has assigned a prefect to help him to integrate. Some bonding has taken place and he was taken out for a day in Harajuku on Sunday as part of a group of youngsters."

"There was a demonstration against Yamada's party on Sunday on the Omotesandō. We do not want him to become politicised. That could be awkward."

"I agree that hardcore activism could be awkward. However, I would argue that his presence as part of a group of enthusiastic youths will simply allow him to belong. This is to our advantage. There is no problem with harmless youthful politicisation."

"See to it that that is all that it is, Stepson-*san*. We cannot afford for him to become a symbol of protest for greater acceptance of migration. Not if this will place us at odds with Yamada's election campaign."

"Please do not worry, Matsubara-*san*. I am in control of the situation. The May family is an ongoing successful project."

"I accept your summary of the situation, Stepson-*san*. Fortunately, Jordan May-*san* is an exemplary worker with strong production data. It is very pleasing to me that he has settled quickly and that there is nothing which can endanger his success at work."

Stepson Struthwin smiled inwardly, choosing to respond with a thoughtful, silent nod. He knew that Matsubara would have been pleased with the data. He also knew that all data of all kinds would have been carefully studied, right down to the names, nationalities and circumstances of the new intake of unskilled workers. None of the names will have been noteworthy, including that of Eric Marks, a FREW migrant from the Yokohama holding camp. False papers had been Struthwin's only option. Smooth was dull and Struthwin did not want dull. He could afford enjoyment when exercising such a high level of control.

It was not until the lift doors closed that Stepson Struthwin allowed himself a smile.

#

At eleven, they sent me away. Pressured to work my way through the system, I did not return for another twelve years. Twelve years of misery in the UK. Who knew then how few years the UK had left as a united kingdom? That miserable country with its miserable climate and its miserable, uptight class system was always going to find a miserable end. I felt that as keenly from its privileged end. You probably doubt me, but it's true.

As a young Marlburian, I would have my well-being and prospects elevated, they said. I would develop friendships for life, they said. I would learn, through boarding, to treat my fellow pupils with the kindness, sensitivity and respect that they would show me. A trio of values, for which read physical and psychological mistreatment, sexual abuse and cruelty. And this, 6000 miles from home.

From a young age I was awkward and sensitive but comfortable in my own company. But these traits which were common and accepted in Japan, were weaknesses to be exploited at Marlborough. Exploited by alpha males and females, pupils and staff, in the menacing environment of Father's alma mater. Alma mater! A misnomer deliberately lifted from Latin to mask the reality of the public school system. Who knew that, even at a co-ed school, you would be buggered by older boys in a packed dorm in the middle of the night? The straggly loner may not have been the most attractive child, but he looked like a victim. The kind of victim who would bite his pillow, stifle his own sobbing and keep his mouth shut. Unless it was his mouth which was being used, of course. I would go to bed praying to be abused by a true coward. At least these surreptitious abusers would not disturb my sleep. All I had to do was wake up early and wash the semen out of my hair before anyone else saw. As I checked the mirror, I saw my father looking back, telling me time and time again how Marlborough would make a man of me.

More and more detached from other humans, the latter years of my education and training were a breeze. Free of abuse I hopped through the VIth Form, skipped to an Economics First at Oxford and jumped into the FCO. In the FCO, you either toe the line or give a very strong impression that you are doing so.

#

Chapter Thirty-three

Another week had passed, another week to get used to school, to get used to life in Japan, life away from Evie. Tomoko had kissed him. Alfie had not been disloyal. Yet. It was what he felt that was tinged with guilt. Another week with Tomoko, breaks, the end of lunchtimes, after school. There had been no repeat of the kiss, but there was no denying that they were getting on better and better. It was a developing friendship but there was also a spark.

The following weekend, Alfie had been invited out again. This time he knew that a sunny Saturday afternoon in the park was not going to be leisure, but his desire to strengthen his friendship with Tomoko would draw him into her activism.

Yellow, white and red, in Alfie's view Tomoko's flamboyant mode better reflected a bright spring day than the darker colours of the previous Sunday. He felt that she lit up the carriage as she joined the train at Hōya, the station his dad came to every day. They rode carefree, stop by stop, further and further from the city. Crossing the border from Tokyo into Saitama prefecture, an altogether greener proposition, they alighted at Tokorozawa station. A change of platform to the Seibu Shinjuku line and they had one stop to travel to Kōkū-kōen station, right in front of Kōkū park. Cherry blossom season was all but over, no *hanami* for them today, though Alfie would allow the late April sun to wash over him as the increasingly large band of activists, which they joined at the park entrance, discussed and colluded and schemed.

Chaotic bowing all round lacked the formality of last week's encounter. Perhaps this was not an occasion, as such, but an informal assembly, a friendly troupe spending an afternoon in the sun, chatting as well as plotting. Finding himself behind Tomoko for the first time, he noticed a discreet back-pack, realised he was one of few without a bag.

"Is this a sleepover?" he whispered, drawing up alongside her.

"What?" A confused smile.

"Why does everyone have a bag?"

"We are going to have a piku-niku," explained Tomoko, American momentarily giving way to Japanese. She knew what his response would be, interrupting before he could begin. "I have brought contribution for two of us. Both of us. I wanted to treat you. You can do it for me next time. No big deal."

She was charming, concise and forceful. And so much more. He could only return her smile and offer a meek *arigatō* which added approving laughter to her beam. They followed the tarmac pathway towards the centre of the park. Wide-open green areas on either side hosted congregations of varying sizes, seated on blankets, often beneath trees, eating and drinking. Some played badminton, football, baseball. Equipped with machine and mic, some sang karaoke, a national pursuit which Alfie had thus far avoided.

Beautiful weather had brought families and youths out in their numbers. Having this morning judged it to be a two-layer day, Alfie found himself removing his retro Superdry sweatshirt to reveal a chest-hugging T-shirt, crisp-white this morning but now sticking to the small of his back. Concentrating on pulling the cotton away from his back and underarms, he missed the appreciative eyes on his athletic torso.

It was cooler for a while as the path took them through a wooded area. They emerged in the centre of the park. Immaculate grass stretched into the distance, a café sat in a central, concreted area and the diverging pathways were punctuated with mobile drink and snack kiosks. Now they left the pathway, walking carefully between bevies of disparate humanity, Japanese humanity, towards the broader areas of unoccupied verdure in the distance. The feeling of unwelcome scrutiny returned to Alfie for the first time since the previous weekend, genteel picnickers of a certain age unable to focus on their *nigiri* in the presence of a paler face and a shock of brown hair.

The chosen spot was beneath a pair of moulted cherry trees, the ground around them off-white with the fading blossom. Alfie counted thirty-three in their company, at least half of whom immediately removed large blankets from their bags. Arranging themselves in a large circle, an array of refreshments began to emerge, systematically arranged on the ground. Alfie did not need to understand the language to sense the warmth of the occasion, the evident comradeship, as the chatting continued and the sharing began. Hunger was addressed before the principal business of the afternoon.

In his time at school, Alfie had started to recognise words and short phrases but he still lacked the confidence to try to use them himself. He could name the vast majority of the food items being shared amongst the coterie of activists and could accept or decline offers with good grace and politesse. The only way to further ingratiate himself with people of his own age would be to learn to converse passably in Japanese. It really was galling that a knowledge of English was quite common in older Japanese, but its rarity in his peers was as much a by-product of the times as his presence in Japan.

Alfie was on the point of steering the idle chit-chat he had been enjoying with Tomoko towards the reason for this gathering, when the assembly began to fall silent. They both looked up, only to be blinded by the sun, which had moved into a gap between two branches. Raising themselves from their semi-prostrate positions, now cross-legged and straight-backed, the sun hid once more behind the tree, revealing to them the unremarkable figure of Jun, readying himself to speak.

Everyone had spoken in the café the previous Sunday, Alfie thought, and Jun had not stood out. In fact, Alfie could not say for sure that he had been there. Today, however, he led. Ordinary was an accurate description. And standard. Ordinary and standard. The standard uniform of a weekend student type. T-shirt, jeans and canvas trainers. What Tomoko would call *sneakers*. Physically ordinary. Short, black hair, average height, average build, narrow eyes and a small gap between his two upper front teeth. His smile was genial, his manner determined, assured and at the same time understated.

For the next couple of hours he would address his comrades at length, then, remaining the focal point of the group, take questions and lead a lively and passionate discussion. Tomoko took a full part, Alfie sat back. The observer, he zoned between the passion of the discussion, picking up very little, and his own thoughts. The pitch of the exchanges slowly but surely transformed, increasingly strident, increasingly animated. Climax after climax, the afternoon progressed towards the final crescendo of what Alfie understood to be Jun's summarising call to action. Occasional whispered comments from Tomoko told Alfie little more, lulls were rare, detail scant, the discussion fast-moving and heated. Elated applause erupted as Jun finally sat down. Conversations broke out across the company, the language irrelevant, the excitement and approval comprehensible. Something had been agreed. Alfie turned to Tomoko and raised a questioning eyebrow.

"*Baddo-min-ton yarimashō!*" enthused Tomoko, jumping up and grabbing two racquets and a shuttlecock. They moved onto an open space and, over ten minutes of to-and-fro, Alfie gradually had his questions answered.

"That was quite a discussion," Alfie expressed the impression which had been made, the impression Tomoko had been hoping for. She wanted him engaged by the atmosphere and the excitement before she gave him the details.

"It sure was. I think we've found a leader."

"He seemed impressive. It sounded to me like you had a worthwhile meeting."

"We did," the brief, mysterious answers forcing him to ask, to show his interest.

"So? What did you discuss? What did you decide?"

"Well, we talked about last Sunday, how we engaged a lot of young people, how we get more each time."

"Last Sunday wasn't the first time?"

"No. We have been gradually building interest, protesting on a small scale, beginning the fight against racist politicians. But we need to be bigger. You saw how there were no journalists. We need an event which is so big that it cannot be ignored. The wider public needs to know what the JSD is really doing and that there is another way. We need to reintroduce humanitarian empathy."

"No reasonable person could argue with you. But can this small group really put on something that big?"

"We think so. Word is spreading through universities and high schools. Everyone expects protests on the Omotesandō on a Sunday. They are predictable and easily contained. We just need to take them by surprise."

"So are you going to tell me the plan?"

"A bigger and better demonstration."

"Last Sunday was pretty big."

"Much bigger than that. Two weeks from tomorrow."

"Two weeks?" Alfie was incredulous. "How on earth are you going to boost numbers in such a short time?"

"We are building a network. We have links to so many schools and colleges. Everyone has agreed to hold secret student meetings. To inspire people to take part. We are all very confident. We have to do this."

"But won't the police get involved, contain us, inform the JSD and keep the press away?" It was not lost on Tomoko that Alfie had used *us* for the first time. He was on board.

"That's why we have to plan in secret. We will publicise meetings but the detail will be delivered in person and in secret."

"And what *is* the detail?"

"We need to surprise them. It will happen on Saturday afternoon on the first day in May. It used to be a day for workers around the world, a day for equality, a celebration. In the morning, some of us will assemble on the Omotesandō. We will draw the police to Harajuku, stage a peaceful march, they will think that it is all over by midday."

"Very clever. And then you'll go somewhere else?"

"To Ikebukuro. East side. We will meet at Sunshine 60 in front of the Matsucorp showroom, then at 2pm we march down Sunshine Dōri onto the Meiji Dōri, forcing the traffic to a standstill. We then begin a long march on the Meiji Dōri to Shinjuku."

"Meiji Dōri?"

"One of the biggest, busiest, most significant roads in Tokyo. We will bring the north-west of Tokyo to a halt and eventually, if the police don't stop us, finish in front of the Shinjuku government buildings."

"Why meet at the Matsucorp showroom?"

"It is the most powerful corporation in Japan at the moment and there is worker unrest. Foreign workers are being given inferior contracts to the Japanese. They are beginning to form unions. We think we can get the unions involved. The demo will not just be students. It could be massive."

Alfie was full of admiration. His breath had been taken by the sheer audacity of the plan, but also by the anxiety in the back of his mind. Potential violence did not concern him, but his activism would place him in conflict with his dad's employer, the corporation which had improved their lives. It was as if Tomoko were able to track his thought processes.

"Many of our fellow students will be involved. Did you know that most of the students at Nerima High are Matsucorp children? You will not be alone. And as a white boy you will not be conspicuous. This march will be huge. You will be one amongst many thousands and there will be other white faces, too. Many non-skilled workers are from Europe and they are being treated poorly. It is racial discrimination, Alfie. We have to fight it."

Badminton was forgotten as Tomoko now walked towards Alfie, her voice softening in intimate proximity. To him, her plea felt tender rather than clichéd.

"We will fight for humanitarian values. Liberty, equality and fraternity. And at the same time," now squeezing his upper arm, "we will look after one another."

Alfie's head swam as they maintained eye contact for a moment longer. It was time to go. They returned the racquets, bowed to a ubiquitous chorus of *gokurosama deshita* and sauntered away for some time alone.

Sitting in a corner of the park café, they retraced their conversation, Alfie needing to clarify the enormity and ambition of the plan in his own mind. His apparent commitment to the cause, or perhaps to Tomoko, lent a greater feeling of intimacy to their friendship. At the small wooden table they sipped cappuccinos, a symbol of bygone European influence, leaning in, their faces close together, their eyes locked, their smiles abashed. Beneath the table, their knees had interlocked as they sat down, neither attempting to break the physical contact. The conversation moving from the serious to the mundane, time passed as they shared more coffee and a plate of roasted sweet potato. Outside, the light began to fade.

Emerging, they followed the path back towards the station, the park now sparsely populated. Their comrades were nowhere to be seen. In the beautiful warm spring dusk, Alfie realised that they were holding hands. It was unclear who had initiated it, but it felt natural. They were both comfortable as they walked through the wooded area, back into the open and through the gate. Neither had noticed the three men who had been seated outside the café, who had got up to leave very soon after them, who followed them out of the park and now stood at the far end of the platform.

Having stood close together on two trains, it was Alfie's turn to alight before his stop, walking Tomoko to the ticket gates at Hōya station. This time the kiss was initiated by Alfie, this time not a surprise, this time reciprocated. A deep, prolonged and affectionate kiss, simple friendship now a precursor to a relationship, consummated by mouths, enveloped arms insulating them against the cooling evening air.

"See you tomorrow," both chimed in concert, Alfie returning to the platform, still oblivious to the attention which would be unwelcome.

Two further stops and he found himself ambling along the edge of Shakuji park, his head still swimming as a black-jacketed arm emerged from a park gate, grabbed his hoody and dragged him onto the pathway around the lake.

Gaijin was the only word he understood in a vicious verbal tirade which was accompanied by blows and shoves which sent him sprawling into the undergrowth. Pulling himself to his feet once more, he began to run in the direction of home, only to be rugby-tackled to the ground, his face hitting the damp grass, tasting the soil. The justificatory invective continued as a rib-cracking kick turned him onto his back. Squinting through the dirt, he recognised his assailants from Akihabara the weekend before. Taking in the hatred on the faces of the three young men, dressed in black, he was lifted several times by the scruff of his overgarment, only to be laid out again and again by punches to the face, punctuated by further kicks to his torso and legs.

In a state of semi-consciousness he saw them running back towards the station, disturbed by a local man of considerable seniority, accompanied by a chihuahua which began to lick Alfie's wounded face. Replying to the man's concerned "*daijōbu?*" with whimpers and groans, Alfie was soon alone again.

The swollen foreign face had told the man all he had needed to know. Within minutes he was knocking at the door of the gaijin house.

Chapter Thirty-four

A beaten child awaited Shaylie when she returned from work on Sunday morning. The old man with his chihuahua had called an ambulance and Jordan had spent the evening with Alfie at Ōizumi hospital, halfway between Shakuji and Hōya, where an x-ray had revealed a broken rib. Patched up, bruised all over and with a badly swollen face, Alfie now lay on his futon in their shared room. A kindly doctor with medical English had managed to impart that Alfie would require a week's rest from school.

The effects of strong analgesics dissipating by Sunday lunchtime, a *compos mentis* Alfie was able to give his parents a patchy account of what happened.

"How many of them were there?" asked Jordan.

Alfie winced as he attempted a more comfortable position. "It was the same three thugs as last week."

Shaylie's questioning face forced Jordan to reveal the truth. At the time he had felt it better she didn't know, but now it was clear to the three of them that they were victims of a targeted racist attack. They agreed that police involvement in the current political climate would achieve little and that, as guests in the country, they did not want to make waves. They simply felt that they would have to be careful.

"I'll stay at home tomorrow and look after Alfie," said Jordan.

"You will not!" asserted Shaylie. "We were brought here because you are a skilled worker with an excellent attendance record. Do what you need to do to make sure our stay is smooth. Besides, tomorrow is my night off. You look after Alfie tonight, then I'll take over in the morning. We carry on as normal and we'll soon have Alfie back on his feet."

And so it was that they tended for Alfie's every need, knowing not that his greatest anxiety was not his cuts and bruises, but the prospect of missing Tomoko tomorrow and the next day and the next.

Chapter Thirty-five

Jordan's head had been so occupied since Alfie's hospitalisation that it was only walking to the station on Monday morning that he remembered something else he had kept from his wife. And from his son. Ethan. His brother, Ethan. His parents' darling younger son who could do no wrong.

Jordan's memory harboured so many examples of his brother's unseen arrogance, but there was one afternoon in particular which he often revisited. It was the afternoon when he had been surprised to return to a quiet house. In his high school days, he always arrived home an hour after Ethan. Middle school finished an hour earlier and he would find his younger brother in front of the TV, feet on the coffee table, with a bag of crisps and a can of pop. For Jordan, TV was an evening treat. After middle school, he had gone straight to his room to battle with his English homework. His brother's *laissez-faire* attitude irritated him. The fact that it was never reflected in his school report irritated him more. Their parents arrived close to 6pm, by which time Ethan had picked up a book for appearance sake.

So the day when Jordan entered a deserted front room, he knew something was up. Then he heard movement upstairs. A door banged and he approached the staircase. "Bye, Ethan," came the female voice and the girl brushed past Jordan on the way to the front door. Jordan looked up and locked eyes with his smirking brother, standing at the top of the stairs in his boxer shorts, arms crossed. He scratched his crotch, winked at his brother and turned back to his bedroom.

Jordan had never felt himself to be in a race to get laid, but he could see that his brother thought otherwise. That arrogant stare was a statement of knowing superiority, of fraternal victory.

By the time their parents got home, both boys were in their books. To this day, Jordan was most hurt by his parents' belief that they had two similar, hard-working sons.

Jordan saw pockets of foreign workers stood deep in conversation outside the gates of Matsucorp. A mixture of orange and green shared common gripes, the activists persuading the wary of the merits of action. He slipped past Kim, who was working a group of skilled workers of Asian appearance. In the distance he noticed the unmistakeable figure of Ethan in a separate huddle. He entered the building and the locker room, preparing himself for his shift. Jordan was happy to assume his boiler suit in the locker room every morning, rather than draw attention to himself as many others did, bright orange on the crowded trains.

Nobody would dare approach him at his workstation. Production line distractions were taboo. Mentally he prepared himself for morning break, another stress to add to that of his injured son and the targeted attacks. Only now he remembered that a first union meeting was planned for that evening.

Jordan could only behave naturally, the way he always was. Understated, unassuming, he went about his life and his work without creating waves. There were advantages to operating under the radar. He joined the stream at the beginning of break, pulled towards refreshment with his colleagues, some of whom opted for a detour to prioritise bladder relief. One orange boiler suit amongst a crowd, he joined a drinks queue a couple of places behind Eguchi, who looked round and aimed a friendly nod in his direction. Returning the greeting, Jordan felt a tap on his shoulder. He turned to find himself nose to nose with Kim, the Korean activist who had been very insistent the previous week. There was no escape.

"So?" Kim did not need to verbalise the question. His voice was urgent, low in pitch but aggressive. His eyes were locked with Jordan's, desperate, almost panicked.

"I'm not sure," responded Jordan. Although there were activists trying to recruit other foreign employees, Jordan was beginning to understand from Kim's desperation and persistence that his was a scalp worth having. The only orange Westerner would add diversity and a sense of universality to the cause.

"Come on, Jordan-*san*. Let's not draw attention to ourselves. You know what I am asking. We have our first union meeting this evening. We are not trouble-makers. We only want equality of working conditions across races. It is not asking too much, I think."

"Everything you say makes sense," pleaded Jordan in hushed tones, "but it puts me in a difficult position. Matsucorp have given me a new life. I'm not sure this is the time to invite trouble upon my family."

"But there is so much at stake. Not just for you, for all of us who are not Japanese. We need to support one another to…"

"Jordan May-*san*, please join us for drink and cigarette." The very deliberate interruption came as Eguchi moved away from the serving hatch with his drink. Once Jordan had responded with a nod of gratitude and a brief *arigatō*, Eguchi withdrew, aiming a look of disapproval at Kim.

The distraction allowed Jordan to turn to the hatch for service, Kim delivering his parting shot in Jordan's right ear.

"We need you, Jordan-*san*. This issue is bigger than you. You know what is right. We will be discreet. We are meeting away from here. Be at the *north* exit of Shiinamachi station at 6:45pm."

Kim did not wait for a response. Jordan did not need a second invitation to the sanctuary of the benign conversation of Eguchi and friends. He soon found himself finishing his break with a barley tea and a Mild Seven, before returning to his workstation.

Head space would have been welcome. Jordan wanted to think, to assess the quandary, but head space was not afforded to him by his job. Back in front of his screen he focused once more. The decision he knew he would have to make became a background irritant. Possible confrontations to come in the impending lunch break also nagged at the back of Jordan's mind, but an active workstation was not the place to resolve anything.

Lunch time came and Jordan left his screen. The sooner he reached the canteen, the shorter the queue. He really wanted to get his lunch and get sat with Eguchi. He wanted to avoid more awkward discussion with Kim. What he had not counted on was an awkward attempt by Eguchi to tackle the issue of foreigners and unions, interpreted by the Japanese as disloyalty.

"I am very sad, Jordan May-*san*," he said through a mouthful of rice. "Staff in this factory used to be united. Even when we started having foreign cleaners, we were a family. What has gone wrong?"

What could Jordan say? It was impossible to respond without becoming embroiled in an unwanted conversation. He wasn't about to argue the case for a union to a man who had welcomed him so warmly.

"I don't know." Jordan felt pathetic. But he knew that all arguments were irrelevant to Eguchi. This may be the usual way to behave in Europe, in China, in Korea, but guests in Japan should accept Japanese culture and live according to Japanese customs. Awkward silences, one-word answers, a shadow had been cast over today's lunch. Fewer words spoken, faster eating, less mastication, more indigestion. An unpleasant aftertaste.

Eguchi and colleagues left Jordan to finish his dessert. They all pointed to the smoking terrace and nodded, as a cleaning operative moved towards their table to clear bowls and plates. Ethan affected friendly brother in hushed tones, his genial greeting met with "What do you want?"

"Don't be like that, Jordan, there's so little time to talk."

"Who needs to talk? What are you even doing here?"

"Working. Like you. Improving my life. Like you. Getting mugged off. Like you. We can't just sit back and let them get away with it, you know."

"Let who get away with what?"

"You've changed. What happened to equality, to working class beliefs? What happened to sticking together?"

The exchange became heated. There were inquisitive looks from adjacent tables as the orange and the green fought hard to remain in control.

"What the fuck do you know about sticking together? You haven't been in touch for years. Since when did you care about anything other than yourself? Equality has never been your thing."

"It used to be yours, though."

"It still *is*," hissed Jordan.

"So prove it. I may have rejected your morality in the past but I always knew I was looking up to you on the high ground. You were right. You *are* right! Don't give in to the big corporations now when we need to be strong."

More orange boiler suits turned to stare as Jordan, without another word, pushed his chair back, more noisily than intended, and stood to eyeball his brother. He opened his mouth to speak, paused, considered, closed his mouth, shook his head slowly and turned towards the terrace.

"See you later," insisted Ethan as his brother distanced himself, as he had been for many years. Always inscrutable, it remained entirely unclear to Ethan what Jordan planned to do. He did not know that it remained equally unclear to Jordan himself.

Chapter Thirty-six

Having checked on Shaylie and Alfie, Jordan was on the citybound Seibu Ikebukuro line. There had been no further incidents until a pop-up message appeared on his screen before the end of his shift. Although it had not surprised him, it had filled him with dread and he had not found three minutes with the wiry toff any less intimidating than before.

"I hope that you are well and that nobody is making life difficult for you."

Sympathy? Or mind games?

"I was sorry to hear about your son. I hope he will soon make a full recovery and be able to return to school."

How did he know?

"At Matsucorp, we want to look after our employees, especially those who have come so far to join us."

Wishing to give nothing away, all Jordan could do was thank him for his concern.

The ordeal was soon over, the omniscient protector having again played his role. Nothing controversial broached, no overt warning, the true reason for the meeting left unsaid, festering behind a facade of employer duty of care. The grand master had given his pawn a cursory health check and released him without instruction.

Approaching Shiinamachi, Jordan was deep in thought. Instinct dictated that he attend the meeting. Influenced by family and community as a teenager, he had formed a set of values which prized social justice. He had lived and worked by these values for two decades as an adult, nurturing his son with the same beliefs. Did fresh circumstances warrant fresh thought, a new approach? It was not too late to turn back. Matsucorp's awkward ex-pat was aware of his every movement. Would he find out if Jordan attended the inaugural union meeting of disenfranchised Matsucorp workers? The notorious *gaijin*. Jordan could be risking this chance at a new life, handed on a plate to his family. Wife and son, relying upon him, settling in, their economic futures assured for years to come. He could cross the bridge now from the platform where he paused to deliberate and take the next train home. Avoid putting their new home in danger. Danger of upsetting his benefactors, danger of appearing ungrateful and, yes, danger of further reprisals from right-wing thugs. Principle drove him through cautionary thoughts to the north exit where he hovered, keeping his distance, following the large crowd of *gaijin* to the venue.

The magnitude of Matsucorp began to dawn upon Jordan as he walked along the street, mingling at a safe distance with homebound workers who had spilled out of the train from Ikebukuro. This anonymous suburb had been chosen with good reason. He recognised few of the Matsucorp crowd. This small heterogenous fraction of the workforce was now removed from its orange or green contexts, their huge Tokyo factory one part of a world-leading operation. A corporation of this size could surely not have much interest in the passive activism of one individual. Nevertheless, Jordan would plant himself at the back of the meeting, an extra in an unfolding drama of conscience.

Kim's faint nod in his direction showed respect for his reticence. He acknowledged Jordan's support for the cause without drawing undue attention. Anonymity was aided by the atmosphere of the meeting room, thick with smoke, at the top of a shabby staircase in a shabby building which stood two floors high. He negotiated his way through to the back of the packed room. He identified the back of his brother's head, positioned at the front amongst the most vocal. But he did not recognise his new-found fervour.

Silence broke out almost at once when a tall, earnest individual stood on the small dais, facing out at the gathering. For the first time since his arrival in Japan, Jordan found himself in a setting where the *lingua franca* was English, and yet in that short time he had rarely felt so uncomfortable. The baritone voice speaking excellent English with a German accent penetrated the noxious fumes.

"My name is Armin. I come from the north of Germany and I have been working for Matsucorp as an unskilled maintenance operative for nine months. They rescued me from the Yokohama holding camp. I am grateful for the opportunity they gave me. They have given me back my humanity, but only conditionally. I am now part of the human race again, but only if I agree to work under conditions which are different to those of other human beings. This differentiation is made according to nationality, one could argue according to race. This cannot be right."

Cheers and applause started at the front and quickly spread throughout the room. Common cause was established. Armin impressed.

"Many years ago in Germany, I trained as a lawyer and I have studied employment law. The Japanese worked hard to rebuild their country after the Second World War and worked together effectively as a society. Trades unions were not necessary. As they became stronger and free-market capitalism led to greater inequality, unions were legal but barely tolerated. Since Japan became the world's leading economy, unions no longer have a place in Japanese employment law. Working conditions did not vary sufficiently for this to be an issue in a society with minimal immigration. We migrants now find ourselves the victims of contractual discrimination. It is a discrimination which has a basis in law. Does this mean that our hands are tied?"

Low-level, grumbling discontent was the response of the *gaijin* workers who had, until now, not understood the complexity of their plight.

"Friends, it would be easy to accept our lot and be grateful. Only by making difficult decisions, by committing ourselves and by fighting for what is right do we have a chance of affecting change."

More cheers and applause, Armin was winning.

"If we wish it to happen, this evening we can agree to form a union, unofficial though it may be, and we can plan action to communicate our views and our demands."

"Strike!" shouted an English voice, Ethan's voice. It was followed by cries of support.

"Striking will always be a last resort, friends," continued the voice of reason, "especially in our situation. Those of us who are working in unskilled roles, the majority of us, can be replaced from the holding camps at the click of Mr Matsubara's fingers. Deportation would quickly follow. We need to be more astute. Every one of us has a platform to speak here this evening. It is time for us to hear your views and your ideas."

Armin stepped down to a rousing reception. There followed a succession of rabble-rousing addresses of little substance, some in accomplished English, most more halting, resulting in a charged atmosphere. By encouraging the input of all-comers, Armin had achieved a critical mass, ready for action. The nature of any action, however, was very unclear. Direction and leadership were needed.

A break was called, the cue for groups of men, mostly men, to discuss and argue the way forward. Jordan stood, alone in a crowd, and observed. A sea of animated workers, a collective, working man's spirit which would once have motivated him but now worried him. He could not decide why Ethan felt such a need to be involved, deep as he was in discussion with Kim. Armin had disappeared but now Jordan could see him at the side of the room, at its only entrance and exit. He towered above two young orientals, listening intently as they spoke. They were certainly not old enough to be colleagues, they cannot have been much older than Alfie. The boy was ordinary, average build, short black hair, narrow eyes, the girl pretty, petite, intense. The boy did most of the talking. There was nodding from all sides and then they were gone.

Jordan watched Armin regain the stage with renewed purpose. The majority of the room had not noticed his powwow during the break, but the assembly was impressed with what he had to say next. Somehow, whilst all-comers had taken the dais to suggest unlikely courses of action, Armin had come up with a winner. Their unofficial union had been invited to be part of a huge demonstration, along with similar groups of disenfranchised workers from other companies. The organisers? A bunch of students. Young Japanese people prepared to face down the authorities to protest against discrimination and the lurch to the right of the Japanese electorate. It was inspiring and it was an opportunity.

For Jordan, it was the chance to be involved but to remain anonymous. At an event of that size he imagined he would be able to blend in whilst satisfying his conscience. He slipped out and disappeared into the night before the meeting ended, his heart less heavy than before. Keen to be back with wife and son, he failed to see what could go wrong.

#

After two years in Whitehall, my relative proficiency in Japanese was always going to land me with a junior posting somewhere in Japan. They could have put me in the Consulate in Osaka, but it was decided to place me under His Excellency, The Ambassador of the United Kingdom to Japan in the British Embassy, Tokyo. So back home I finally went.

This was not a fact I broadcast to my fellow graduates. They were all boasting on social media about the status, starting salary and kudos of their first posts in a variety of very much establishment careers. Having been particularly outspoken in debates, both official and ad hoc, in debating halls and pubs, expressing my distaste for the privilege and nepotism of the old boys' network, here I was, unwittingly the biggest fraud of them all.

It was time for some independence. Of course, Mother wanted me to move back into the official residence, into my old bedroom, that single bed. Imagine that! As I towered over her, did she not get the feeling that I had outgrown that room? Twelve years later, she wanted to revert to my early childhood, having opted out of bringing me up through my teenage years. That was not going to happen.

I got myself a swish flat in Roppongi. His Excellency helped with the key money, of course, three stops on the metro from work or from a weekend visit to Mother, but on the doorstep of Tokyo's most cosmopolitan nightspots. I could make friends, well, acquaintances anyway, and entertain. I could even think about dating if I could work out whether I had any sexuality and, if so, which way I swung.

At work it was easy to impress. You would not believe the intellectual limitations of some of those who get into the FCO. I was surrounded by Russell Group Desmonds, and I benefited from the nepotism which had placed them, rather than worthier graduates, as my rivals.

Though I say so myself, eloquence, intelligence and the subject matter of my Geoff Hurst soon afforded me a trade portfolio and easy access to powerful contacts in Japanese industry.

#

Chapter Thirty-seven

By Tuesday, Alfie was able to inch around the gaijin house, empty other than his mother and the two Israeli girls sleeping in preparation for their shift. His dad was less troubled on departure for work that morning and he, himself, was not bothered by his own absence from incomprehensible lessons. But he did miss Tomoko.

He wondered whether he could really have more intense feelings than he had had for Evie. Evie, friend then girlfriend, his first girlfriend. Bright and pretty, she had helped him with his homework, invited him for tea, held his hand in more ways than one, kissed him, sometimes affectionately. She had looked after him, in some ways like his mother. Unlike Tomoko.

Perhaps that was not quite true. Tomoko had been looking out for him. That is what she had been told to do. That was her role. But this was not some longstanding friendship which had matured. She was a ten-tonne truck, crashing into his new world, making his head spin and his stomach churn. Chance and circumstance were propelling him into an emotional bond with a mature, attractive and independent human being. His new girlfriend was not a girl. He had wandered into the adult world. Trepidation told Alfie that he needed to prepare to experience life, to develop sophistication and culture, to measure up to a relationship with a young woman a little older than him. He had felt what she was feeling through their kiss. He could be a child no longer.

Early afternoon he had been drinking tea in the kitchen when the knock came. He used the table top to lever himself out of his chair and padded along the hallway to the front door. He cried out in pain as Tomoko, no less beautiful in her school uniform, flung herself at him and hugged him. She stepped away, sympathy replaced by concern.

"I've cracked a rib," explained Alfie, holding his side with his right hand, then stepping forward and gently enveloping Tomoko with his left arm.

"Poor Alfie," she said, kissing his neck tenderly and carefully returning his embrace. "We mustn't let those bastards win," she added, ever the firebrand.

"Why aren't you at school?" he asked with concern, taking her hand and leading her to the kitchen. "And how did you find the house?"

"I was really worried when you didn't come in yesterday, so I asked at the office and they said a doctor had informed them you would be off for a week. No idea why. I worried all last night and when it got to lunchtime today I couldn't stand it anymore. I had to see you. You told me you lived near the park, so I just asked in the street and they pointed out the gaijin house."

"You shouldn't miss school. You'll get into trouble."

"They told me to look after you, so that's what I'm doing. The headteacher likes me. It won't be a problem. So who did this to you? JSD thugs?"

"I don't know who they are, but they were the same blokes who pushed me and my dad down the stairs in Akihabara. Young blokes dressed all in black."

"You didn't tell me about Akihabara. You are being targeted. When did this happen?"

"On my way home on Sunday, just outside here."

"Oh, Alfie, I'm so sorry. We must have been followed. This is my fault, involving you in politics."

Alfie was defensive. "I decided to come with you, you didn't force me. It's not your fault."

"But I feel responsible. You look different and I have helped to make you into an easy target. I would understand if you wanted to keep away from me."

"No way," said Alfie, almost too quickly.

Tomoko smiled. "Then you must let me help you to get better. I will come every day after school. I will nurse you!"

Sat at the kitchen table, Alfie allowed Tomoko to serve him with tea and snacks as they chatted time away. Leaning back, then forward. Feet touching, occasionally stroking. Hands coming together on the table top amongst the mugs and plates. Eyes always locked. Until Shaylie broke the spell.

The sliding door from their room opened and Alfie instinctively withdrew his hands and sat back, as if concealing a terrible secret. He blushed and attempted to keep his cool. His eyes now focused on his tea mug. The two women broke the silence with their laughter whilst Alfie remained unmoved.

"Aren't you going to introduce me to your friend, Alfie?" asked his mum, still amused at his diffidence.

Before Alfie could speak, the ever-smiling Tomoko stood and bowed.

"I'm Tomoko."

The name registered with Shaylie. "You are the prefect from school who is helping my son, aren't you?"

"Yes, I am."

"So how's he doing?"

"Very well. I'm not sure he needs so much help any more. Would you like some tea?"

"Yes, please." As Tomoko turned to the stove, Shaylie aimed a beaming smile and two thumbs up at Alfie. Words were unnecessary.

Tomoko turned to face them again. "I hope you don't mind, but I said I would visit Alfie every afternoon this week, just until he is well enough to come back to school."

"That's very thoughtful of you. I'm sure he'll love that. So, how old are you Tomoko?"

"Seventeen. I'm in my last year at high school."

"So, two years ahead of Alfie? Where do you live? And what are you going to do next year?"

"Too many questions, mum!" interjected Alfie.

"It's fine," said Tomoko, "I don't mind. I live in Hōya and next year I'm hoping to go to *Tōdai* – Tokyo University," she explained.

"What does your dad do?" Alfie cringed at another prying question.

"He's a businessman in the car industry."

"Just like Alfie's dad!" Alfie had never asked that question before, but he knew that industry employed many parents of students at their school. It was no surprise and of little interest to him.

"Well, it's very nice to meet you," Shaylie sat down and spent some time exchanging further small-talk with Tomoko. Alfie was a spectator for the time it took to drink a cup of tea, then Shaylie was again on the move. It was already mid-afternoon.

"I need to do some shopping for tonight's dinner. Will you stay and eat with us, Tomoko?"

"I have to be back by six. My mum's cooking. But thanks for the offer."

"Another time, maybe. Alfie, I'll be about an hour. See you both soon."

With that, she was gone. The two of them alone again, Tomoko pointed out that he had not yet shown her around the house.

"It'll be a short tour," said Alfie. "Upstairs is just other people's rooms. We only live down here. You've seen pretty much everything already."

"I've seen your kitchen!"

So Alfie showed Tomoko the toilet to one side of the kitchen and the bathroom to the other.

"And that's our room," he said, pointing at the sliding door from whence Shaylie had emerged fifteen minutes earlier.

"Show me!"

Alfie shrugged. "It's nothing special," he said, drawing back the washi door to reveal a six-mat tatami room, two futons laid out for his parents at one end, one for him at the other. They had not been observing the daily Japanese practice of packing the futons away in the wardrobe, because Shaylie slept during the day, but this did not bother Tomoko.

He heard the door shut behind them and, turning, she had dropped her blazer to the floor and was removing her long white socks.

"Is it comfortable?" she asked, her voice soft as she stepped close to him, put her left hand behind his head and

179

pulled him into a long, tender kiss. She interrupted it by pulling his T-shirt up over his head then, careful not to touch his injured midriff, she gently towed him down onto the futon.

#

Dazed from an unexpected seduction, his first seduction, Alfie did not respond to Tomoko's question at first. Raising her head from his chest, she asked again.

"What time will your mum be back?"

Suddenly frantic, Alfie lifted himself onto one elbow, then winced.

"I don't know, I've lost track of time, pretty soon, we need to get dressed."

Unabashed, she quickly got to her feet, her naked beauty not lost on Alfie, even in his panic. She dressed and then helped him retrieve his clothes. She straightened the bed and, when Shaylie walked in five minutes later, they were both sitting at the kitchen table drinking tea.

"You two certainly get on well. You haven't moved," said Shaylie. The young couple smiled at one another, wondering without concern whether Shaylie would notice reddened cheeks or tousled hair.

"We find plenty to talk about," responded Tomoko for the sake of answering, realising after a pause that Alfie was not going to break the silence. "But I really should be going now."

In his semi-concealed disappointment, Alfie walked Tomoko to the front door. They faced one another.

"Thank you," was all he could think of.

"Thank you?"

"That was lovely."

"You don't need to thank me. It was lovely for me, too."

They kissed a long kiss, each feeling fondness in their embrace. Still smiling, Tomoko stepped into the street and waved.

"See you tomorrow."

Consumed by tenderness, neither noticed the man, dressed in black, standing inside the park gate, watching Tomoko's progress towards the station through his sunglasses.

Chapter Thirty-eight

By the third Thursday, Shaylie knew what to expect. Having caroused for an hour with two ageing salarymen, she was relieved by a colleague. Along with Aaliyah, she was directed to Ken and his drunken co-workers in their habitual booth.

The initial conversation was the usual set-piece. Fripperies from the rest of the crowd and stray hands to brush off from one side as the familiar verbal jousting took place to her right. Ken probed for personal information, she avoided direct responses by reciprocating his questions and, in turn, he raised his own barriers.

There was something peculiar about this man, more peculiar than simply his sober, measured behaviour which distinguished him from his companions. There were moments when she thought, *I quite like this chap, he's nice.* A realisation followed, *I don't know if I like him, how can I? He has avoided telling me anything about himself.*

Whether he was different or whether he had created a devious facade which others were too drunk to fashion, she continued to explore. The physical evidence was compelling. Darker than his cronies, his complexion suggested an altogether more exotic provenance than Tokyo. Shaylie's knowledge of the local geography was scant, but she supposed that he hailed from further south than the capital. He did not have the brash demeanour of a city man and she could imagine a simple, sun-drenched upbringing on a farm, surrounded by labourers working crops or tending to cattle. She wondered what could have brought him to the world of business and to such a frenetic city.

She thought back to her own childhood in Colchester, much smaller than Tokyo but not the country upbringing she imagined for Ken. Still she envisioned some similarities, some common ground. Perhaps his family had also had a simple existence, struggling to make ends meet with both parents in manual work, providing for children who were quite happy to amuse themselves in the absence of more affluent pleasures. And against the odds, Ken had found himself comfortable in this very different environment, successful in business, frequenting hostess bars but impervious to the drunken behaviour of those around him, immune to the stereotype of the salaryman.

But Shaylie had adapted equally well, perhaps too well. She had assimilated a huge cultural shift to live in Japan, but now she was succeeding in a double life within a new culture, wife and mother by day, hostess by night. She, too, was different to her colleagues, more mature and visibly western, a curiosity to whom Ken was drawn.

Only when she thought about the particular attention he now lavished upon her did she begin to feel nervous. She knew that the pressure for her to date him could only mount and wondered whether she was playing with fire. A couple of hours in a restaurant? No big deal in itself, but it could raise the expectations of a man who was used to getting his way. It would also necessitate, for the second time in her married life, a secret from her husband.

Ken read her thoughts.

"Don't worry, Shay-ree-*san*," he said, "*Dōhan* is normal part of hostess duties. You can be sure that I will treat you well."

"I'm not worried, Ken. You seem to be an honourable man." She took a deep breath. "I would be happy to go on a *dōhan* date with you."

Ken smiled with humility. "That is excellent news. How about this evening?"

Shaylie was taken aback. "This evening? That's very soon. I am expected to finish my shift."

"I am sure that Tsubasa-*san* would say yes. After all, it is work during working hours. I'll be right back."

Shaylie knew that this was not the usual way to go about organising a *dōhan*. It was usual for these to take place outside of working hours and, if not, advance notice was required.

When Tsubasa returned to the booth to grant permission for Shaylie to part immediately, it was clear that Ken possessed more sway than the average client. Before she knew it, Shaylie was in the lift, shaking inside.

For the second time, Shaylie experienced a capacious black sedan. They stepped out in front of an Italian restaurant in fashionable Ginza. Her hand resting gently on Ken's biceps, they entered a stylish yet comfortable atmosphere of chic black and silver décor. It was quite clear that the *maître d'* knew to treat Ken with discernment and discretion as they were seated at a well-located table away from prying eyes.

Shaylie was confident that she was displaying a calm facade but Ken, as if he could hear her racing heartbeat, attempted to reassure her.

"Please relax and enjoy meal. No string attached. I know this is your first *dōhan* and I am honoured, but there is no need to worry. I will enjoy your company and then my driver will take you back to bar. Now … allow me to order for you?"

Shaylie had understood nothing of the menu other than the two Michelin stars, boldly placed on the front of the black leather binder with silver debossed characters. She understood equally little as Ken ordered drinks and food before returning his attention to Shaylie.

"So what do you think of restaurant?"

"It's beautiful. I'm looking forward to the food."

"You will like food. It is excellent. You have noticed stars, yes? It is best Italian restaurant in Tokyo. Next time I will take you to eat Japanese food."

His eyes bore into Shaylie's as he suggested that there would be a future occasion, but she gave nothing away. He smiled and sat back.

"You are hard to read, Shay-ree-*san*. And you are very discreet. I know so little about you."

"I know almost nothing about you, either. You are very good at telling me nothing."

Ken laughed.

"I cannot deny this. Maybe we can exchange a little more information this evening. Why don't you tell me about your childhood? I am interested know more about you and your country."

For the next half an hour, Shaylie talked. She talked through the aperitifs and she talked through the starters. She talked about her parents, about Scotland and its subsequent independence, about the Colchester she was born into in 2020. She talked about life as an only child, the struggle of her parents and of the country as the UK ceased to exist and she found herself growing up in an impoverished FREW. She talked about primary school and modest academic success, leaving school and becoming a legal clerk. And then she stopped.

"What a delicious starter!" The change of subject was a little clumsy, as if Ken needed attention drawing to the fact that Shaylie had talked about the first twenty years of her life but had ignored the rest. Ken had suspected that this was a woman in her late thirties. Now she had given away the year of her birth.

"I'm glad you enjoy it. Main course will be even more impressive, I am sure."

"So, Ken-*san*, you were going to tell me about your childhood?"

Ken smiled again. He would probe for more later, but he had already convinced himself of one detail. She was married. She may even have kids. He could see no other reason for her to stop her account. She was protecting the more private details of her life.

"Well, I was brought up in very different place to Colchester. And very different to Tokyo. Have you ever heard of Ōshima Island?"

She shook her head and leaned in with interest.

"It is in Sagami Bay, 100km south of Tokyo. It is close to Pacific Ocean with simple people, farmer and labourer. It is society where everyone help everyone. Not like Tokyo. My father was rice farmer without modern machine. He employ many local people in rice paddy and use water buffalo to till field and to provide milk for local community. It take long

185

time for Ōshima to catch up with modern way. When I come Tokyo to go university, it was great culture shock.

"So you have a degree," supposed Shaylie.

Ken smiled, a smile tinged with regret.

"No, I not stay long at university. I wanted earn money and become involved in local business by work many hour on door of club and pachinko parlour in Kabukichō and run errand for my boss. I often work all night so I cannot maintain my study."

The main courses arrived, the portions small but immaculate.

"So, what kind of business are you involved in now?" asked Shaylie, thinking of the motley crew which came to the club with him every Thursday.

"I have always involve in entertainment industry. I work my way up. I am part of group which run many establishment in Kabukichō in Shinjuku. We are very successful."

In turn, Shaylie felt that he, too, had omitted plenty of detail. She had an idea of the kind of places he worked, but no more than that. Silence fell for a while as they finished their divine mains, both speaking only to compliment the food and to agree that desserts were surplus to requirements.

Having asked for the bill, Ken decided that now was the time.

"So," he asked, "are you shingle?"

His odd pronunciation did not delay her comprehension. Shaylie had thought through the possibility of this question and nervously delivered the answer she had rehearsed in her head, the answer she was sure he wanted to hear.

"Yes, I gave up looking for the right man in England. I came to Japan with no commitments. I wanted to find a new, exciting life."

She fought to retain eye contact, to validate her dishonesty. She did not have the nerve to reciprocate the question this time. He did not simply hold her gaze, he looked through her and into her soul, seeing all he needed to see.

Stilted pleasantries, conveying nothing and everything, took them back to the car. Shaylie sensed his disbelief and anger, but he remained polite as he accompanied her back to the club entrance in the lift.

"I had wonderful evening, Shay-ree-*san*."

"So have I. It was very kind of you to invite me to dinner."

"It not kindness. I enjoy your company. I hope you will accompany me on *dōhan* again. It would be great honour for me. Perhaps you would like to eat at my *lugzhuri apaatomento*."

His final suggestion crossed the boundary of what was considered safe for a hostess on a working date. Both guilt and fear prevented Shaylie from responding with a courteous rebuff. Her hesitation sealed her fate as she could only smile, head slightly bowed, and tell Ken how pleasant that would be.

Chapter Thirty-nine

Alfie returned to school at the beginning of the following week. If fellow students noticed the vestiges of facial bruising, none of them mentioned it. He was left alone, Tomoko's appointment to his charge having offered him not inconsiderable protection. She had been to visit him every day, but greeted him at the gate that Monday morning as if reunited after a long break.

"Alfie, how are you doing? You're looking better every day."

The hug was brief but it was the first time it had happened in public. Another first was about to materialise.

"I'm glad you're back," she smiled, dimples pronounced, then suddenly a serious face, a deep breath and the following.

"My mum really wants to meet you. I've told her I'll bring you home for some food after school today, OK?"

She was about to apologise, when his frown broke into a broad grin.

"Yeah, why not? My Japanese is still an embarrassment but I'll do my best."

"Don't worry, Alfie, mum's English is pretty good."

"Cool. Well, this is unexpected. I did think you'd me dragging me off to meetings this week to discuss and organise the demo. Only a few days to go."

"We are pretty well organised. We did a lot of that while you were in bed last week. We have one final meeting on Friday."

"Friday? OK," Alfie had returned to his monosyllabic ways.

"I know it bothers you, Alfie, and you don't have to be involved, but I'd love it if you would."

"I know. Don't worry, I'll be there."

As they approached the school entrance, smiling Tomoko became serious one more time.

"I almost forgot," she said. "About the demo …"

"What about it?"

"Don't mention it to my parents."

Alfie nodded and, before he could ask why, she was off to her first lesson. He was curious. He hadn't discussed it with his parents yet, but he would. Only now did he begin to wonder what type of people Tomoko's parents were and how they would react to her *gaijin* boyfriend.

#

A ten-minute walk away from the railway line and they found themselves, hand-in-hand, amongst bigger and bigger houses in deepest Hōya. Tomoko stopped in front of a pair of ornate, cast-iron gates. She presented her forefinger to a small sensor set back into the adjacent brickwork and looked into an iris scanner. The double security measure created a fortress. The gates swung open for long enough to allow them access to the long drive, leading up to a grandiloquent residence which was modern in structure and could have been located anywhere in the world. Alfie had thought that Tomoko, like most of his fellow students, came from a comfortable Matsucorp family, but he had not imagined her with her revolutionary politics to be issue of the superrich.

Fingerprint and iris recognition once more at the front door allowed them entry to a very large house, or perhaps a small mansion. There were obvious western influences, melanged with typical Japanese effects.

"*Tadaima!*" called Tomoko as they removed their shoes at the *genkan* and heard Tomoko's mother's response, "*o kaeri nasai*", from the kitchen.

They walked through to be greeted by the bow of an attractive woman, a fifty-year-old version of Tomoko. She was elegant in her floral dress and pastel blue jacket. Alfie's bow was awkward beside that of Tomoko.

The older lady immediately eased into passable English, less grammatical than her daughter's but well accented nonetheless.

"Please to meet you, Alfie-*san*. Tomoko spoke a lot about you."

"It's very nice to meet you, too."

"Please. Sit down."

The table in the spacious kitchen was replete with a spread of cake and pastries and cans of Japanese fizzy pop to tide them over until dinner. As Alfie made to sit down, he glanced through the window to see a beautiful garden, large by Japanese standards, where two gardeners worked to maintain the idyll. The lawn was a white carpet, indicating the end of cherry blossom as Japan moved into the sweaty end of spring.

"We like to keep in pretty condition," Tomoko's mum had caught Alfie's curious eye.

"It's beautiful," replied Alfie, aware that it was polite to address an older Japanese person by name and suddenly all too conscious that he did not know what to call her, did not know Tomoko's family name.

"Thank you. Tomoko will give you tour when you have eaten snack."

Alfie could not work out why he had begun to question his presence here. There was no reason to the sense of caution which now suppressed his appetite as well as his conversation. He had three times been the focus of anti-migrant attacks but had got over that, settling into a new life with greater comfort and an attractive and intelligent girlfriend. They had become intimate. He loved her and he thought she loved him. Now he was being introduced to her mother. But he didn't know their name. It wasn't so important; he struggled with Japanese names anyway. Tomoko's mother awoke him from his moments of self-doubt and broke the awkward silence.

"You are not hungry, Alfie-*san*?"

He raised a smile in response. "I'm saving myself for dinner."

"Come on." Tomoko spoke for the first time since they'd sat down. "I'll show you round."

An oasis of affluence in an ever more impoverished world, Tomoko's family home was a maze of clean, decorative rooms which were anything but Japanese in size. The parquet flooring was international, but the occasional tatami room lent the house an unmistakeable national identity, although Alfie did not spot a single sliding shōji door of washi paper. They began at the top in Tomoko's Western-styled attic bedroom, then descended to the main upstairs floor, its four en-suite bedrooms and a huge shared wet room with sunken bath at the end of the landing. A spiral staircase led them back to the ground floor where, in addition to the kitchen, Alfie counted two large reception rooms and a beautiful dining room. At the back of the house as they made their way out into the garden, they passed a closed wooden door which Tomoko referred to as the study. Drawn towards the heavy door, he was not invited to enter and could faintly hear one side of a telephone conversation, the voice male, and the sporadic tapping of a keyboard. Evidently old-style, Tomoko's father, like many of his generation, rejected the now ubiquitous smartscreen technology.

As they toured the garden hand-in-hand, Alfie was reassured that Tomoko did not feel the need to avoid physical contact in the presence of her parents. They chatted about school and politics at length, but he was made to feel a little indiscreet when asking about her dad's job. She dealt with this question briefly, he worked for Matsucorp. He had assumed as much, though found it strange that her dad was at home so early in the evening. He did not keep the hours of a typical Japanese salaryman but earned enough that his wife could dedicate herself to voluntary service and charitable works.

From the top of the garden, they heard the gong and made their way back across the carpet of blossom for the evening meal. Re-entering the house, Tomoko withdrew her hand from his, either for ease of passage through the doorway or for the benefit of her father who, at that moment, emerged from his study and, without a glance in their direction, made his way through to the kitchen.

The snacks had given way to place settings, chopsticks, napkins, plates, bowls and myriad condiments and culinary accompaniments. For the first time, Alfie faced Tomoko's father. He was short, stocky and grey. Half a size too big, his well-worn suit trousers, shirt and tie presented a comical contrast with his slippers. His serious countenance did not slip for a single moment and, chastened, Alfie tried in vain to match his formal bow and garbled set-piece greeting.

"*Yoroshiku onegaitashimasu.*"

Alfie's "*dōzo yoroshiku*" in response could have been straight from a phrase-book in the days when Japan was a viable tourist destination for Westerners.

If the earlier silence in the kitchen had been awkward, it was nothing compared to the initial unease as the head of the household sat down and, eyes down, face in bowl, began to eat to the exclusion of all else. Once plates had been changed, the mood was broken by Tomoko's relentless positive attitude, drawing first her mother and then Alfie into an animated conversation which endured throughout the meal.

To Alfie: "Sorry about dad. His English isn't much good."

To her mother: "This is a lovely dinner, mum."

This initiated compliments from Alfie, followed by a discussion on the relative nutritional value of Japanese food and the ease with which Alfie had adapted to eating it. Alfie was the centre of attention, questioned on school, his parents and various aspects of Japanese society. The regular slurping of noodles was the only contribution from Tomoko's father.

By the end of the meal, spirits were high and Alfie felt the warm glow of Tomoko's mother's approval. She stood and this was the cue for Tomoko to lead Alfie through to one of the reception rooms.

"We take green tea in the living room after dinner and watch the TV news."

As Alfie sank into a plush sofa, Tomoko turned on a home cinema screen. She went to help her mother with the tea, leaving Alfie to watch the beginning of the news. He did not need to understand the commentary to recognise the placard-bearing hordes, protesting against the presence in Japan of Alfie and his kind. The crowds collected outside various ports of entry and the launching of various missiles towards non-Asian immigrants were not news to Alfie. As his mood again became deflated, an unexpected invitation in broken English came from behind.

"Aru-fu-ee May-*san*," the diction was halting, "would you like to visit my office?"

Pulling himself out of the plush settee was quite an effort and, as he turned to face Tomoko's father, he was unnerved by a forced smile and an absence of eye contact.

The older man who, Alfie thought, could easily have been Tomoko's grandfather, stepped back and gestured with an open palm for Alfie to enter first. "*Dōzo*."

Briefly taking in the magnificent room with wood-panelled walls, carpeted floor and a large oak desk, Alfie soon focused his mind on the fact that this man stood in front of the closed door. As he waited for him to speak, Alfie wondered whether he was imagining an atmosphere of menace.

"You have a beautiful office."

"*Arigatō*, Aru-fu-ee May-*san*, you are kind. I know you, Aru-fu-ee May-*san*. Matsucorp invite you to Japan. I know. It's OK for me. I know."

Alfie waited.

"You are guest in my house. I know. It's OK, too."

The short English phrases were taking their time to come out. Alfie waited some more.

"My child is also kind. And pretty. And clever. She help you. I know. *Gaijin* friend is OK. You know *gaijin*?"

Alfie nodded slowly.

"*Gaijin* friend, but not *gaijin* boyfriend. Tomoko help you in school, but not your girlfriend. OK, *desu-ka*?"

Another nod. This time less convincing.

"I think you are not clear. Outside school, you not with Tomoko. Stay away. Not touch my child."

Alfie was expressionless.

"I make life difficult for you. And your father. And your mother. I promise."

Alfie was spared a response as he heard Tomoko calling him from the living room. As the old man opened the door and stepped aside, Alfie half ran through the fixed stare and out of the office.

The door closed behind him and he accepted the offer of green tea with Tomoko and her mother.

"Has my dad been showing you his study? You're honoured. He's very proud of it."

"It's lovely," said Alfie, attempting to mask his discomfiture and despair with a feeble smile.

Accompanying him back to the station, Tomoko was unable to shake Alfie's mood. He would only hold hands when they were well clear of the family home and she could only guess what had been said in her father's office.

As she walked back to the house alone, she knew she would not give up on Alfie. If her dad was going to be difficult, so be it. He was making her more determined to fight for what was right. If Matsucorp was damaged in the crossfire, he had it coming.

Chapter Forty

Struthwin remained inscrutable as he entered Matsubara's office that evening. The unexpected presence of Yamada did not knock him from his stride. Matsubara would engineer meetings where he saw fit and Struthwin would deal with every hand which was dealt.

"*Kombanwa futari-sama*," was the smooth greeting, reciprocated by both Japanese with a curt, single-worded *good evening*.

Matsubara sat back in his chair with his cigarette, waiting for the discussion to begin, a mediator in waiting. Struthwin sat. He would not be drawn into the furious pacing which would accompany Yamada's frantic delivery. Yamada would not have been there if he did not have a gripe. And he would not be able to keep still until it had been aired.

"I am concerned, Stepson-*san*, deeply concerned."

The big city politico delivery soon gave way to reveal a distinct lack of composure.

"I do not think that you are in control of the May family. There are too many risks you are not nullifying. Matsucorp needs me. It will be my presence in the Ministry which will best protect Matsucorp's interests for many years to come."

"We are all on the same side, Yamada-*san*. I can assure you that all aspects of our migration programme are well under control. Our positive focus on Japanese labour, combined with our human face, presented by the selective introduction of migrant workers is a winner across the political spectrum. We all agreed that this would create an ideal platform for your election, were you to associate yourself with us."

Yamada postured in the face of Struthwin's deliberate artistry, stamping his left foot as he turned to face Struthwin for the first time. He raised his voice.

"That may be the case. But, respectfully, you ignore the potential difficulties which the May family are presenting to us. You cannot sit back and hope that matters will be resolved in a way which does not upset the status quo. You brought them here to work hard and to present a positive image of how we can be sensitive to the economic misfortune of others whilst having the good sense to use the best foreign workers for the good of Japan. You have achieved this in the case of the individual migrant workers you have selected, but you have taken too great a risk with this family. We cannot have our migrant workers involving themselves in political causes which target the establishment. You are allowing this to happen."

Struthwin was the son of a diplomat.

"I can understand how it may look to you, Yamada-*san*, but *respectfully* you cannot be aware of the day-to-day manipulation which I am able to affect upon these three individuals who, I am certain, pose no threat to our strategy. However, if you have questions with regard to the Mays, I am happy to elaborate."

"I have reliable sources."

"As do I, Yamada-*san*," cut in Struthwin.

"*My* sources tell me that there is a protest movement gaining momentum amongst the migrant workers. A movement which Jordan May could easily be drawn into."

"*Could*. But ultimately won't. He has too much to lose."

"You may think so. But he attended a union meeting a few days ago."

"Union meeting?" Now Matsubara's interest was piqued.

"Yes. A union meeting. Politicisation of the workforce which I was assured would not happen."

"Such abortive attempts at workforce power are inevitable but will be confined to manual workers and will ultimately hold no weight."

"Your confidence is unfounded."

"It most certainly is not. The pressure placed on Jordan May will fail. He knows where his loyalty lies and he will not dare to show anything more than a passing interest to appease his colleagues. In the eyes of the voter, this will be a discredited protest led by resentful individuals from our Asian neighbours. The electorate will wish to protect Japanese individual strength against the perceived envy of Korean and Chinese entryists."

"You have introduced Eric Marks to the maintenance staff. A single Englishman with an uneven temperament and nothing to lose. He was seen in heated discussion with Jordan May, shortly before May attended the union meeting."

"You are aware that unions have no legal footing in Japan. May is curious, nothing more. He will not risk the new life he has secured for his family by becoming active. You have my word."

Yamada sought support from Matsubara, but saw in his countenance only confidence in his closest advisor. Yamada could not understand how he was failing in his attempt to prompt Matsubara to join him in his probing of Struthwin's strategy.

The CEO sought to move the discussion onwards. "Do your sources have anything else for us to address, Yamada-*san*?" His use of *us* further fuelled Yamada's displeasure.

"Yes, they do," he railed. "The boy could also be a problem."

"I have heard that the boy has settled well, Stepson-*san*. Do you know otherwise?" asked Matsubara.

"You have heard correctly. Teething trouble at school has been dealt with by assigning a senior student mentor. He struggles with his Japanese but is now well integrated into his new life."

"But he is also integrating himself politically. There is a youth movement which has held demonstrations against my party. He has been seen on the streets of Harajuku with this rabble. A sizeable body of kids who think they are owed something. He stands out like a sore thumb, one white protester, a legitimising symbol in a pro-migrant, pro-*gaijin* movement."

"As you say, Yamada-*san*, a lone white symbol. What do you really think one child can do? One child who knows he cannot jeopardise the considerable improvement to his family's life. We control the media. We kept the demonstration out of the news. We have succeeded in nullifying what these students are doing and, even if it were reported, it would look to the electorate to be exactly what it is. A rabble, as I believe you called it. We have kept him suitably quiet, despite the best efforts of right-wing thugs from your party."

Struthwin turned the conversation towards an ugly detail of which, he knew, Matsubara was oblivious. Until now. Yamada hesitated and Matsubara launched into this momentary lapse, for the first time leaning forward in his chair.

"Right-wing thugs? What do you mean, Stepson-*san*? I thought that Alfie May-*san* had been hit by a missile thrown by a misguided student on his first day at school. I would hardly refer to him as a right-wing thug. I also know he took a hit from demonstrators outside the airport on arrival, but we were satisfied that this was a one-off."

"Those two incidents were, indeed, unfortunate, Matsubara-*san*. However, he has also been attacked twice, deliberately targeted by JSD boot-boys in public places, once with his father in Akihabara and once alone in Shakuji Park, where he was beaten badly enough to have a week off school."

Matsubara turned to Yamada, the look of guilt belying his protestations.

"Why are you trying to discredit my party? You have no evidence that these thugs were anything to do with me!"

Now was the right time. "On the contrary," responded Struthwin, reaching to his inside jacket pocket. He laid the manila envelope in front of Matsubara.

"My sources are extremely reliable and my web is widely spun. In that envelope, Matsubara-*san*, you will find the names and profiles of the band of goons who are paid-up members of the JSD and who are employed by Yamada-*san* on an *ad hoc* basis to mete out violent warnings and what the JSD sees as rough justice."

"Is this true, Yamada-*san*?"

"What do you expect me to do? If you will take risks with our project, one of us has to put some resistance in place. You have forced me into this, Stepson-*san*."

This time, Matsubara's defence of Struthwin went beyond blind loyalty.

"Yamada-*san*," came the sharp response, "I cannot think of anything which will better propel Alfie May-*san* into political activism. Your heavy-handedness can only endanger the progress of our alliance. We need migrants who are settled and content, not a *cause célèbre*."

Struthwin's work was done for another day. He had been carrying the fruits of his network of informants around for days, knowing that a confrontation was likely. Now he relaxed and watched a useful but potentially dangerous political ally silenced and humiliated. Without another word, Yamada left Matsubara and his closest advisor in their bubble of complicity and smoke.

Champagne receptions were ten-a-penny in those days. The diplomatic service managed to hang onto the luxuries of colonialisation for as long as the UK remained both in one piece and inside the EU. But that was nothing compared to the wining and dining by directors in the great Japanese companies. They loved me for my ability to communicate with them in Japanese and they kept inviting me back. I had a blast.

At the time, technology was still Japan's blue riband industry. The giants of audio-visual, wireless and satellite electronics were unrivalled. I schmoozed with them and built unprecedented links, but I had a penchant for cars. Fast cars. I communed and parleyed with industrial all-comers, but I took particular care to cultivate close relationships with those in the world's most highly respected automobile industry.

Nobody needs a car in Tokyo, but I wanted to bum a freebie for weekend drives out to the hot springs. Toyota was top dog then, highest sales, image as the most reliable, but I was amazed at the Mazda coupé I was leased at a rock bottom price. I became known as the car industry's man in the British Embassy and they courted me all the more.

Initially it was corporate parties with Japanese beer, Japanese whisky and Franco-Nipponese wine, of course. But I got to know some of the top bods really well and spent an awful lot of time at out-of-town weddings, anniversaries and birth celebrations. Swanky hotels in the foothills of Fuji were more often than not the venue.

It was at one such event that I decided to take myself back off to my room for an early evening break, having felt ill in the ballroom following supper. Raw fucking fish. I excused myself directly to Suzuki-san, eponymous CEO of the great company, whose daughter was getting married. As I turned to close the door of my suite behind me, I caught sight of Suzuki-san's wife, mildly dishevelled, exiting the room opposite in a hurry. It was the room of a man not that much older than me, a man destined for the top, with whom I was pretty well acquainted. Suzuki's brightest young director was shagging the boss's wife. His name was Shinji Matsubara.

#

Chapter Forty-one

It was a shaken Alfie who turned up at school the next morning. A new obstacle, a new element of risk arose every time he thought that he had gone beyond the inevitable teething troubles of his new life. As usual they greeted one another at the school gates, the unspoken bond between them remaining strong, despite its muted nature.

The first lessons of the morning were a haze and Alfie soon found himself with Tomoko at morning break, sat on *their* bench, overlooking the games of football and basketball on the shale playground. As they snacked, Tomoko attempted to kick-start the conversation.

"Are you OK, Alfie?"

"Yeah."

"Are you sure?"

"Yeah."

Has something upset you?"

"No, I'm fine."

"You were quiet yesterday."

"I'm always quiet."

Tomoko laughed.

"True, but last night you were especially quiet. My mum enjoyed meeting you. She loved you."

"She was nice. It was a nice afternoon."

"How about my dad? What did he say to you?"

"He just showed me his office. It's a great office."

"Nothing else?"

"No, not really."

Tomoko did not buy this for a moment, but it was not the time to press. He placed his daughter on a pedestal and could be protective, but she knew that the old bastard had a Machiavellian side to his nature and she was now convinced

201

that, one way or another, Alfie had experienced a certain level of threat.

The psychological intensity of their monosyllabic conversation had rendered them oblivious to their student colleagues gathering around them. In their tens, they had assembled in two distinct groups.

Hirata-*kun* was the first to take advantage of the pause in the couple's conversation. From the middle of the smaller group, political support for Tomoko was evident.

"So you want us to meet at 1pm on Saturday in Ikebukuro?"

"Yes, in Mosburger, opposite the East Exit."

"I hope there will be a big turn-out."

"You can bet on it. There's a lot of support from high schools on this side of Tokyo and it won't just be students. Asian and Western workers are starting to unionise. It will be too big for the media to ignore this time."

"Is he coming?"

Alfie was aware that Hirata-*kun* was pointing at him but was unable to follow the conversation.

"Yes, of course. We are fighting for Alfie and his family and many thousands like them. We are fighting for our fellow human beings."

"We Japanese are human, too," came the interjection from Komatsu-*kun*, stepping forward with ill-disguised aggression from the larger, male-dominated group. "You are protesting to disadvantage our families, to hijack our economy. Why do you want to give Japanese jobs to foreigners?"

Hirata-*kun* took a step towards Komatsu.

"What are you talking about? You are just parroting the right-wing press. Foreign workers are doing jobs no one else wants and they're being expected to do it for low wages. Our economy is the world leader. We can afford to share, to pay properly and still our parents will keep the best jobs."

Now Komatsu had his face centimetres from that of Hirata.

"*His* dad has a skilled job. A job which a Japanese could have. That is proof that this wave of immigrants is taking over. I don't need the newspapers to tell me that."

Tomoko stood as the mood became uglier and thrust herself between the two boys.

"You are entitled to respect for your views, Komatsu-*kun*, as I'm sure you respect our right to *peaceful* protest." The emphasis was on non-violence as her eyes turned to Hirata. Then, addressing Komatsu again: "I have the right to engage politically in my free time. While I am at school, I have a responsibility to help Alfie to integrate. You do not have to like him or to like the fact that he is here, but he has been accepted by our headteacher and you will not interfere with my role as student ambassador."

The bell rang and the students dispersed. It was Alfie's turn to show concern. "Are you OK?"

The strain showed in the frail response. "Let's go to class."

#

The remainder of the day passed without incident and Tomoko waited for Alfie at the gate longer than usual as the student body filed out after the final period. Ten minutes later she was still waiting, concern rising within her.

Raised voices and general commotion drew her out into the street where she saw Alfie, back to the school fence, hemmed in by a semi-circle of angry youths. She arrived running as Komatsu, at the centre once again, stepped into Alfie's personal space. Tense and immobile, any fear experienced by Alfie was well hidden.

As Tomoko stepped into the mix, the volley of racism faltered. Komatsu looked round.

"Ah. Our student ambassador is here to hear the grievances of her fellow students." Komatsu smiled. An unconvincing smile. A smile laced with malice.

"You are expecting me to support your racism?"

"Racism? What are you talking about? You recognised earlier that I have a right to my opinion. I am a patriot. Our country is strong because we have always had a strong immigration policy. Your American friends gave us that a hundred years ago. Now is not the time to let all these foreigners in. It's not good for our country. Be a true ambassador and accept views other than your own."

"Let's look past your views and deal with your actions. You are intimidating my charge with threatening behaviour. He doesn't understand your words, only your violence."

"He should learn Japanese, then."

"He *is* learning Japanese and your behaviour is unacceptable."

"We are outside school now. You are not the headteacher's official *gaijin*-lover out here."

"In that case, I am also not the student ambassador who listens respectfully to all views. Get out of our way."

Tomoko grabbed Alfie's hand and led him through the mob. Hightailing hand-in-hand towards the station, Alfie dared, once well clear of his aggressors, to look at Tomoko.

"Wow!"

"Wow what? We're not going to be pushed around by them."

"I can see that." A pause. "But you have crossed a line."

"A line? What line?"

"The line between student diplomat and activist fighting her boyfriend's corner."

Tomoko smiled. "It was a line worth crossing."

They both smiled as they stepped onto the platform.

Chapter Forty-two

"Eric-*san*!"

The demonstration was one day away and Ethan had been spending every moment of break and lunch reinforcing the message, supporting his Korean and Chinese comrades by recruiting Western employees. He had reached the morning break on Friday without attracting unwanted attention, but now a supervisor wanted a word.

"Eric-*san*!"

"Yes, boss?"

"I watch you today. A little cleaning, a little tidying, a lot talking. What you doing?"

"I'm helping, making sure my comrades are OK."

"Comrades?"

"Colleagues. Friends. Co-workers."

"Ah! Co-worker. Yes. Please to let co-worker relax. They have break for relax."

"No problem."

Ethan was determined. Ethan had work to do. He could be more discreet but he could not stop. It was too important. The message was simple. Do you want to improve your contract? Do you want to stop exploitation? Meet at Kirin City on Sunshine Dōri in Ikebukuro straight after work tomorrow.

He kept his head down as he buzzed around white and black faces alike. Mopping up spillages, collecting empty plates and glasses, delivering the message. Brief the workers. Get them on board. Brief the workers. Get them on board. Improved contract? Yes. They were unanimous. End exploitation? Yes. They were unanimous.

Meet tomorrow. A pause. Every time an anxious pause. Unanimous anxiety. I don't want to lose my job. What will they do to us? What can they do? Safety in numbers. Safety in numbers. Safety in numbers. Ethan could only hope that the will would be matched by commitment.

Chapter Forty-three

"My parents are going out tonight."

After food, they spent the end of lunchtime together. Tomoko and Alfie were sitting on a bench, isolated on the far side of the playground.

"So?" replied Alfie.

Tomoko smiled at Alfie, unfazed by the self-imposed segregation her outburst had brought them. The lame-duck student ambassador was now focused on her boyfriend and the imminent events of the weekend rather than her standing amongst her peers. Plenty supported the cause, supported Alfie even, and would attend the demonstration. They would stand up to a faceless regime but recoiled in the face of a dominant, aggressive and sizeable minority of anti-migrant pupils. Tomoko knew that a triumphant display of adolescent political power would return her to a position of strength by Monday. She was prepared to bide her time.

"So we can have the house to ourselves for a few hours. It might be fun."

"Are you sure?"

"Sure? Of course! I know from experience that it will be fun!"

"No! I mean, are you sure that we will be alone? It would be more than awkward if your dad came home early."

It was clear to Tomoko that Alfie was worried not about her parents but about her dad. It was still unclear what had been said in his study, but she knew not to dig further.

"I'm sure. They have been invited to a theatre box at the Kabuki. This is a great and rare honour and my parents will not miss it. They will be gone by seven and won't be back until after midnight. Come after dinner and take the last train home. It will be worth it!"

Alfie remained slightly anxious but what could go wrong? It was not an opportunity he wanted to pass up. He smiled and nodded.

Chapter Forty-four

The diary was light that afternoon. Always plenty of work to do, but not every day was filled with meetings. Matsubara had received an intranet message from one of the Tokyo supervisors, complaining of mutinous mutterings by some of the foreign workers. He had no choice but to trust Struthwin, didn't he? But the seed of doubt was there. He needed thinking time. He needed space. He needed his office at home.

Checking out with his holographic PA, he soon found himself in the lift, which took him below ground level into Ikebukuro station. The express train, less busy early in the afternoon, took him to Shakuji-kōen in two stops. A change to a local train, two more stops and he stepped from the station straight into a taxi. Within half an hour of leaving HQ, he was home.

Jacket off, tie loosened, window open onto the garden, he sat back and closed his eyes. Thirty minutes later, his head rolled off the side of the headrest, awakening him and cricking his neck. Refreshed, he reopened the message which had bothered him earlier and began to think it through.

Matsubara was pleased to be able to employ a wide range of migrant workers. He was, and always had been, a hard-nosed executive with humanitarian tendencies. Profit and success were top priorities, for him, for his company and for Japan. His desire to ensure that foreigners were also able to benefit was good for PR. It was also well-meaning, if patronising.

Offering the three skilled positions, normally reserved for Japanese nationals, to the three recent arrivals from the FREW had been a stroke of genius. Matsubara felt only a slight regret that it was not *his* genius, but his enforced loyalty to Stepson Struthwin over the years had only benefited the business. The hard right of the JSD had not been impressed, but the wider public saw Matsucorp as sympathetic to the plight of the rest of the world. These Westerners who, in barely more than a century, had transformed themselves from war victors into an economic disaster zone. Over that time, Asian economies had gone from strength to strength, but the Japanese people were not undignified in their superiority. It was unfortunate that incompetence was genetic.

Unskilled workers were different. Although a degree of positive publicity could be gleaned from employing cleaners, catering assistants and maintenance staff from around the world, this was born of necessity.

The buoyant economy had grown more quickly than the population. Migrant workers were essential as well as cheap, even in times of such low unemployment.

We need them, thought Matsubara. *The Chinese, the Koreans, the Europeans and the Africans. We need them and they need us. They work hard, they accept low pay, they do as we ask. I have discussed their working conditions many times with Stepson-san. There have never been any problems. I trust Stepson-san. So why does this e-message worry me?*

>>Matsubara-*sama*

There has been much talk amongst migrant workers recently in the canteen. Not idle chat, but heated debate and discussion. At least, this is my impression. I don't understand much of what they say, but Chinese and Korean workers seem to be trying to spread a message, trying to persuade. There is also a new worker from the FREW, Eric Marks-*san*. He has a lot to say in English. I can understand a little. There is talk of some kind of meeting tomorrow shortly after work in Ikebukuro. I know nothing more.

I thought you should know.
Yoroshiku onegaishimasu.
Hanada<<

Takaki Hanada was reliable and loyal. And Japanese. Struthwin had assuaged Matsubara's concerns about unionisation, but mass meetings and adverse publicity he could do without.

There was no need to doubt Struthwin. There was no need to overreact. But Matsubara was not content with inaction. Struthwin was the master manipulator, but it would not take much for Matsubara to put a spanner in the works, just to be sure.

It came to him in a flash and he quickly typed his reply.

>>Hanada-*san*

Thank you for your message and your loyalty.

This is nothing for you to be concerned about.

I would, however, like you to communicate to our maintenance and cleaning staff that tomorrow has been designated as a deep clean day. All such staff in the Hōya factory will work until 6pm and will be paid double time.

Please thank our staff for the excellent job they are doing.

Yoroshiku onegaishimasu.

Matsubara<<

Chapter Forty-five

After school, Alfie was relieved that Tomoko insisted on walking him to the station. There remained a perceivable threat from a vocal group of thugs amongst the student body and he was grateful not to take his chances alone. He could not shake the feeling of being watched as he alighted in Shakuji-kōen and he ran out of the station and across the square, slowing to the gait of a race-walker as he hastened alongside the park to the front door of the gaijin house.

Shaylie was waiting in the kitchen with a mid-afternoon snack and dinner on the hob. Post-school pleasantries were exchanged and Shaylie saw no significance in Alfie's reticence in imparting information on his day. This was quite normal. She asked after Tomoko, who was "fine", but she was not apprised of Alfie's plans that evening. She was going to work. Therefore, she did not need to know. Jordan would be there for Alfie.

Alfie attempted some homework while Shaylie readied herself for her shift. When Jordan returned, she left them with a Japanese-style curry and sticky rice, a dish they had both come to love. Jordan's reserve that evening made an impression even on Alfie. In a reversal of roles, the son tried hard to engage the father in conversation.

"You're pretty quiet tonight, dad."

"Am I?"

"Yeah."

"Not usually chatty, am I?"

"Well, not like mum, but you do usually ask me a few questions about my day. You seem … different to usual."

"Sorry, Alfie. I'm a bit preoccupied. That's all."

"Is it work?"

"Yeah. Kind of. There are a lot of unhappy foreign workers. A bit of trouble between them and the bosses."

"Does that include you?"

Alfie chose not to reveal that he knew something about this issue. He did not want his parents knowing about the demonstration and his involvement.

"Well, I am a foreign worker, so I should be on their side. But I'm also on an enhanced contract, so if I want to keep what I've got, perhaps I shouldn't seem ungrateful. It's tricky."

Alfie nodded sagely.

"What are you up to this evening, Alfie?"

"I'm going round to Tomoko's for a bit."

"Nice. You seem to be getting on really well. She's a nice girl."

"Yeah, she is."

"You will be careful, won't you?"

Alfie was abashed, prompting Jordan's swift qualification.

"I mean, on the journey there and back. In the dark. Keep your eyes open. We don't want more trouble, do we?"

"I know, dad. I'll be careful. I see men in black wherever I look at the moment. I'll keep moving."

"Good."

Alfie stood and cleared the table, navigating around fellow residents as the kitchen's evening rush hour began.

"I'll do that," said Jordan, before Alfie could begin the washing-up. "You get ready for Tomoko."

"Thanks, dad," Alfie said, moving towards the sliding doors to their room. Hesitating to enter, he turned back to Jordan.

"What is it?"

"Dad, I think you should stand up for what is right."

"What do you mean?"

"I know you are trying to protect what we have, but you should support other foreign workers. Because it's the right thing to do."

Astonished, Jordan found no response before Alfie had closed the sliding doors behind him.

Chapter Forty-six

In cases such as this, when a message from the top was not to be delivered in dramatic style through hologram, it filtered out language by language. Matsubara was happy for a slow and understated dissemination through the workforce. It was posted in the canteen in time for afternoon break and soon made its way through Japanese into Chinese and Korean. It was almost time to return to work for the final session of the day when it was converted to Hindi and English.

Ethan turned from the site of a spillage, just missing Kim with the handle of his mop.

"Have you heard?"

"Heard what?"

"They're doing a deep clean tomorrow. We're all here 'til 6pm."

"Since when?"

"Just been announced."

"This can't happen. This is bullshit. It's not a planned deep clean. They've heard about the demo. This is fucking sabotage!"

Ethan's face was red. The veins on his neck stood out. He was the embodiment of an imminent myocardial infarction. Microbeads of saliva sat on his lips as he considered his next move. Kim took a step back.

"It sounds like it came from the top."

"Matsubara?"

Kim nodded.

"Get me his address."

"You've got to be joking."

"I want his address. Who can get it?"

Kim exhaled.

"No one's going to give you the home address of the CEO."

"Someone must know where he lives."

"I know roughly where it is. They all live around here. It's a well-to-do area and further from the train line where the houses get bigger and more expensive. There's an exclusive neighbourhood about fifteen, twenty minutes walk away. I've taken my kids there to look at the big houses before. I don't mind showing you the area, but I'm not door-knocking with you."

"That's good of you, but what's the point if you can't identify the house?"

"The Japanese have their names on the front of their gates. All you need is to be able to read *Matsubara* in script. Get one of the Chinese to write it down for you."

Ethan did not know how he was going to approach this, but he wouldn't let it go. There was no cool-headed planning. Find the house. Then decide what to say. As soon as they had clocked off, Ethan and Kim marched through the ever richer suburbs in search of confrontation.

As the houses started to grow in splendour, Kim returned to the station and Ethan soon spotted the Matsubara family name on an iron gate. There was no mistaking it. It matched the carefully written characters provided to him on a slip of paper by colleague Wen Bo. The old lady, almost bent double, who eventually answered the door was confused. She shook her head a number of times and jabbered away in Japanese as he repeated, "Matsubara-*san*? Matsubara-*san*?"

It was a false start and he continued his search, the ornate houses becoming mansions, spaced further and further apart. The next Matsubara household he found had its nameplate on a dark metal postbox, next to a doorbell button some twenty or thirty metres from the front door of a beautiful residence, surrounded by trees and shrubs. He chided himself for thinking that the old lady's house could have been big enough for the owner of Matsucorp.

Soon after he pressed the bell, an ageing male voice spoke through the intercom.

"*Dare?*" Who is it? "*Dare?*"

In his ignorance, Ethan could only repeat his question "Matsubara-*san*?"

Eventually a frustrated Japanese man, perhaps in his sixties, began the walk from his front door to the gate. As he got closer, there was no mistaking the match between this man and the framed photographs distributed throughout the factory. Ethan had struck lucky at the second attempt.

Matsubara clearly knew that he was going to have to attempt English.

"Who are you?"

He seemed to recognise the name Eric Marks as he immediately placed his forefinger on the sensor, looked into the iris scanner and allowed Ethan access. Unspeaking, Ethan followed the company boss up the driveway and in through the front door. Not a word was uttered until Matsubara had closed the office door behind them and both men were sat either side of an impressive desk.

"Yes?"

"I work in your factory in Hōya. I am a cleaning and maintenance operative."

"I know you. I gave you job so you can have better life."

"I know. Thank you. I am grateful for the opportunity."

Matsubara nodded an acceptance of gratitude shown.

"So why you come to my house?"

"The deep clean day tomorrow. We only found out about this today. This was not planned."

"Everything is planned. Company decision is mine."

"But this is short notice. The workers have a right to their own lives. I have plans for tomorrow afternoon."

"This is Japan, Eric Marks-*san*. In Japan, workers are loyal to company. You work when I need."

"But I don't think you need me to work tomorrow afternoon. I think you are trying to obstruct legitimate union activity."

"Obstruct? Legitimate? What is this? I don't understand your long word, but I know *union*. We do not have union in Japan. That is why our economy is number one."

Matsubara had suddenly become more animated, for the first time sitting forward in his seat, elbows on his desk. He reached for his cigarettes, lit up and offered his packet to Ethan who waved them away.

"Companies work better with happy workers. Because you are number one, you can afford to pay us properly. We work just as hard as Japanese workers."

"We do not have to let you come. If you come, you have to accept Japanese pay, Japanese rules, Japanese way of working."

"But you can choose to be more reasonable."

Now Matsubara was on his feet, voice raised.

"You do not tell me what to do! You are ungrateful! I run company my way. You accept or leave. Union is not legal here. You stop union or you don't have job. No job, no visa. No visa means deported. Back to poor country."

Now Ethan became incensed and joined Mastubara on his feet.

"Unions are international," almost shouting now. "Our contracts discriminate according to race. You are breaking international law. That is why we have to demonstrate tomorrow. Your deep clean will have to wait!"

Ethan made to continue but was shouted down. The significance of tomorrow had become clearer to Matsubara and his displeasure escalated his fury.

"No! We do not make success by follow ancient international law. We show kindness by offer jobs to foreign worker. You are not grateful. You *will* do deep clean. If you do not come, I sack you all. Now, get out!"

Suddenly, Matsubara was more formidable. He moved towards the younger man and propelled him to the office door. Ethan turned, opened the door and exited alone into Matsubara's house, the door slamming right behind his heels.

Much as we were on good terms, I could not believe my luck. Gold dust of the blackmailing variety. I was still wondering what to do with it when I got home on the Sunday night, but it was relegated to the back of my mind on Monday morning when a major scandal broke.

This was back in the days of fossil fuels. We still look back in wonder at how governments and energy companies continued to promote and sell their poison in the face of such convincing data on human causation of climate change. How experts were disregarded and discredited! The fake news brigade was certainly on top there for a while.

Anyway, let us not leave you hanging. There was a major scandal which had initially surfaced in Germany, but it now emerged that in Japan too, major players in the car industry had been installing software in diesel engines which could defeat emissions testing. Results were artificially improved and the life of diesel was prolonged.

Diplomacy had never been so prized. For months I was thrust into the position of intermediary between the Japanese motor CEOs and the British government and import market. My contacts turned on the hospitality and ramped the charm up to eleven and I worked my magic with the folks back in the UK. I saved some contracts and limited damage on some reputations. I worked pretty hard there for a few months and I cemented my own reputation as a protector and facilitator of trade for a long time to come.

The Japanese were grateful, boy were they grateful! It often takes years to erode the ethics of a junior diplomat, fresh out of university, however desperate for advancement. I had the advantage of starting without any such encumbrance. Favours and backhanders were a perk of the trade.

Call me arrogant, but I really was rather good at it. I had all the sushi in Japan and a little something up my sleeve for when I needed it.

#

Chapter Forty-seven

"Do you ever feel that you're being watched, Alfie?"

Jordan was walking Alfie to Shakuji-kōen station as darkness fell.

"All the time. I thought I was just being paranoid. Why? Do you feel it, too?"

"A bit," replied Jordan. "Anyway, you shouldn't dismiss it as paranoia. Best to be alert. Keep your wits about you."

"I will, dad. Don't worry."

Odd looks were drawn by their hug at the ticket barrier, sound-tracked by the cries of the *yaki-imo* man, selling charcoal-roasted sweet potato from his mini-van. Jordan turned away as Alfie rounded the corner onto the platform. Only now did the potential difficulty in finding Tomoko's house begin to trouble him. The worry lasted until he stepped onto the platform at Hōya and found Tomoko sitting on a bench. She grinned.

"I didn't think I could trust you to find my house again."

"You're right not to trust me," said Alfie, visibly relieved, then soon tense again, as he remembered his concern from earlier. "Have your parents gone out yet?" he asked.

"No, but they should be gone by the time we get there."

"*Should?*"

"Yeah, well, if not, they'll be about to leave. I told my mum you might call in. It's no big deal."

"What about your dad?"

Alfie looked at the pavement as the root cause of his anxiety emerged.

"Don't worry about my dad, Alfie. He's a big softy really. I know he comes across as a hard case and I regret the fact that you don't want to tell me what he said to you in his study that time. Probably something about my honour! But he has no more problem with you than any other father would have with his daughter's boyfriend. Don't sweat it."

Finally, Alfie looked up at her and smiled. They joined hands and increased cadence as they waded ever deeper into the affluent suburbs. Alfie felt like a celebrity with security, accompanied to and from stations at each end of his journey, happy that he would not arrive alone at Tomoko's door.

Fingerprint and iris technology had them inside with efficiency. It was evident that Tomoko's parents' departure had been delayed.

Her mother greeted them as they entered the kitchen to get a drink.

"Hello, Alfie-*san*," came with a bow of moderate depth, reciprocated with *gaijin* clumsiness.

"Your father is delayed by business meeting, Tomoko-*chan*. We will leave very soon."

"No problem, *okāsan. Daijōbu*," a response now within Alfie's comprehension.

"So," came the pleasant attempt at polite conversation, "what plan for this evening for you and Tomoko?"

"Popcorn and a movie." Tomoko's hasty response masked almost all of Alfie's awkwardness as he sought a cover story.

"Great! Why not take tea in the lounge?"

The three of them moved to the patent leather sofas in the adjacent room and maintained a level of polite conversation. The atmosphere became awkward as voices in the nearby study were raised. It was an argument in English, evident from the occasional word, rather than the detail, shouted first by the familiar pidgin Alfie had experienced from Tomoko's father in that very room, then by his adversary who was a male native English speaker.

Tomoko's mother decided that now was the time to precipitate the end of this meeting. They were running late. This would not do. As she raised a fist, Alfie watching in slow motion, they heard heavily accented Japanese, shouting "Get out!" The door flew open, Tomoko's mother stepped back and a Westerner in green Matsucorp overalls was propelled into the lounge, the door slamming shut.

Bewildered, the man briefly took in the mixed race family scene before him, then made for the front door. Seconds later, he was gone.

"This is not like your father," Tomoko's mother mused, propping her hands on the sofa back where her daughter was seated. Both women were visibly shaken, Tomoko wondering in silence what had driven such anger in her father. Alfie had his own questions, preoccupied with the identity of the departed Westerner. For as long as he could remember, he had only seen photographs, but he was struck by this man's resemblance to his uncle Ethan.

As one, they turned to face Tomoko's father, his face red as he emerged from his study. What happened over the few minutes between the altercation and the departure of Tomoko's parents happened in Japanese. An exchange between the older couple was followed by a family row, triggered by Tomoko's interjection. Alfie was left in the house with a crying Tomoko, her tearful mother and angry father having left for the theatre. Tomoko stood and, through the snot and the tears, said "I'm going to pack my bag."

Chapter Forty-eight

Since her first night, Shaylie had not been this nervous. Friday was busy. It was not the usual night for Ken and his colleagues, but somehow she knew he would be there.

Ken was not her only preoccupation as she worked the first few hours from booth to booth with different combinations of the other girls. It had struck her before leaving the gaijin house that evening that both Alfie and Jordan were quieter than usual. Coincidence, or were they complicit in their reticence? She could not help but wonder whether they were keeping something from her.

She was alone in a small side booth with two young besuited men with goofy teeth when she noticed Ken arrive, this time with just two companions. She observed Tsubasa's involvement in ejecting a larger party from Ken's habitual booth which was far too big for three. A hand on her thigh propelled her back to the job at hand. The squeeze was tight and was not dislodged by a gentle nudge. By the time Shaylie had slapped the young man's hand, she felt sure that there would be some bruising which would require explanation at home. She scolded the salaryman, little more than a boy, who understood her face, if not her English. She had expected this to be an easy hour, but their complete lack of English made it very hard going. As the rather too forward man hung his head in a shameful bow, she leaned across his friend to replenish his drink. With equal disregard for the rules of the game, he gently ran the back of his hand along the outside of her breast as she withdrew from her lean.

Shaylie snapped and stood, looking him in the eye, shouting "*Dame!*" It was the one expression of prohibition she knew. Tsubasa was there in seconds, flanked by a compact and brawny doorman. Before he could ask, a flustered Shaylie blurted, "He touched my breast." Tsubasa could see that it was not the occasion to encourage one of his most popular hostesses to overlook a silly impropriety. And thus, she was fast-tracked to the company of a more familiar client.

She was shaking as she sat down next to Ken.

"Are you fine, Shay-ree-*san*?" A rhetorical question she felt no compulsion to answer.

He continued, "I see you are not fine. You shake."

"I'll be OK," she said, her hand trembling more as she made a mess of topping up his glass.

"Don't worry," he reassured her, taking his handkerchief from the breast pocket of his suit jacket and mopping the spillage himself. "You will spend evening with me. You will not be with silly boy again tonight."

Grateful for the respite and the familiarity, Shaylie settled into idle small talk with Ken and his two younger colleagues, the latter mostly talking amongst themselves, assuming the role of chaperones.

Ken had retreated into the small talk of their early meetings and Shaylie could not help but wonder whether he had decided to reserve his prying for occasions when they were alone. Another *dōhan* invitation was surely not far away. She felt that she, too, had to respect his approach and therefore steered the conversation towards the trivial, a task which she found particularly onerous that Friday evening. Their previous discussion of the personal made their pleasantries so false. Ken allowed Shaylie to lead and she felt herself trying to drag the context of the chatter back from the line which they had so recently crossed. She forced Ken to talk about the geography of Japan, the people of the countryside, how the country's politics worked and the few countries he had visited. Only the plight of the newly and so violently reunited Korea ignited his interest. His responses were otherwise forced through a veiled preoccupation.

Abruptly, he excused himself in a lull in the conversation, ostensibly to visit the bathroom, and Shaylie watched the detour he took in the direction of Tsubasa's office. The struggle to engage Ken's colleagues was brief, as he returned minutes later.

"Come with me, Shay-ree-*san*."

"Where? Where are we going?" she stuttered, faced with a sudden and unexpected instruction.

"You are not fine this evening. Tsubasa-*san* agrees to our *dōhan*. We will eat Tokyo's most excellent sushi. In Ginza."

It was an opportunity for Shaylie to escape the claustrophobia of an arduous evening, one which she could not envisage completing as a popular hostess. Their first *dōhan* had been fine. What could possibly go wrong?

Leaving Ken's co-workers in their sizeable booth, awaiting a new hostess, Shaylie and Ken took the lift and were picked up outside by Ken's chauffeur. On the back seat, Shaylie became monosyllabic as Ken was suddenly animated, describing the extraordinary culinary experience which awaited them.

Understated luxury and a pictorial menu in leather-bound folder told Shaylie than this *sushi-ya-san* was indeed exclusive. Space between tables and capacious booths in the depths of the restaurant afforded considerable privacy to the wealthy customers. Cost was inconsequential to nonchalant diners who ordered from a menu without prices. Bombay Sapphire and Schweppes had a calming effect and Shaylie was relieved to sit back and allow Ken to order. The *carte image* was of little help to a sushi amateur, but Ken was an *amateur*.

There followed a feast with Ken's enthusiastic commentary. He explained each microdish and complimented Shaylie on her chopstick dexterity. Relieved of the onus for table talk topics, Shaylie relaxed and listened, enjoying a meal she could never expect to afford.

Sated and mildly intoxicated, they sat back, drained their green tea and accepted a post-prandial *atsukan*. The high-grade, hot sake quickly permeated the lining of Shaylie's stomach and hastened to her brain. The effect was empowerment, the removal of inhibitions. She could sense Ken's desire to resume questioning, so boldly acted first to turn the conversation onto him.

"This really is a beautiful restaurant. You must have a really good job to eat in places like this."

"Last time I tell you, Shay-ree-*san*. I work in entertainment. We control many bar and pachinko parlour in Kabukichō. That is very popular area of Shinjuku. Some our bar is hostess bar like Tsubasa-*san* his bar in Okachimachi. I know this industry very well and you are right. There is much money in entertainment in Tokyo. So I have much money."

Shaylie took a deep breath.

"So do you live in a big house with your wife?"

Ken's smile was tight, his stare direct.

"I have no wife, Shay-ree-*san*. Like you, I live alone." It was almost a question.

"So," a pause, "I do not need big house. I live in luxury penthouse in Ikebukuro. It is very expensive place to live."

Guarded with most details of his personal life, Ken was nevertheless keen to impress with details of his wealth.

"Would you like to see?"

Shaylie wanted the ground to open, she wanted to bring an awkward moment to a close. Blurred by the sake, desperate to evade a return to the claustrophobic ordeal of the night's hostessing, Shaylie jettisoned judgement and agreed. The need to return to complete her shift was a useful caveat. The safety rules of the hostess lay broken for the evening, another line crossed.

Chapter Forty-nine

She emerged from the stairs wearing a rucksack, with a coat draped over her left forearm.

"We have to go," now calmer.

"We've got all evening. Sit down and explain. I don't understand."

"I've been kicked out."

"Kicked out?" Alfie was incredulous. "Why?"

"For disloyalty to my father."

"Disloyalty?"

"That man was one of his workers. My dad is one of the company owners who have put foreign workers on inferior contracts. That man is one of the people who we are demonstrating for this weekend. My dad is trying to make them work tomorrow afternoon so that they cannot demonstrate. He has found out about our demo. Mr Marks came to protest."

"Mr Marks?" Alfie could barely disguise his disbelief.

"Yes, Mr Marks. Why?"

"But ... he was wearing a Matsucorp overall."

The yen had dropped.

"Yes, because ..."

"You've never told me your surname."

"What?"

"What's your surname?"

"Matsubara. I am Matsubara Tomoko."

"Matsubara. My God. I never knew. I never asked you. My dad works for your dad."

"I know. Does it matter?"

"Well, no, but you're demonstrating against your dad. Does he know?"

A resigned sigh. "He does now. I stuck up for Mr Marks and all his co-workers. So he asked me straight out. I'm not going to lie. We are fighting for what is right."

Alfie's shoulders dropped, his gaze switching from Tomoko to the floor between his feet.

"What's up?" asked Tomoko. "You're not the homeless one."

"It's you."

"What's me? What have I done wrong?"

"Wrong? Nothing. You're amazing. So brave. So strong. I could never have done that. What are you doing with me?"

"You have started a new life in a strange country and now you are going to take to the streets, one white face in a sea of Japanese students. That's brave. And strong. You're amazing, Alfie."

Abruptly, Alfie stood. "Right. Come on then."

"Wait. I've got to phone round some friends, find somewhere to stay."

"No way. You're staying with us. I'm not leaving you alone and homeless."

"Alfie, your family lives in *one room*!"

"We'll manage. Let's go back and talk to my dad. It's time to come clean. We've got a demo to plan."

Shinji Matsubara was an interesting chap. Still is. There was I, junior diplomat with trade portfolio; there was he, up-and-coming junior director with Suzuki. I made strong contacts in the boardrooms of companies across a variety of industries, but, as party-goers of a similar age, you could almost say he became a friend.

Our backgrounds had little in common, but then who the hell outside of the UK had an upbringing like mine. I'm a clever bloke, but even I doubt that I would have found myself in Japan with the FCO if it weren't for the ridiculous privilege of my outmoded, ostentatious, archaic education. Matsubara had to work for his success, but with his brain and ambition, he was always in with a good chance.

He was in it for the long haul. A company director in his mid-twenties: that was never going to be enough for Shinji Matsubara. He had endurance. Physical and mental endurance. He could work, he could party and he could run. He was one of an extraordinary generation of university endurance athletes who ran times which bordered on the elite, but which, in Japan, Kenya and Ethiopia alone, were unremarkable. He was a sight to behold, straight of back, slight and graceful, popular with the girls and the gays, and he was a winner.

I was a passenger in his life for a while, filling the gaps around the rather long working day with training, individual races, the ekidens and parties. I would watch these extraordinary team road relays with thousands of others, then be dragged off to a celebration, usually in an izakaya with a nomihōdai. Drink all you can, drink some more, end up on your knees in the station. Matsubara stood up to alcohol better than most of the locals. He was, in every respect, a conquistador.

I admired such a very good acquaintance for his many qualities. His greatest attribute, however, was his foresight. For who could have known what was coming?

Chapter Fifty

Another trip in the purring sedan, an interminable ride in a lift and within half an hour Shaylie was sitting on the balcony of a 42nd floor apartment, looking across the bright lights of an enormous city. Without asking, Ken fixed another generous gee and tee for each of them and sat next to her. He would save the grand tour until later. By then, she would be beyond squiffy and oblivious to the lack of personal effects that one would expect in a permanent residence.

"So. What do you think?"

Shaylie could only massage his ego with congratulatory set-pieces. His flat was magnificent. He had done so well for himself.

The unrelenting traffic sounded distant as Shaylie's compliments abated and they enjoyed their drinks in comfortable silence. Ken had promised her the full tour, but she was happy to relax, a state of mind only achieved, given the circumstances, through alcohol.

Past midnight, the temperature dropped, the traffic continued. There was no music and, in the silence, Ken noticed gooseflesh and raised hairs on Shaylie's forearms. He withdrew momentarily into the flat and returned with a cashmere shawl. He decorated Shaylie's upper body with dragons, his lightness of touch palpable.

Drinks refreshed one more time, Shaylie fought for her consciousness, eyelids heavy, sight increasingly blurred. From above, she watched Ken support her from beneath her elbows as she struggled back into his flat. In the warmer environment, she ached for the sofa, for horizontality, for sleep, but she was led towards the entrance hall and past the front door.

"I promise you tour, Shay-ree-*san*."

Shaylie did not have the strength to respond, able only to focus on Ken's interminable pronunciation of *tour*, his elongation of the word to *tsū-a*. She barely saw the magnificent kitchen, the height of technology, the capacious bathroom with its large sunken Jacuzzi, the spare rooms and, finally, the ornate master bedroom with its beautiful en suite wetroom.

Now close to collapse, Shaylie did not even question the suggestion that she should have a lie down and was soon in a deep sleep on Ken's four-poster bed.

Chapter Fifty-one

Half an hour of hiking, Alfie with Tomoko's rucksack on his back, had them entering the gaijin house. They walked in on Jordan, alone in the kitchen, making two cups of tea. There was time for a brief greeting and a questioning look from Alfie's father, directed towards the rucksack, now unloaded. The girl, who seemed a little familiar to Jordan, was introduced as Alfie's girlfriend. They were soon interrupted by the flush from the adjacent toilet.

The green Matsucorp uniform emerged from the water closet and there was another introduction.

"Alfie," said Jordan, "meet your uncle Ethan."

Only Jordan was confused at the understated greeting, restrained handshakes between Ethan and the teenagers.

"Well, I thought you'd be more surprised."

"We've already met briefly this evening," said Ethan, "but I have to say that I'm surprised to see *you* here." The comment was aimed at Tomoko.

"Uncle Ethan, Tomoko is my girlfriend."

"I've not really merited that title, have I, Alfie? Just call me Ethan, and then perhaps explain why you are consorting with the enemy."

Now Jordan was involved again. "The enemy? Already met? Would someone tell me what is going on?"

Ethan got there first.

"I told you I had an altercation with Matsubara this evening."

"Yes. So?"

"Well, he threw me out. And as I walked from his office, through his lounge to the front door, guess who was sitting there on his sofa?"

"You two?" Jordan turned to Alfie and Tomoko, incredulous.

"Yeah, us," said Alfie.

"But … but why? How come?"

Alfie assumed the narrative, explaining who Tomoko was, that Matsubara was her father.

Jordan resumed questioning.

"And you never thought to tell me this?"

"I didn't know, dad. I only found out tonight. Japanese names are a struggle. I never thought that it was important to know Tomoko's surname."

It was Tomoko's turn to be shocked when Alfie recounted previous meetings and decided that Tomoko's estrangement from her father now allowed him to tell of his own ordeal in the study.

"Why didn't you tell me, Alfie?" she asked.

"The man's a monster," interjected Ethan.

"He really isn't," retorted Tomoko, turning back to Alfie.

"I didn't want to bother you with it. I thought it was no big deal. I didn't want to upset you."

"Of course I'm upset. He is only trying to protect me, but you didn't have to deal with it alone. I could have spoken to him. But not now, not any more."

"He may not be a monster, Tomoko, he's your dad. But he needn't have kicked you out. And now you're homeless?" Jordan was at a loss to know what to say.

"About that, dad. Tomoko has stuck her neck on the line for me. She's looked after me and helped me to settle in. I said we'd find room for her to stay with us for a bit."

Jordan hesitated but, realising the gravity of the situation, agreed.

"Well, I'm glad that's sorted," said Ethan, "because we have another pressing matter to discuss."

"The demo." Alfie took the words right out of the mouths of the other three.

It was another surprise for Jordan. "What? How do you know about that?"

"That is my responsibility, Jordan-*san*," said Tomoko. "I am involved in organising student involvement. I have encouraged Alfie to take part. There is a large movement of young people who want to protest against poor treatment of foreign migrants and the rise of the JSD. I am one of the organisers."

Now it was all out in the open. No more secrets.

"So you are fighting against your dad and his company? My employer? Ethan's employer?" Jordan could barely speak.

"I don't think I am directly fighting my father. Really my father is fighting against himself. In his own head. He is in favour of limited economic migration. He wants to help foreigners. But Matsucorp is a massive company. Its success depends on political support.

"Yamada-*san* is a key JSD member. He is on Matsucorp's board and so the JSD have a lot of influence. He needs to compromise and it is frustrating for him. Sometimes too frustrating. And then he gets angry. He has to do what is best for Matsucorp and it is not easy to know what is best. For me, it is much simpler. I love my father, but I am doing what is right."

A pause.

"Wow!" Ethan was first to respond. "Impressive. And correct. Demonstrating is the right course of action. It is morally right."

"Agreed," said Alfie.

The three of them turned to Jordan.

"You all make it sound simple."

"It is!" In unison.

"It isn't!" Now Jordan was more animated.

They all waited as he collected his thoughts.

"I'm very grateful to Matsucorp. I have to be. We were facing a life on unemployment benefit in a broken economy. We would have lost our house. We'd have been living on nothing. They have gifted us a new life, financial security, comfort. We were chosen over many others and fast-tracked to economic migration. Throwing it back in their face could put all of that at risk. I don't want us to appear ungrateful and be on the first plane home."

"It's the same for me," said Ethan. "I may not have as good a job as you, but it's still better than what I'd have at home. We have to do what is right. They haven't given us jobs out of sympathy for us, but for good PR and convenience."

Tomoko cut in.

"You are right up to a point. But my dad does have sympathy for people in the collapsed economies. That's why he is torn."

"OK, I get what you are saying. But he doesn't like us standing up to him."

"As I said, he is torn. He doesn't want the negative PR of the demo, but he knows we are in the right. He will have to accept it. It will be a mass demo and we have safety in numbers. He can't sack everyone. And he won't be able to sack all those who demonstrate. He won't have an attendance list thousands of names long."

Alfie was impressed by his dad's determination to argue his case.

"He may not have an attendance list, Tomoko, but many of the workers at the demo and all of the students will be Asian. There will be lots of Africans, too. White faces will stick out like a sore thumb. Alfie will be the only white student. And I will be, in a small number of white workers, the only one who has been put in the privileged position of having a skilled job. My presence will be a kick in the teeth for your dad. He's given me a job which could have been taken by a Japanese person. He can't replace thousands of cleaners, but he can easily replace me."

"And take the adverse publicity which comes with it," said Tomoko. "He wouldn't take that risk. He would look like a hypocrite. This is not about defeating my dad, it's about making sure that all employers who benefit from economic migration treat foreign employees equally. It's also about defeating the JSD anti-migration politics and weakening the influence of Yamada on the Matsucorp board. If we all stick together we will achieve our goals and we will be too numerous for individuals to be singled out and dealt with."

"This girl is really switched on," said Ethan, impressed again. "What do you think, Alfie?"

"Yeah, she is."

"No," laughed Ethan. "I mean what do you think about what she says?"

"Oh, yeah." A sheepish reply.

He turned to his dad.

"I've been worried about this too, dad. For the same reasons. I didn't want to put your job at risk. Didn't want to seem ungrateful. But I've been to gatherings which have been getting bigger and bigger." Jordan looked surprised. "There are thousands and thousands of students coming out on the streets tomorrow. And yes, I'll stand out amongst *them*, but we won't stand out once all the migrant workers come into the mix."

"Exactly," continued Tomoko. "It will be a huge display of solidarity."

"They're right Jordan," said his brother. "We are where we are because Matsucorp's board agreed that we would be good for their public image. Matsubara will only be able to draw one conclusion from this mass display of solidarity. Non-discriminatory contracts will emphasise their human side, show them to be a benevolent corporation and it will allow them to dilute the influence of that weasel Yamada. The far right may have a following but it's still a minority. We could improve our contracts and dent his election prospects at the same time. It won't be a defeat for Tomoko's dad, it'll be a defeat for *him*."

Alfie served more tea and Jordan sat back in his seat, looking around the table. Little attention was paid to the house rat as it made an appearance on top of the microwave.

He smiled. He had his reservations, but he had nothing to trump what had been offered across the table. First thing tomorrow morning he would ensure that Shaylie was on board. That wouldn't be a problem, though, not with Tomoko there to talk it through.

He set his mind to a simpler issue: how to sleep four in a room that was a squeeze for three.

Chapter Fifty-two

It was still dark when she awoke, although she thought she could distinguish the very beginnings of a dawn glow. She struggled to roll from her back onto her side. Head pounding, she was panicked by her inability to move either her legs or her arms. The position of her arms above her head felt unnatural. Forcing her eyes to open she discovered, in the half light coming from elsewhere in the flat, that her wrists and ankles were tightly bound and attached to the bed frame.

Stifling her instinct to cry out, she struggled to no avail. Beads of sweat running down her temples, she ceased her wrangling and regained her composure as Ken re-entered the bedroom. She promised herself rational thought in anticipation of an imminent need for diplomacy. Ken, now dressed in a *yukata*, an opulent Japanese dressing gown, spoke first.

"I have wonderful time with you, Shay-ree-*san*. I am very happy you accept my invitation to come back my home."

"It was a nice evening, Ken-*san*, but why have you tied me up?"

"Our evening is not finish, Shay-ree-*san*. It is good you are now rested. But you are not happy about ties. They are too tight for you?"

"Yes. No. It's not about how tight they are," she said. He sat on the side of the bed, his look of concern seeming genuine.

"So what is problem?" he replied, freeing her ankles from their constraints.

"I came here of my own free will. I don't understand why you have tied me up at all."

Ken had constructed his own account of their circumstance in his head.

"We are single adult spending lovely evening together. Now we come to bedroom. It is natural."

"Tying me up is ... natural?"

"Adult in bedroom can do many thing. *Essu-emmu* is very popular. Most of people enjoy this now. Not you?"

Neglecting to free Shaylie's wrists, Ken was now stroking her cheeks and her arms as he spoke. She ignored this as she quickly deciphered *essu-emmu*. Ess emm. S and M. S&M pornography was certainly popular and the sexually inexperienced interpreted this as both common and normal in the real world.

"This is not something which I think I would enjoy, Ken-*san*. Would you please untie my wrists?"

"You have never try?"

He was now running the back of his hand over her stomach towards her hips.

"Maybe you like if you try."

She had retained a relaxed aura until now, but her body tensed as his hand continued over the side of her hips, beyond her dress to the bare, smoothly waxed flesh of her thighs. Ken was intent on physical intimacy without the complication of freeing Shaylie's hands. She knew now that avoiding rape would not be easy. She forced herself to relax again, knowing that her best chance was patience, a clear head, the right moment and engendering a sense of security in her adversary.

She choked back tears and looked at the ceiling as he now leaned in and kissed her upper chest, moving in and out of her cleavage. He was now lying next to her and his hand stopped its descent of her thigh, moving upwards and taking her dress with it. He stroked her knickers and her lower stomach, occasionally running his fingertips along the inside of her knicker elastic. She began to feel physically sick as she felt him stroke her pubic hair.

She fought her gag reflex, but suddenly he stopped. Stopped the kissing and stopped the touching. Avoiding eye contact, he placed his hand on her right shoulder, pulled her onto her side and unzipped her dress at the back. She felt pain in her right shoulder as the rest of her body moved away from it, but she was soon returned to her back as he set about pulling her dress down over her torso and then her bare legs and feet. Now she regretted the strapless dress.

Seconds later, Shaylie craned her neck, bewildered, as she observed Ken's unmoving body on the floor between the bed and the door. Her head was playing catch-up. Now she congratulated her own instinct. She had seen perhaps her only opportunity. As her feet were freed from her dress she had managed one almighty kick with her right foot, planting her heel into Ken's temple.

Her reflection was momentary as a groan from the floor underlined the fact that she needed to free herself before he regained consciousness. She hauled herself into a seated position and worked at the tie on her right wrist with her teeth. Her right hand came free as Ken raised his head and opened one eye. He slumped again. Shaylie untied her left wrist.

She dismounted, retrieved her dress from the floor, stood tall and turned towards the bedroom door. There in the doorway, supporting himself on the frame, was a groggy businessman, staring into Shaylie's mind. He wore the same tight-lipped expression she had experienced when she had denied her marriage.

"Please come back to bed, Shay-ree-*san*. We can be happy. We don't need *essu-emmu*."

Shaylie's only escape was a partial one. She ran into the en suite, slammed the door and saw that her prayers had been answered. There was a lock on the door.

#

Looking back, it's obvious. Fossil fuels were not renewable, nor were they inexhaustible. They would run out and then, well, we'd have to use something else.

But that was where Matsubara's foresight gained him a huge advantage. Still in his 20s, still a director of a major user of fossil fuels, he saw the end coming. When major automobile manufacturers and their supporters in the West were dismissing the environmental lobby, disregarding incontrovertible scientific evidence and pooh-poohing all experts, Matsubara knew it was time to get ahead of the inevitable new phase of the game.

Not only did he know exactly what he needed to do, he recognised the opportunity when it arose. He needed a team of scientists to work on the commercial development of the hydrogen engine and he needed to have extensive manufacturing facilities in place. The diesel emissions scandal could not have come at a better time. The car manufacturers began a downward spiral on the Nikkei, there were redundancies in all departments and a couple of the less popular names on the market went to the wall.

I had contacts in all of these boardrooms, I had the inside track and with it my discretion was a given. Matsubara greased my palm, he trumped my discretion with a handsome payment which I lacked the moral fibre to refuse and, in return, I tipped him the wink. He knew when there were facilities about to be liquidated and he stepped in and met the derisory asking price. His business plan was excellent, his bank manager astute, his real estate advisor eloquent and crafty. All that he needed he had in place himself, using his extraordinary prescience and his corrupt diplomat ally.

I can remember the conversation verbatim which established our relationship for decades to come. A courteous bow accompanied the manila envelope.

"You are mine now, Stepson-san, and this will stay between us."

His poker face slipped as I replied.

"I prefer to think that we will collaborate as equals," I replied, "and nobody will ever know of your affair with Mrs Suzuki."

#

239

Chapter Fifty-three

Struthwin followed the obligatory *Ohayō gozaimasu* and bow with an immediate question as he entered Matsubara's Ikebukuro office early Saturday morning.

"No Yamada?"

The question was rhetorical. After the last meeting of the manipulative trinity, he fully expected the absence of the holy ghost. Matsubara did not feel the need to answer. He had more pressing concerns.

"I have always trusted your overseas recruitment, Stepson-*san*. But now, at this crucial point, I am led to question your judgement."

Struthwin was taken by surprise.

"Please stay calm, Matsubara-*san*. I am fully in control of the entire May family."

"My concerns about the May family have become secondary. There is a loose cannon amongst our newer maintenance operatives. His name is Eric Marks. You signed his papers."

Struthwin was unsure whether his boss spotted the momentary look of surprise, suppressed by a confident smile.

"Ah yes, Eric Marks, I have had my eye on him. It is true, he has a lot to say for himself, but he does not carry authority, he holds no sway with his co-workers."

"He is an added complication who could further ignite the activities of the Koreans and the Chinese."

"From what I have seen he is a jumped-up pussy cat who can be manipulated like the rest. They will have their little demonstration, we will pacify them and then we will all carry on as normal."

Matsubara stood, lent forward over his desk, raised his voice.

"You knew about this, this anarchy?"

Struthwin bridled, cleared his throat and paused to regain his composure as Matsubara lit up.

"Yes. I mean, it is my job to know."

"And to inform me!"

"I have only just found out. When you called me this morning I was about to call you. I am here to talk through this benign and insignificant act of foreign ungratefulness, in which Eric Marks will play a minor role."

"I do not intend that any of my co-workers will have a role to play in this, this insurrection."

"We cannot stop it. We have to manage it."

"That is where you are wrong. And that is where Eric Marks is wrong, too."

"Hold on a moment. There's something you are not telling me here. You've spoken to him?"

Matsubara fell back into his chair, exhaled a long trail of smoke in Struthwin's direction and told the story of his deep clean announcement and Ethan's subsequent visit to the leafy suburbs of Hōya. Matsubara was at once inwardly amused, at being one step ahead of Struthwin for the first time, and outraged that his right-hand man was no longer ahead of the game.

Having heard Matsubara explain his heavy-handed attempt to scupper the demonstration, Struthwin was afforded some thinking time as the tale of an angry showdown became background noise. As the dander rose to a crescendo, he suppressed a smile and awaited the inevitable subsidence.

"A typhoon in a tea-cup," he offered, as Matsubara lit up again. "You are right, I hadn't expected him to get quite so involved, but this really isn't out of character. He has much to say, but he has neither the charisma nor the nous to affect change. He is an upstart, not a leader of men. He is easily dealt with, as are the rest of them."

Appeased by Struthwin's confidence, Matsubara was momentarily calm.

"So what do we do, Stepson-*san*?"

"As always, we take the intelligent option. We do nothing."

"Nothing?!"

Struthwin extended his hands, palms to the floor, waiting for Matsubara, out of his seat again, to sit.

"This is another opportunity for positive PR."

"How so?" was the disbelieving response.

"A hard line on this will align us with the JSD. If we look beyond the hard right views of the few, the public will appreciate a benevolent corporation which shows empathy with our unfortunate foreign cousins, whilst continuing to prioritise the skilled Japanese workforce. We can further sideline Yamada, denting his hopes of a landslide and cementing our place as the number one contributor to this country's GDP."

"Whilst handing the advantage to a pro-immigration mass movement."

"No. Quite the opposite. We magnanimously allow them their public display of concern, make minor concessions which strengthen our popularity across the board and go on to even greater prosperity."

"Minor concessions? They will not settle for minor concessions."

"Of course they will. They are not stupid. People like Eric Marks may want to take the issue further, but the majority are like Jordan May. They want to protect what they have. They will be delighted at any deal, accept it and get on with their lives. They will not believe their luck."

"I am not in the business of handing out deals when faced with strong-arm tactics."

"Offer them an arrangement to win their loyalty. A small pay rise of no consequence to Matsucorp. An amount which we can easily afford which they can be persuaded would be in line with what an unskilled Japanese worker would earn, if we had any Japanese unskilled workers. A couple of extra days holiday per year. And unionisation."

"Unionisation? We allow them to form a union?"

"A union in the context of Japan. A union which is strictly regulated by us. With no right in law to strike. With an elected leader who meets regularly with our board and is kept in check. An elected leader who we can use to keep them under control. It will be seen as a highly progressive move. But it will allow us to continue to use cheap foreign labour whilst strengthening our control."

Not for the first time, Matsubara was rendered speechless. He would never have believed that Struthwin had invented it all on the spot.

Struthwin knew to allow him to finish his cigarette in silence. Finally, the boss said exactly what Struthwin knew he would say.

"So, what next?"

"So, now all that *you* have to do is call off the deep clean."

I was happy to sell my silence to the only bidder. Life was good and Matsubara was a fine acquaintance. Almost a friend, I suppose. We rubbed along just fine. We each had enough dirt to sink the other, so we were able to operate on equal footings.

Diplomats on the make were not, I would hazard, rare, but few were as good at it as I was. There I was in the background, making sure Matsubara had all the information first, making sure he was well placed to buy the right people and the right premises and, when the time was right, advising him on his launch and setting up trade links with the UK.

But it wasn't all me. Matsubara was magnificent. Intellect, foresight, ambition; he had it all. He set up offices in Ikebukuro and acquired manufacturing premises in suburban Tokyo as well as two other Japanese cities. Other than me, he told no one. Leaving personnel until last, he kept it quiet. He wanted maximum impact. I had stolen the data on redundant skilled workers and engineers. When the time came, recruitment would be swift.

Finally, he bought the time of two graphic designers from a small company of renown. We took them away for a week in Okinawa, away from prying eyes, and did all of the branding. The media was tipped off for a press conference the following Monday at midday, we flew back in with our artists that morning. No time for any leaks.

Matsubara delivered his resignation by email at 11:30am, stating his intention to honour his one month's notice.

Boom! Matsucorp was launched to the world's media. To everyone else, the hydrogen engine was for a better future, decades down the line. Matsubara accelerated us into that future single-handed. Well, almost single-handed.

As expected, he was put on gardening leave. Time to get set up. One month to the day from Matsucorp's launch, production began. Also in that month he had successfully poached some of the youngest and brightest executive directors from rival firms. Add into the boardroom one advisory non-executive director on a very comfortable salary. This role was not advertised. There could only ever be one right-hand man.

#

Chapter Fifty-four

In a semi-awake haze, Jordan contemplated the reappearance of his brother and the weak genes that they shared. Shaylie's parents had gone on well into old age, dropping in now and then, living a healthy retirement. Jordan and Ethan had a higher than average likelihood of a malignant cell mutation. They had lost both parents within months of one another. He did wonder whether his mother might have been stronger, but when his dad went, she seemed to give up.

Given Jordan's strained relationship with his brother, his mother's funeral was as sober an affair as could be. No friendly wake, sharing amusing tales and anecdotes of a life well lived. The spectre of Ethan's ill-won good reputation put paid to that. Extended family members paid their respects and disappeared.

Their mother had held their father's funeral together, but this time Jordan did not have the fortitude to play his role. Shaylie's out-of-character pointedness and haste to leave did not help, and Ethan's smug attempt at a fraternal handshake as they departed was met with a curt rebuttal from his older brother. Jordan did not expect to see Ethan again.

#

Ethan had left shortly before midnight and the three of them arranged themselves on futons with a morally acceptable space between them. After a fitful night, heads full of anticipation, it was getting on for 9am when they finally came around. Jordan was surprised at the empty space next to him at this late hour.

"*Ohayō gozaimasu,*" came from Tomoko's corner of the room.

Jordan was too preoccupied to reciprocate.

"Where's your mother?" he directed at Alfie.

"I don't know, dad. She's usually back before now."

Jordan sat bolt upright.

"This isn't right," he said. "She should've been back a couple of hours ago, latest."

"Maybe she's had to work late."

"It's not like office work. Surely these clubs have a closing time. She's always home at around the same time. It doesn't make sense. Today of all days."

Tomoko doused the flames of panic with calm.

"I'm sure she'll be back soon. Let's get ready. She'll be here by the time we've finished breakfast."

The May men remained unconvinced but had no choice other than to have faith in Tomoko's good sense. Jordan went off to the shower first, Tomoko laughing off Alfie's suggestion that she go next.

"Did you forget I had a shower before bed?" she grinned. "That's how we do it here. No need for one in the morning"

Beneath her duvet, she pulled on her clothes and jumped to her feet. In seconds her bedding was folded and packed away. She stooped to give Alfie a kiss and tried once again to set his mind at rest.

"I'm sure she'll be back soon. Now get yourself up. I'm going to get the food out for breakfast."

Tomoko knew she was not going to make the decoy event in Omotesandō. Off she went to the kitchen and, by the time that the Mays joined her, the table was set and tea and toast were on offer.

By ten, they had finished and cleared away. Still no Shaylie.

"So," Tomoko broke the silence again, "we need a plan."

"What can we do?" asked Jordan. "This city is enormous. We can't just go out and look for her. All I can do is stay here and wait for her while you two go to the demo."

"Sitting here isn't going to help," said Tomoko. "If she's not back by the time we leave for the demo, there must be something wrong. And then what will you do, Jordan-*san*? Is your Japanese good enough to call the police?"

"No," was all that Jordan could muster.

"She's right, dad. If anyone needs to be contacted, we need Tomoko to do it. We need to do something while she's still here."

"OK, right, I see that, but what can we possibly do? What's the use in calling the police now? An adult woman is a couple of hours late home. They won't be interested."

"But, dad, they might want to know when we tell them she works as a hostess. She could come into contact with some dodgy people."

"They might say that it's a risky job. They might call it irresponsible. They might say that an adult has to be away for 24 hours before they'll consider her missing."

"So," said Tomoko again, "we *do* need a plan."

Jordan was slumped in his seat, his shoulders low, his eyes focused on his busy thumbs, turning above the single fist formed by his intertwined hands.

This time, the silence was broken by Alfie.

"Elisa! Elisa and Aaliyah!"

A glimmer of hope lit Jordan's eyes as he raised his head to face son and girlfriend.

"What?" asked Tomoko.

"Not 'what'," replied Alfie. "Who. Elisa and Aaliyah introduced mum to the hostess bar. They work together. And they live here."

"And they will have been in bed for a couple of hours by now," said Jordan.

"So what?" replied Alfie and Tomoko together.

"If they came home," Alfie added, "they are here and might know where mum is. If they aren't here, she's probably gone for breakfast with them. There's only one way to find out."

"What, wake them up?" The two younger people were beginning to be frustrated, to find Jordan obtuse.

"Dad, this might be an emergency. The only thing we can do is go bang on their door."

Minutes later the three were on the upstairs corridor, assembled outside the door which, they were fairly sure, was Elisa and Aaliyah's.

"Let's hope they're not here," said Jordan. "Let's hope they're with mum."

He prepared his fist at face height and carefully knocked on the wooden frame of the sliding door, avoiding the delicate washi paper.

No response.

He tried again, slightly louder this time.

Still nothing.

He turned to Alfie and Tomoko.

"So what do we do now?"

Tomoko responded. "We make absolutely certain they're not here."

She knocked, much harder, again and again and again.

They all listened.

"Let's go," said Jordan.

"No," said Tomoko. "We have to look."

"We can't go in their room," said Alfie.

Tomoko was determined.

"We *have* to look."

She placed her hand on the door, removing it immediately.

"Did you hear something?" she said.

Alfie had heard it, too. A sniff, or a snort, perhaps a faint yawn or a snore.

He called out. "Elisa? Are you there? Aaliyah?"

Finally, there were footsteps, a slow pattering on tatami. The door slowly drew back, far enough to reveal Elisa's sleepy head, hair awry, eyes swollen and barely open.

"*Nani?*" growled Elisa, still in Japanese mode from a long night shift. Jordan ignored both her language and her tone.

"We're looking for Shaylie."

"She's not here."

"No, not here. I mean, she hasn't come home. Do you know where she is?"

The realisation that Shaylie was missing raised Elisa's eyebrows and widened her eyes. Her recovery was almost immediate.

"No, sorry, she didn't travel back with us this morning."

"I thought you always came home together," persisted Jordan.

"Well, usually we do, but when we left this morning, Shaylie wasn't there."

"What do you mean 'she wasn't there'?"

"She wasn't there. She'd left before us."

"Why would she do that?"

Elisa shrugged and then the door was closed again. They redescended in silence and returned to the family room.

"What now?" asked Alfie.

"What can we do?" replied Jordan. "Wait here and hope she comes home. You two can go to the demo. I'll wait for her."

"No way, dad. I'll wait with you."

Tomoko stood, placed a reassuring hand on Alfie's shoulder and, without a word, left the room.

Chapter Fifty-five

Pota, pota.

Drip, drip, drip from the tap over the sink. Shaylie awoke on the bathroom floor. She shut her eyes again as her movement activated the lights.

Pota, pota.

She tried to move again, her body creaking from a night on a hard floor. A night? Not really a night. She had sat shaking for what must have been hours, having escaped from Ken's assault. It must have been four or five in the morning by the time she had drifted off. Or six.

\#

Guilt transported her back in time. She found herself at Jordan's mum's funeral, the scene of what had previously been her only transgression and her only secret from her husband.

She had tried to hold things together for the family. What remained of the family. Jordan had accepted his dad's death and Alfie, small and resilient, was barely affected by it. Jordan had comforted his mother, tolerated his brother and Shaylie had spent the day entertaining their son. But to lose his mother within months was hard to bear. Alfie acted up, he could sense the change in his father's mood, and Shaylie tried to be there for her husband, her son and the small number of distant cousins and friends who, after the service, had accepted their invitation to a modest buffet at their house. Despite Jordan's animosity towards his brother, it was Ethan who had helped Shaylie to maintain a brave facade for the gathering. She could not help but appreciate it.

When Shaylie had needed respite from the role she had been playing, she had run up two flights of stairs to their tiny shower room. She stepped inside and the tears came. She was so glad of the comfort as he entered, pulled her into him and held her tight. Their mouths met and the grief became passion. He lifted her skirt and pressed her into the door now closed. She could no longer remember at what point she realised that this was Ethan and not Jordan, but she had needed this release. Less than a second after her orgasm came shock, regret and self-loathing.

Now, for only the second time in her life, she felt it again.

#

She squinted at her watch. 12:00pm. Later than she had expected. Now she realised that it would be light outside and that she was incarcerated in a windowless room. She recalled the views from the balcony and reflected that a window would not aid her escape. She needed to wake up and consider her next move.

Pota, pota.

The apartment was silent. She could hear no movement outside the bathroom. She wondered how Ken was. She'd kicked him hard, but he had come round. He couldn't have had a relapse, could he? And no, she was almost certain that she couldn't have kicked him hard enough to kill him. Her foot was sore, but not that sore.

With her elbow, she levered the top half of her body from the floor. Her head swam, she gagged, she slumped back to the floor. Had he drugged her? Not necessarily. Last night she had drunk far more than she was used to. She reflected on her own stupidity. Had there been signs? He wasn't the drunken fool. He was the quiet, calculating one, the one who kept his cards close to his chest, the persistent one. Ken had the air of a man who got what he wanted. Should she have been more careful?

Pota, pota.

Reflections which would have to wait until she got out of there. If she got out of there. She needed to know whether Ken was at large. She levered herself up for a second time and sat with her head on her knees, this time overcoming the gag reflex without resuming horizontality. A deep breath in to stem the nausea, then slowly out. In, and then out. The third time in was accompanied by a distant metallic noise. She held her lungs full, waiting. There it was again. She breathed out, long and slow. There it was once more, a loose, metallic sound, approaching the bathroom door.

Chapter Fifty-six

The doorbell rang.

Alfie and Jordan sprang to their feet and rushed to the door, where they found a dishevelled Ethan, soaked through from a morning shower. He was the first to speak.

"Don't look quite so disappointed," was his response to the extinguished hope on the two faces which greeted him. "I've called in sick. I thought we could all go from here today."

Ethan rubbed his hands with anticipation of the day's excitement as he followed them through. They sat in the kitchen and explained Shaylie's disappearance, her job and its inherent dangers. Within five minutes, Ethan was as concerned as Jordan, whilst Alfie now had the extra worry that Tomoko was nowhere to be seen.

The ensuing silence was brief, soon broken by a speedy trip-trap on the stairs. Tomoko appeared in the kitchen, her breathless face suggesting promise.

"I just met Elisa's roommate." Tomoko could barely contain herself.

"Poor you," said Alfie. "Elisa's the nice one."

"Aaliyah can be a bit sullen," added Jordan.

"She may be sullen," said Tomoko, "but she also has principles. I *knew* Elisa was hiding something."

"She was lying?" Jordan was standing, ready to return to the women's room upstairs.

"She didn't lie. But she didn't tell us everything she knew either. There is a reason Shaylie-*san* wasn't there when they left. She went on a *dōhan*."

The three men requested more information.

"A *dōhan* is a date with a client. A date like going out for a meal, it's part of the job."

Tomoko qualified each detail in an attempt to neutralise Jordan's mounting outrage.

"So if it's all part of the job and it's not dangerous, why is my wife not home?"

"It can be risky, Jordan-*san*, but usually not, because the bar will only allow these with trusted customers. However, there is never 100% safety when the job is taken outside of the club."

"So what else do we know?"

"We know that Shaylie-*san* went out for a meal before midnight and never returned. We know that it was not the first time she went on a *dōhan* with this client. A wealthy and highly valued client called Ken." Tomoko paused. She battled the apprehension and continued. "A client with a missing pinkie."

The room reacted. Jordan and Alfie turned in confusion to Ethan, whose expletive suggested he knew what the missing digit signified. Something negative. But before he could say *yakuza*, a throat was cleared and they all turned to face Aaliyah, dressing gown held shut with one hand, piece of paper in the other hand.

"Shaylie might have stayed out of her own free will. You have to accept that as a possibility," she said to Jordan. "But there is also the possibility that she is not still out of her own free will. That is why I phoned Tsubasa-*san*, our boss. He will take it seriously because bad publicity could destroy his business."

Aaliyah was thanked by all, as if to move her on to the salient facts.

"This man, Ken, is an important client. He is always given the best booth. His missing pinkie points to mob involvement, either past or present, and he tells us he is in the entertainment industry in Kabukichō. This also suggests mob involvement. But he is always polite and friendly to the hostesses. He is not one of the gropers."

Jordan bridled again. Alfie, too, exuded discomfort.

"He has been requesting Shaylie recently. She is his favourite hostess. He took her out for a meal once before, but they were back inside three hours. Last night Shaylie was in a funny mood. She had reacted to some poor behaviour and then Ken had come in. Soon they were gone and they didn't come back."

"So we need to find where this Ken lives," said Ethan on behalf of them all.

"Tsubasa-*san* has an idea. He knows that it is in an exclusive apartment block in Ikebukuro. It will be a case of circumnavigating security, perhaps bribing the concierge. He will meet you outside the East exit at midday."

Ethan foresaw the only problem.

"It's a very busy place and today it will be especially packed."

"Don't worry," said Aaliyah. "With my description you will not be able to miss him."

#

Turning up late for Tsubasa was not an option. They caught the express train from Shakuji-kōen in plenty of time and alighted at ground level a good ten minutes early. Through the ticket wickets and soon onto the street, Ikebukuro was busier than ever. Besuited men and women were in a minority on a Saturday, outnumbered by weekend shoppers in casual dress.

Amongst the usual crowds, there were clearly some individuals and groups of people who were in a more purposeful frame of mind. Jordan could identify Matsucorp workers of Asian appearance, making their way early to the agreed meeting place, a bar called Kirin City in Sunshine Street. There were few European or African faces so far, but they would show up closer to the mobilisation time of 1:50pm.

Tomoko and Alfie were tuned into the presence of larger groups of younger people, chatting as they advanced towards the branch of Mosburger opposite the station. It was the Japanese burger brand which had benefited the most from Ronald Macdonald's ejection from the island nation for refusing to transition to factory-synthesised meat. Many of these students were carrying banners and placards, the words and images covered for the moment with plastic bags. Tomoko was pleased to see so much activity so early, also anxious to be able to join them. Alfie was otherwise preoccupied.

A couple of minutes before 12, Tomoko gestured towards a man who was dressed in a very particular style. Aaliyah had been right. The mixture of purple, yellow and orange, the simple clothes, the brothel creepers, it had to be him.

"*Tsubasa-san desu ka*? asked Tomoko.

Tsubasa answered in his best English, the language he was forced to use for much of the time.

"Hi. Yes. I'm Tsubasa." A brief bow. "Please to meet you. I am worried that Shaylie-*san* did not arrived home. Let's try find her."

"Do you know where she is?" asked Jordan, not immediately warming to the man who was their only hope.

"I know who she was with. Very powerful man. Valued customer. I trust him to look after Shaylie. I expect them to return from meal, *deshō*."

Jordan grabbed his arm and looked into his eyes. Tsubasa could feel the words which were spat at him from a matter of centimetres.

"And I expect you to return my wife to me. Unharmed."

Ethan was quick to step in.

"He's here because he wants to help us. Let's work together. You can discuss the way he runs his bar later."

A short brisk walk along Green Ōdōri and they stopped in front of a very modern, high-rise apartment building. Tsubasa turned to face them.

"We need plan."

Chapter Fifty-seven

A couple of hundred metres away in Sunshine Dōri, Kirin City was getting busy. *So* busy, in fact, that it was standing room only and the pavement outside was now crowded with groups of workers, discussing in hushed tones the risk that they may or may not be taking.

Contrast the branch of Mosburger opposite the station. Louder and brimming with enthusiasm, young people about to have their first significant involvement in the politics of protest. A few were wondering at the absence of one of their leaders, who had also failed to show at the morning's event in the Omotesandō, but the majority stood smiling, laughing and checking the time in the late spring sunshine. They willed time on. They could not wait to make their way to the Matsucorp showroom.

One or two of the factory workers wondered aloud. *Jordan has bottled it, hasn't he?* They had known he wouldn't come. A skilled worker with ideas above his station. He was one of *them*.

But, whilst Jordan was closer than anyone realised, his mind was elsewhere.

Five non-residents entering the foyer together, three *gaijin*, two not, had the potential to raise suspicions. The five of them took time to compose themselves, resolving to allay the concierge's wariness for as long as possible. Each was conversant with their hastily constructed plan as they approached the front of the building.

Automatic doors whooshed to reveal a palatial vestibule, akin to that of a five-star hotel, dominated by an anachronistic gothic water feature. The strange choice of style by the interior designer was overshadowed by the favour granted them by the central position of the fountain. The concierge was based at a reception desk to the left, his view of the front doors obscured. He may or may not have watched their approach on a monitor, but he remained calm as Tomoko approached him, Jordan and Alfie reeling clockwise around the fountain. Followed by Ethan, Tsubasa branched right and made for the banks of mailboxes, complete with biometric security, on the wall next to the security doors.

Tsubasa knew that rich residents in an exclusive building like this would be well protected. He also knew that the reputation of his business would be destroyed by a single unedifying incident involving a pretty Western employee. He would gain access stage by stage, and step one was to learn the suspect's flat number.

In the meantime, Tomoko was engaged in the performance of her life at the front desk, flanked by her two white mimes. In broken Japanese, she attempted to confuse the concierge sufficiently to buy Tsubasa the time to look at the names on the hundreds of mailboxes. Through her faux-Korean accent, the concierge could make out just enough detail with his narrow eyes and ears.

"I Korea. Kankok?"

"Kankoku?" nodded the concierge.

"My friend Yoroppa." Tomoko pointed to her companions.

"Yoroppa? Europe?"

Tomoko smiled and nodded, encouraging this curious little man to buy into her story. He looked at Alfie with a confused smile, then across to Jordan who, for good measure, grinned, nodded enthusiastically and repeated "Yoroppa!"

"Looking for friend of Yoroppa friend," Tomoko continued, therewith launching into an imaginative description of a fictional person with exaggerated characteristics.

Tsubasa was over half-way through his task when he hit upon Ken's name. What to do now? It was a pretty common name, not inconceivable that there could be more than one. He turned towards the front desk. He could not see the concierge but, observing the pantomime in full swing, he assumed he had time to complete the scanning process.

Five minutes later, Tomoko was beginning to run out of steam. Glancing across to her right, Tsubasa made the OK sign with thumb and forefinger and moved towards the residents' security door, separating them from the lifts and stairwell.

The custodian of the luxury high-rise was sure that he had not seen the Yoroppa friend.

"Thank you," said Tomoko, her untidy bow as heavily accented as her speech. "We check mailbox name."

Pleased to be at the end of an ordeal, the old man allowed them to move towards the mailboxes. What harm could it do? The three performers collected in the corner of the lobby, greeted by the hushed, victorious tones of Tsubasa and Ethan's broad smile.

"He is on 42nd floor, *ne*. There are 45 floor and there is only one *apāto* on each of top five floor, *deshō*. He is in luxury penthouse. No next-door neighbour. Only neighbour above and below, *ne*.

"Shall we ring the bell?" asked Jordan.

"No way!" was the quadraphonic response.

"Let's give him no warning, *ne*," said Tsubasa earnestly.

"Let's go up!" said Alfie.

"Biometric technology operates this door," Tomoko began to explain, "so …"

"Walk naturally," interrupted Tsubasa, as he spotted a lift door open on the other side of the glass.

The exiting resident reciprocated the smile and shallow bow of the five strangers who walked through the open doors a fraction of a second before they whooshed shut behind them.

Their triumph was short-lived. Biometric technology provided access to the lifts and to the stairwell. Once again, they could only wait.

Chapter Fifty-eight

One eye clamped tightly shut, a grimace, then fast blinking to dissipate the drop of sweat which had fallen into her eye. A warm bathroom in a warm flat? Or simply local corporal conditions?

The inhabitant of the body could not fathom why it was so desired by its pursuant. It felt neither desirable, nor even compliant. She needed it to be prepared to resist, it was ready to call in sick.

Shaylie had navigated the nausea, just, but could feel the concentration of alcohol force its way through her pores. Clammy and aching, she worked to control her breathing as she approached the bathroom door on all fours.

The metallic rattling approached, soon accompanied by footsteps, slipper on floorboard. Ken's shadow was now cast through the gap in the door, affording Shaylie even less light. He stopped outside the door, a final metallic jolt terminating his approach.

Shaylie shuddered as she identified the sound in her head. Her fears were soon confirmed as Ken reached into his tool bag and began to work on the hinges with a manual screwdriver. Grateful for time to think, provided by the lack of power tools, Shaylie looked around the bathroom for the wherewithal to defend herself.

In the half light, precious little presented itself. She wondered at the effectiveness of a razor but grabbed it nonetheless. She then put it down again when she spotted a packet of new replacement blades. She lodged one with care between knicker elastic and love handle. Now what could she use to fight whilst maintaining a little distance between them?

As Ken worked his way through the numerous screws, Shaylie began to work loose the shower head and hose from the wall outlet.

It could only be a matter of time before the concierge raised the alarm. They couldn't see cameras, but cameras could be hidden. Their behaviour had been suspicious enough to provoke difficult questions. They had already had one break, thanks to an exiting resident, but they needed another.

The general anxiety was dwarfed by Jordan's internalised rage. He would not be able to contain himself once he got his hands on this Ken character. He stopped himself from chewing on the inside of his lower lip, only to recommence, instinct undeterred by the taste of blood. His fingernails dug into the palms of his hands, cocooned from the nervous chat of the others as he willed the unwitting intervention of a high-rise dweller.

It came covered in lycra, from the staircase, at the end of an interminable two minutes or so. The five smiled and nodded gratitude in as normal a manner as possible, before slipping past the young, affluent athlete into the stairwell. The lift would have been more convenient, but that choice was not available to them. There was a silent feeling of unity as they embarked upon the climb.

Sweating more than most, Tsubasa arrived last on the 42nd floor. Catching his breath, he followed his comrades along the short corridor to Ken's front door. It was a plain, pale green door with a doorbell and the inevitable spyhole.

They stood and looked at the door, then at one another. Now what?

"We need to knock," said Jordan.

"He won't answer," said Alfie.

"Perhaps not, but Jordan-*san* is right," said Tomoko. "We must at least interrupt him, let him know we are here, keep knocking."

"She is right," said Tsubasa. "And she must do this, *ne*. If he looks through doorhole, he is not worry about this Japanese girl, *deshō*. We men hide."

They all looked to Jordan.

"I can't think of a better plan. Let's get on with it."

The four men stood flat against the wall a few metres along the corridor.

Konkon. Konkon. Tomoko administered the first set of knocks to the door of the luxury apartment.

#

Konkon. Konkon.

Unscrewing and knocking at the same time. Shaylie was confused. Confused about exactly how far Ken had got through the hinge screws. Confused at the sound of knocking which came from beyond the immediacy of the bathroom door.

There it was again. *Konkon. Konkon.* Then, in the ensuing pause, a sudden clatter as the entire upper hinge assembly fell to the wooden floor of Ken's bedroom. *Gatagata.*

Shaylie could tell from the shadow that he had now started on the bottom of the three hinges. He was playing the long game. He wanted to get to Shaylie but he wanted to do it without damaging his door.

Now brandishing the shower hose, a rather heavy shower head intact at one end, Shaylie wondered how effective her only weapon would be. She had incapacitated Ken once. She would only do it again with the same combination of surprise and one single accurate strike. Her failure in this respect and the ugly reality which would ensue began to cloud her thoughts. Until the next distraction.

Konkon. Konkon. This time followed by an aggressive utterance from Ken. A single word, under his breath. His response to the knocking sound was a swear. Now the possibility dawned on Shaylie that someone was knocking at the door.

#

Tomoko looked left. Alfie and Jordan, backs to the inside wall, smiled back.

She looked right. Tsubasa and Ethan attempted to look encouraging.

She had knocked three times with no response. They had all had their ears to the wall, to the door, and heard nothing. They knew, however, that this was a penthouse apartment, well constructed, large, undoubtedly with carpets and soft furnishings to deaden sound.

"What now?" whispered Tomoko.

"Keep going," said Jordan. "We have no other option for the moment. We have to try to flush him out."

Tsubasa agreed. "We keep knocking. We can annoy him, *deshō*. So only way to stop knocking is open door, *ne*."

Tomoko grimaced, shrugged and knocked again.

#

Konkon. Konkon.

Gatagata. The clatter of the lower hinge unit was unable to mask the fourth knock at the door. Ken had begun to work faster. He now had a big decision to make. Several big decisions. Every move had to be right.

Konkon. Konkon.

He could not risk going to the door now and trying to get rid of whoever was knocking. Shay-ree-*san* might shout out. No, he would have to get to her first, gag her and secure her.

Besides, there was something amiss here. After a couple of knocks, you would assume no one was in and give up. If it were urgent, the knocking would be more desperate and less uniform. He doubted the wherewithal of Shaylie-*san*'s fellow *gaijin* to find his flat and get through security, but there was an unsettling element to this knocking.

Konkon. Konkon.

There was now one screw left on the final hinge unit. Ken pressed himself against the door and allowed the final hinge to drop. Maintaining pressure on the door, he stood and, with one hand either side, lifted the door and leaned it against the side wall.

His peripheral vision clocked Shaylie at a safe distance. The blow to the side of his head was a surprise. He immediately felt blood from his right ear. His delayed reaction afforded Shaylie a second shot. This time with an accompanying battle cry, Shaylie swung the hose around her head and landed the showerhead on his forehead.

#

"Shaylie!" shouted Jordan, joining Tomoko at the door.

To the others, the bloodcurdling shout was indistinct but Jordan was convinced of its origin.

"Shaylie!" he shouted again, banging the palms of his hands against Ken's front door.

"Please stay calm," offered Tsubasa.

"Are you mad?" asked Jordan, turning to go nose-to-nose with this rather effeminate man.

"Not mad. But think clearly." Even in this turmoil, Jordan noticed him struggle with *clearly*. "We need plan, *ne*."

With that, Tsubasa took a run-up and delivered a kung-fu-style kick to the door, close to the edge, half-way up.

He turned back to Jordan, bowed, said "*Jumban ni dōzo*" and indicated the door with an open palm.

Jordan did not need Tomoko's translation. By the time she had said "Your turn", Jordan was already launching himself at the door. The five of them took turns. The door was solid. It was unclear if progress was being made. But it was their only hope. For the moment.

#

Ken was stunned by the second blow from the showerhead whilst his hand tended to the flow of blood from the initial hit.

Buoyed by the knowledge that the cavalry had arrived, Shaylie knew that all she now had to do was open the front door. Breaking into a run, she shoved Ken into the wall, ran around the bed and into the hallway. She was close to rescue.

She thought she had tripped on the bedroom threshold, then realised that Ken had caught her as she entered the hall. He flipped her onto her back, sat on her stomach and pinned her wrists to the floor on either side of her head.

"Aaaargh," she screamed in frustration. The thumping on the door intensified. It was a few metres away.

"Shaylie!" This time it was clear. It was Jordan.

"Mum!" Now she heard Alfie.

"Help me!" she screamed back to them.

Ken released her left hand to check on the blood flow from his ear. She slapped his face with zero effect. Her metal whip lay on the bathroom floor. He quickly recovered her wrist and pushed it down all the harder.

She cursed her impotence. She hurt. Her wrists hurt. Her stomach hurt. Her head hurt. Dehydration. She also had a sharp pain at the top of her left buttock. Inside her waistline, something was digging in.

Blood continued to drip onto her top from Ken's right ear. The loss of blood was significant but slow. They could remain in this stalemate for quite some time. At least it would be difficult for Ken to secure Shaylie well enough to rape her. Unless, of course, he knocked her unconscious. As she thought this thought, she wondered whether *he* had, too.

This time, she foresaw the release of her left wrist. As Ken tended once more to his ear, she slipped her hand under a slightly raised buttock and recovered Ken's razor blade. She had nothing to lose. Before he could recapture her wrist, she plunged the blade into his neck and pulled it hard across neck towards chest.

It was Ken's turn to scream and, in the momentary shock as Shaylie created a flap of skin, she dropped the razor and shoved him hard in the chest.

As she reached the door, a bloodied Ken grabbed her ankle and pulled her back to the ground, a fraction of a second after she had released the catch.

#

Jordan was the first to push his way in. As Tomoko and Alfie followed and picked Shaylie up, they saw Jordan wrestle a retreating Ken to the ground. With one knee and most of his weight in the small of the back and the heel of his hand pressing the head deep into the pile, Ken was going nowhere.

Tomoko and Alfie stood with a snivelling Shaylie in the entrance hall.

"Thank you," she choked through tears and snot. "Thank you so much for coming. But how did you find me?"

Alfie began to explain. "It was all thanks to …"

"Shhhh!" Tomoko cut him off as they now looked around at an alarmed Tsubasa, peering in at them from outside the flat, shaking his head and placing an erect index finger vertically over his lips.

Now Jordan piped up. "Can we call the police now?"

Now Tsubasa looked even more concerned, shaking his head with vigour. Shaylie, now calming down, suggested it was time to leave.

"Sweetheart," she addressed her husband, "the police will not be interested in a *gaijin* hostess who's wilfully got herself into a dangerous situation."

"So he's going to get away with it?"

"Apart from today's humiliation, yes, I suppose he is. That is what happens when you are rich and powerful."

Tomoko added, "…and Japanese, I am so sorry you are treated differently, Shaylie-*san*."

Now Alfie joined in. "So let's go demonstrate for equality."

Tomoko checked the time. They had all forgotten about it. The demo was starting in under ten minutes.

"Ethan!" From within the living room, Jordan summoned his brother who had, until now, stayed out of sight.

Having recovered once, Shaylie was again in shock at the re-emergence of her long-lost brother-in-law. On the day that Jordan learned of the foolishness of her dating Ken, her longer-held and more deadly secret had raised its ugly head. She needed to hold it together.

Jordan had little time to consider his next move. Stronger than Ken and fuelled by adrenaline, he pulled his wife's attacker to his knees by the hair. Ethan knew what was required. As Jordan stepped back, Ethan hauled Ken to his feet, spun him round and lifted his head up to face his apartment full of people.

A split second before Jordan's fist broke his nose, Ken's submissive face became wide-eyed with recognition. From behind Jordan, a young female voice exclaimed, "Yamada-*san*!"

As the darling of the JSD crumpled into his plush flooring, the May family and Tomoko joined Tsubasa in the corridor, slamming the heavy door on Shaylie's short-lived *dōhan* career.

Chapter Fifty-nine

From the inside, fingerprints were not needed. Six-strong, they remained silent until they were in the lift. As soon as the doors closed, the four members of the May family found themselves looking at Tomoko.

Shaylie, her head now more together than she looked, broke the silence.

"So, Tomoko, you know Ken? This man you called *Yamada-san*? Who on earth is he? Why do you know someone like that?"

The lift picked up speed.

"He is a very important politician in Japan Social Democrats. They are a nationalist party with a misleading name. We are demonstrating against them today."

A few floors to go.

Jordan took up the interrogation.

"You don't just know him from the TV, though, do you?"

Tomoko's face dropped.

"No," she admitted.

It was Alfie's turn.

"What? You know him personally?"

Jordan stepped into the silence to reinforce the point.

"He recognised you, didn't he? I saw it in his eyes."

As they stepped out of the lift, Tomoko hesitated, then told them more.

"He has been to my house a few times. To meet my father. They are business associates. I have never had a conversation with him, but I have met him briefly several times."

"*NANI YATTERUN DESU KA?*"

Deep into the discovery of Kentarō Yamada's identity, they exited the building without acknowledging the shouts of the concierge, discovering a security breach after the fact.

Ethan's angry mind was working overtime.

"So why can't we phone the police?"

"They wouldn't take it seriously," said Shaylie.

"Why not?"

"Hostesses are foreign women who are providing a service for Japanese men. We are seen as not far above prostitutes. In fact, in some people's eyes, we *are* prostitutes. That's why people like Ken think they can make me get into bed with him."

"He might have got that impression when you went out with him and agreed to go back to his place," countered Ethan.

Jordan turned to confront his brother, Shaylie quickly diffusing the situation.

"Though I have no idea what he's doing here, Ethan has a point everyone and I'm sorry you were all put in this situation today. Going on dinner dates is considered part of the job, but I was far too trusting and I should never have agreed to come here. The police would be right to say I had taken an unwise risk. My face would be in the newspapers as a stupid foreign whore, titillating respectable Japanese businessmen. And Tsubasa's club would take a hit. He would lose clients. He's been very good to me."

"So," stated Ethan, "we are going to allow a sex criminal to get away with it."

Finally, Tsubasa found the gap in the conversation which he had been waiting for.

"We must not call police. But this is not protecting business, *deshō*. This is protecting all us. Tomoko is not telling you, but Yamada is not only politician, *ne*."

They looked at Tomoko. She looked back. She knew what was coming.

"You have met Yamada," continued Tsubasa. "You have seen his hand, his small finger, no?"

Tomoko shrugged and then nodded, now accepting what she had tried to ignore. They had all now stopped in their tracks and stood at the side of Green Ōdōri, waiting for the reveal.

"He is *yakuza*."

A sharp intake of breath from Tomoko, then the realisation that the four Mays did not know this petrifying word. She took up the explanation.

"*Yakuza* is Japanese mafia. They are very organised and very dangerous. If we call police and put Yamada in gaol, we will be in big danger. His associates will kill us."

Jordan and family accepted this. Ethan was one step ahead.

"You've already told us that your dad is one of his associates. Will he kill us? Does this make you part of the mafia?"

"No!" Quick to deny, Tomoko's eyes welled.

"Why should we believe you?"

Ethan had gone too far for Alfie's liking.

"Enough!" he shouted as he stepped closer to Tomoko. His voice became tender as he spoke to his girlfriend.

"I know you are nothing to do with the mafia, but what about your dad? Surely he must know?"

"I think you are right. He must know. But I know from the way my dad greets Yamada that they are not friends. Yamada is useful to my dad."

"How can the mafia be useful to your dad?"

Alfie had seen the hard side of Tomoko's dad.

"Not mafia. JSD. Yamada wants political success. He needs support of industry and he can help industry when he is part of government. My dad is powerful man. He wants the support of any government. Yamada thinks my dad's company can help his election."

Shaylie was in the dark. "Who on earth is your dad, Tomoko?"

"His name is Matsubara. He owns Matsucorp."

#

The seconds it took for Shaylie's mouth to close again seemed like minutes. So many questions had been asked, so many more presented themselves.

In the distance, they all heard a rallying cry and the beginning of a drum-beat. The demo was beginning to assemble. Thousands of workers and students were making their way to the Matsucorp showroom.

Shaylie had expected more surprise from the others.

"It's like … It's like you knew," she said to Jordan.

Ethan started laughing. Alone. "We found out last night, Shaylie. I've thought of little else since."

She soon composed herself enough to question her son's girlfriend, cynicism in her tone.

"Tomoko, you are a nice girl, you are Alfie's girlfriend, but why are you here? To demonstrate against a Mafioso politician and your father's own company? I mean. How does that work?"

"I have my own opinions. JSD is a nationalist party. It is racist. My father's company has been supporting these beliefs by underpaying foreign workers. It is the Japanese way. But many people my age believe this should change. I am against discrimination. My opinion does not change because of my father's job. I don't want to break Matsucorp. I want to force it to operate without discrimination. And I want it to break away from Yamada's influence. We all need JSD to fail."

With no immediate response from Shaylie, who could find little to dispute, Alfie put a proud arm across his girl's shoulders.

"So now you know, mum. We're all on the same side, we all agree. We've talked enough. Now it's time to act."

Alfie and Tomoko led the way into the top of Sunshine Dōri.

Chapter Sixty

They could never have imagined the sight that met them as the length of Sunshine Dōri came into view. The demo was bigger than anyone could have imagined. They could not get near the Matsucorp showroom at the far end of the street. Many, many thousands of activists faced them, the direction of Ikebukuro station. At 2pm they would file out of Sunshine Dōri and turn south towards Shinjuku, where the government buildings were the terminus of the demo. Usually little over an hour walk, they were counting two hours for the march, another half-hour demonstrating in Shinjuku and bringing traffic to a standstill, all done by late afternoon and ripe for the Saturday evening news and the Sunday press.

Towards the front was an impressive congregation of youth. As they walked along the pavement, Tomoko was touched by how few of them she knew. Word had spread far and wide. Further back, they found the workers, many of whom had decided to sport their company uniforms. Most, but by no means all, were Matsucorp workers wearing green boiler suits but there were a few in orange, too. Events had overtaken Jordan this morning. He was glad that he hadn't had to take the decision whether to stand out even more.

"Jordan May-*san!*"

On tip-toe, he caught the eye of the Koreans who were at the head of the Matsucorp group. Good. He had wanted them to know he had turned up.

"Come on," said Shaylie. "Let's go and join them."

Jordan turned to face his extended family.

"I think we should all stick together today, don't you?"

"In that case," said Tomoko, "come with me. I need to be at the front."

Jordan and Shaylie shrugged their submission as they returned to the front of the demo.

By a quarter past two, they were crawling along the Meiji Dōri, the magnitude such that only the front half had cleared Ikebukuro station.

Close to the front, the party of five were surrounded by students, encircled by Tomoko's associates, buzzing at how well the mock demo had worked that morning. Some of their comrades were Alfie's classmates. They were shoulder to shoulder with the organisers and the most vociferous activists.

The atmosphere was charged but not threatening. The white faces soon relaxed and blended into a common sense of purpose. All except Jordan, who still wondered who might be watching.

Chapter Sixty-one

Shoulder to shoulder, Struthwin stood with Matsubara at the CEO's office window, looking down onto the throng.

"Ōkisugiru!"

Matsubara lamented the size of the demonstration which was protesting against the way he ran his company. Struthwin sympathised.

"It is bigger even than I thought. You must see now that trying to force our local operatives to work this afternoon would have made little difference to the numbers."

"I get that, but this is a demo against us, against Matsucorp, against me. We'll never keep this one out of the press."

"No, Matsubara-san, this demo is against the JSD and against Japanese employment law. Many companies are implicated. But we don't want to keep this out of the press. Matsucorp is going to come out on top."

Thus far, they had been unable to drag their regard away from the demo, but now their eyes locked.

"Stepson-san, if we are going to look good after this, it's going to cost me, right?"

Stepson Struthwin smiled his wily, superior smile.

"Mochiron! Of course it's going to cost Matsucorp, but it will be a drop in the ocean for the world's leading corporation. We can do what smaller companies can't. Bring up the pay rate of manual workers and ensure that all workers have the same terms of employment, regardless of nationality. Give the skilled workers a small pay-rise across the board to sweeten the pill. Everyone is happy, we get great press and our ethical brand will receive an advertising boost the world over."

Smoke exited nose and mouth as Matsubara responded.

"You sell the plan well, Stepson-san. In the face of a demo of this size, I can do little else."

"You will knock the students off the front pages. And Yamada will be nowhere. As long as this goes off peacefully, Matsucorp's benevolent CEO will be news item number one."

They turned back to the spectacle below, a well-organised mass of students and workers, no sign of nationalist campaign vans and very little police presence. Little could go wrong.

#

Until Matsucorp, my involvement with Matsubara was a nice little sideline, a supplementary income. But as the only non-Japanese company director in the whole of Japan, it was no longer possible to stay under the radar.

My resignation went to my father first. He was, as always, pragmatic and distant. He knew that the FCO could not match what Matsubara was paying me. Not even close. Not in the same dohyō.

Father passed news of my abandonment back to London. Undoubtedly pissed off, London never shows its hand. Those people truly believe in the stiff upper lip. No persuasion, no pleas, not even any compliments to keep one on board.

>>Insignificant diplomat with trade portfolio tempted by private sector.<<

Hardly a headline of note, is it?

Mother was less impressed. Not only had I chosen not to live in the Embassy, but now also not to work there. After all they'd done for me! They removed me from a happy childhood and packed me off to the other side of the world for an altogether more abusive upbringing. I didn't bother telling her that. I just stood there and nodded. They didn't get it. They thought that sacrificing your childhood and their bond with you for a posh education was normal. What would you expect from people called Isabella and Jeremiah?

Mother's surprise and disappointment were mirrored in a weird way by many of the locals. Once word got out, there was some borderline racist guff in some of the papers. Why wouldn't there be? There were chief reporters praising Matsucorp's inception on the one hand, whilst questioning the boardroom presence of one single non-Japanese on the other. They knew I was non-executive, so demanded to know why I was there at all.

Hilariously, the same question was being asked in whispered conversations within the boardroom. And they have never stopped wondering. Nobody understands my influence nor Matsubara's loyalty to me. As long as he keeps paying me, nobody ever will.

At least, not for a very long time.

#

Chapter Sixty-two

Jordan cowered in awareness of the Matsucorp building which they passed to the right as they entered south Ikebukuro. If Tomoko was aware of the irony, she was not fazed by it and neither father nor daughter could have been aware of the proximity of one another. The noise increased and placards were waved at the Matsucorp HQ, but Jordan was focused on the *7Eleven* on the next block. It would be a relief to reach the point in the Meiji Dōri, fifty yards ahead, where it snaked around to the left, away from the railway line and towards Mejiro. They would be out of sight of Matsucorp and it would be plain-sailing all the way to Shinjuku.

He felt a squeeze on his left hand and turned into the reassuring beam cast by Shaylie's smile. Behind the smile, however, was a question. She knew how he felt about this demo, all the uncertainty in his head, but she was, in turn, unsure about his reaction to the discovery that her job had taken her on dates. Not only that, she had broken the rules, taken a risk, put herself in danger. Drawing his wife into him, arms around one another, Jordan understood, forgave and comforted, all in that single, sun-drenched moment.

The *7Eleven* came and went and the bend on the Meiji Dōri approached. Having made their feelings known in front of Matsucorp HQ, the students raised their pace. Press photographers working the pavements on both sides had to scuttle a little faster. Jordan was not the only T-shirted activist, wet with sweat, to shiver as the sun disappeared behind unforeseen clouds. Spring was shorter and muggier every year, but however early summer came and however long it became, it was always preceded by a humid rainy season. Several hundred thousand demonstrators hoped that it would hold off for a few hours more.

Looking ahead, they saw their son and his girlfriend, gesturing and chanting in unison with the crowd. Alfie was a model of integration and he needed to be. This was not going to be a brief posting abroad. Europe would take decades to recover. This was the Mays' opportunity to make a comfortable living and they were going to take it. The Japanese were going to have to accept them. And they would. Jordan was confident of that. Shaylie and Alfie were at home here now. He had to follow their lead.

Contrast Ethan. Further ahead, close to the very front of the demo, waving, gesturing and shouting in English. He stood out like a sore thumb. It was difficult to see him losing his rough edges, fitting in anywhere, and Shaylie for one desperately hoped that he wouldn't be staying. It was difficult to imagine what could shake Ethan out of his fanatical posturing. But suddenly, stop he did.

Ethan stopped in his tracks, as did those around him, as they hit the apex of the bend and saw what awaited them.

They had managed to stop the traffic, the road ahead remained clear, but the pavements ahead were lined with iron-clad automaton riot police, sporting helmets, shields and batons. Behind them stood a smattering of gun-toting human policemen. In the distance, on the road ahead, an army unit was moving slowly in the direction of Shinjuku with water cannon at the ready. It was flanked by soldiers on foot, armed with rifles. As far as the demonstrators were concerned, the authorities were really misjudging this action. A peaceful demonstration merited light-touch policing. Yes, it was large, but nobody had expected it to be this large. A police and military operation of this magnitude had been organised well in advance. On what grounds? What reason was there for large-scale violence?

"Yamada!" exclaimed Tomoko.

All around her turned towards her.

"I wondered why there was no JSD presence," she explained, translating furiously into English as she spoke. "Rather than be outnumbered and lose out in the press to a huge peaceful demo, he has decided to stay away and make anonymous tip-offs to the authorities. No wonder he has found the time to pursue other hobbies this weekend."

Shaylie blushed and Tomoko quickly apologised under her breath.

She raised her voice again.

"We've done nothing wrong. As long as we do nothing wrong, they will have no grounds to act. The TV cameras are our evidence. We continue, peacefully, all the way to Shinjuku!"

Cheers and whistles and the demo began to move again. They chanted, they sang, they laughed and smiled, ignoring the riot police on either side. As they moved south, through Mejiro and on towards Takadanobaba, the authorities moved with them.

Chapter Sixty-three

The tail end of the demo moved into the distance, watched from a height by Stepson Struthwin. Matsubara had lost interest quite some time ago and sat at his desk, deep in thought, contemplating how to trump this triumphant, peaceful display of popular dissent.

Struthwin turned to face his boss who was ready with a question Struthwin had heard many times before.

"What now, Stepson-*san*?"

"Let's put together a press release. I'll draft, you put it into formal Japanese."

"Are you sure we are doing the right thing? The shareholders will want to know why we have increased expenditure. On foreigners."

"And you will be able to justify it. You will be able to point to countless examples of companies playing hardball with workers' groups and gaining nothing from it. You will be able to point to tomorrow's number one trending news story and the ongoing positive publicity it generates. And you will be able to point to increased profits and the consolidation of Matsucorp's position as number one profit maker in Japan and number one car manufacturer worldwide."

They set to work. Matsubara always worried about his company, his baby. But he also felt that he was at the top of the tree because he had the best adviser in the business. Ironic that his adviser was a foreigner.

They always went through the charade of talking those big decisions through. A charade and not a charade. Matsubara may not have had any choice but to go along with Struthwin, but until now, Struthwin had pretty much always been right. Whenever Matsubara had misgivings, it always turned out for the best. In fact, in all their years of working together,

Struthwin's most recent significant import, Eric Marks, was the only unresolved question mark in Matsubara's head.

But forget Eric Marks. Struthwin had made some momentous decisions over the years. That mixture of Japanese and European experience and mind-set had cultivated such an astute business brain, complemented by a lack of ego. Working in the background, he left all the plaudits to Matsubara.

Matsubara's thoughts panned around his boardroom. Struthwin was non-executive, but he gave all the advice necessary for Matsubara to lead the directors in the right direction. Yamada was the only dissenting voice, but he had political ambition, an ulterior motive transcending the good of the company.

Matsubara smiled as Struthwin wrote. He was glad to have distanced Yamada. Together they had slapped him down, blunted his influence. He would have them fight with workers' rights and with foreigners. With Struthwin's help he had taken the board with him, freed the company from implication in nationalist politics, blunted Yamada's toxic influence.

Matsucorp was generating positive press and there was little Yamada could do about it.

⚘

I know my own mind. I listen to no one. The world is full of people who want to give you their advice. And if you listen to it all, it is almost always conflicting.

When I handed in my notice to the FCO, many congratulated me. But there were doubters, those who will always champion a secure career with a good pension. It's true that those jobs for life had become rare by then and are even rarer now, but I can trump that. There is no place more rarefied than that of an Englishman in an all-Japanese boardroom, being paid an Emperor's ransom to advise the CEO. Especially where that advice is followed to the exclusion of the executive directors. I love to watch their frustration.

The doubters mysteriously disappeared when the UK broke up, not long after I jumped. All of a sudden, nobody thought I'd made a bad move. Those interminable Brexit negotiations were only going to end badly, and who could blame the Scots for wanting out?

So, for a short time we had a smaller queendom, then the northern Irish got fed up and a change of monarch sealed the deal. A bloodless coup, then we were a republic. The Federal Republic of England and Wales was born an orphan, isolated on the edge of Europe, geographically at least, and abandoned by its European patronage. All of this happened as Europe was beginning to struggle, too. Years of neo-liberal capitalism morphed into a brief flirtation with fascism across the Western world, before its inevitable decline and eventual collapse. Following a model of massive state investment, full employment and a duty of care to all citizens, China, India and Japan moved into the driving seat.

The FREW did not have the world standing based on past glories which Britain had lived on for so long. The lifelong career offered by the UK FCO no longer existed. As the fabric of society in the land of my fathers went to shit, I was sitting pretty.

#

Chapter Sixty-four

At the front of the demo, the students were working hard to keep the mood uplifted, in spite of the overbearing armed presence to either side. More police joined the ranks to their left as they moved past Totsuka Police Station towards the great crossroads with Waseda Dōri.

The chanting and good-natured shouts and jeers continued, contrasted for a moment by cries of derision, negative in tone, and the sound of a scuffle. Jordan and Shaylie were propelled forwards into Tomoko and Alfie as the two young men emerged from the pushing and shoving. Intent on being closer to the front, they pushed through the May family and installed themselves behind Ethan. Eyebrows were raised, but all were intent on a non-violent demonstration. No challenge was made and order was restored.

Jordan and Shaylie had learned the chants and slogans and were joining in. Ahead of them all, Ethan was doing the same. Alfie and Tomoko, however, were now deep in discussion.

"Those two bother me," said Alfie, nodding towards the men who had pushed towards the front.

"Forget it," said Tomoko. "They are just over-enthusiastic."

"Do they look like students to you?"

"No more than your mum and dad do. It isn't students only."

"I know, but there is something familiar about them. Familiar and sinister."

The men were late teens, early twenties, small of build and square of shoulder. Dressed in black, black jeans, black T-shirts, black jackets and shades, it was like they were in uniform, in a secret club with no obvious logo. Each time Alfie caught sight of a profile, he became more convinced of his feeling of foreboding.

As the tightly packed demo moved into the overwhelming breadth of the Waseda Dōri – Meiji Dōri intersection, Alfie watched the men in black look at one another and nod. It was an affirmative and definitive nod.

They then reached into their jacket pockets, grabbed a handful of large stones each and flung them at the riot police on either side of the demo. The chaos caused at the centre of the demo, as the two thugs shoved their way back from whence they had come, was insignificant when compared to the charge of the police who now closed in on the front and sides of the demo.

#

A moment of lucidity. It was clear that this was a set-up. Tomoko knew straight away and Alfie only added evidence when the penny dropped on the bogus, black-clad demonstrators.

"They were in the gang who attacked me and dad in Akihabara," he shouted over the growing calls of distress. "And they beat me up in the park."

"That makes sense," cried Tomoko in Alfie's ear. "JSD thugs. Yamada has paid them to start trouble today and then tipped off the police."

There was an immediate squeeze on the front of the procession as the authorities closed in on the source of the projectiles. It was clear they had been told not to hold back.

Tomoko and the Mays were first shoved this way and that as police robots from either side shoved the demo in towards its centre with their shields. The reaction of the crowd was not to react in the face of its aggressors. Concerns turned to lifting those who had been knocked over, to avoiding trampling their comrades. Soon it was not possible to fall, as they were squeezed in from either side.

"*Itai!*"

Tomoko joined in with the many around them, letting the police know that now they were hurting them. *Gyuuuuu.* Tighter and tighter. Tighter and tighter. They were being crushed and nobody knew how far the police were prepared to go.

From the front, the army moved in, their water cannon trained on the front of the demo. Tomoko and Alfie were stuck, arms pinned to their sides. Jordan and Shaylie were in an identical situation behind them.

"Come on!" was the cry in English from their left. Ethan had wriggled through to the side and was encouraging a group of students around him to push back. This was about to get ugly and for those without an appetite for conflict, there was no escape.

Shoulders and arms delivered blows to the riot shields. A few cyborg police were knocked backwards, but soon recovered their position and came back harder. Batons began to rain down. Heads were avoided, but the selection of body targets was indiscriminate. At this point, the army decided to fire water at the peaceful but irate demonstration.

As unbearable pressure was being placed on those at the front of the demo from three sides, the many thousands who had not yet reached the crossing were beginning to realise that their demo was under attack. As those at the front attempted to retreat, those further back reversed to accommodate their comrades.

Tomoko, Alfie, Jordan and Shaylie were able to begin their retreat. Despite the withdrawal, the water cannon persisted, as did the police baton charge. Then they heard a gunshot. Then another. And another. Students fell, clutching at chest, arm and leg, then got up again as rubber bullets bounced around the tarmac. They got up again and they ran. They ran and they ran. Now even Ethan ran. He caught them up. He ran. And then he fell.

The four turned to help him up, but Ethan was not moving. They were now withdrawn from the crossing, the riot police had stood back and Ethan was not moving. The water cannon had stopped, police and army were now spectators and Ethan was not moving. Fellow demonstrators had escaped further back along the Meiji Dōri. They stood alone in the middle of the road and Ethan was not moving.

Jordan was first to approach his brother, who was prostrate, face down in the white line. Head to one side, his eyes were open. Open and glassed over. Glassed over and dead.

Shaylie knelt by her husband, at once feeling his pain and not a little relief of her own.

Once turned over, face up, chest up, the entry wound of the bullet was clear. Surrounded by rubber bullets in the middle of the Meiji Dōri, one of the bullets had not been rubber. Lead, plated with cupronickel, clean entry, now embedded in the upper left thorax. A solitary, deadly bullet, shot cleanly into a crowd with mortal accuracy. Choreographed chaos, the police and the army had played their part, but a well-paid sniper had finished their job, delivered the message.

Struthwin's well-spun story of Matsucorp conciliation would be relegated to the inside news pages tomorrow, by the warning of the far right.

Trouble-making Westerners had been warned, unionised foreigners and students had been warned, somebody had signalled his intolerance to tolerance.

Uniforms slipped away, the Mays and Tomoko sitting in the road as the crowds receded. They remained silent until the arrival of emergency vehicles. Tomoko translated for Jordan as identities were communicated and Ethan's body could be removed. They were escorted to the side of the road and the traffic began to flow again.

Jordan looked lost as he had done on that Thursday in March when he had come home with news of the Bathside factory closure. Shaylie knew that it was time to take control.

"Take me for a beer, darling," she said, squeezing her husband's midriff.

"What about Alfie?"

"He'll be fine with his girlfriend. We've got some catching up to do. I disappear for a few hours and all of a sudden your brother is here, in Japan, with you!"

"And now he's dead."

"I know, sweetheart, I know. It's been a tough day. Let's drink to his memory."

Tomoko guided them to the nearest station and onto a train back to Ikebukuro, where Shaylie and Jordan wandered off to share a beer or two. She then stood with Alfie on the Seibu-Ikebukuro line platform.

Tomoko hesitated as they slowed into Shakuji-kōen station. Return to the Matsubara residence? Or support Alfie? Rebuilding her relationship with her father could wait. They both got off.

That evening, sat on a bench in Shakuji Park, Tomoko told Alfie that his life was in Japan. She would work hard to ensure that the Mays did not leave.

Chapter Sixty-five

"I didn't know," lied Struthwin, so accomplished in his mendacity.

Matsubara avoided the piercing eye contact.

"You didn't know that Eric Marks was actually Jordan May's brother?"

"No. But it matters little now. His death is an attack on Matsucorp. An attack on our good news story. An attack on company policy. This demonstration was hijacked by someone who had the power to do so, the money to do so and the political will to do so."

"We have to shoulder some of the blame for this, Stepson."

"No. We are not going on the defensive. We both know who did this."

"We can't go public and blame Yamada. They'll never pin it down to him. He has officials in his pocket. I don't want to be seen as a mudslinger."

"You won't be, Matsubara-*san*. But, with respect, you don't know how to play this game like I do. I will brief the press. We will hint at JSD involvement, we will tarnish them and we will relaunch our pay-rise and improved contract story with a sympathetic piece on the bereaved family."

Resigned, Matsubara nodded and lit up.

"I know you are unsure about this, Matsubara-*san*, but believe me, you will continue to enjoy the ride."

Struthwin turned and smiled. Stepping into the lift, he tapped out a brief reply to an email. Time to set it up. Another false name, another divertissement, the next scene in the final act. If Evie was desperate for a job in Tokyo, then who was Stepson Struthwin to disappoint?

Economic and political upheaval in the FREW was less kind to Father. He was no so far from retirement when his employer, the UK FCO, ceased to exist. Promises were made by the new FCO of the FREW to honour pensions and posts abroad as far as possible, but promises were made which couldn't be kept. Staff were made redundant all over the world and ambassadors had to run their embassies almost single-handed.

Father retained Mother as his administrator but everyone else left. The team of bright, young junior diplomats, including the one who had replaced me, were sent home and paid off. Although I had not been close to my parents, it was sad to see Father struggling to maintain what he had built up over decades. A skeleton staff was never going to allow him to serve the FREW with status and deals in the way he had done for the UK.

Mother and I both tried to persuade him to retire early. By this stage he was only about three years short. I wanted him to cash in while the federal government was still good for the money it had promised. Who knew how long it would be before they were bankrupted.

But Father hung on until the day that the bombshell hit. It was not the disaster served cold from London, as I had expected. Oh no. Tokyo was responsible for finishing off Father.

A failing economy and almost zero international influence rendered the FREW a burden, even a liability. Tokyo no longer felt it had anything to gain from the presence of this minor player and its poorly staffed embassy, housed in these beautiful buildings of my childhood. And so it was an oil-rich Scotland which took over the ex-British Embassy.

At the time I got it and I still get it. Tokyo had its reasons and its priorities. But there are ways and means. They evicted my parents at very short notice, with no recognition for Father's achievements and service, and forced the FREW to downgrade him to a small consulate in Osaka. There he spent little more than one miserable year, dying shortly before his retirement.

The Japanese humiliated Father. My Mother did not last much longer. They were both killed by the country we had all served. And here they are now, sitting pretty, top of the league, a booming economy, a fantastic infrastructure and the top technological and automotive corporations.

They are going to pay. One day soon. Intelligent intervention will destabilise the economy. A wobble in confidence in the top automobile corporation in the world could play merry hell with the Nikkei. What if that allowed one of the Korean manufacturers to take over Matsucorp? Can you imagine the shame?

Some would regard that as comeuppance, retribution, revenge. All it would require would be for the CEO to be fed convincing but damaging advice. Plus dedication to a long-term goal and a not insignificant quantity of patience.

Shaylie May's secret is an interesting plot twist which she thinks has died with her brother-in-law. But it still lives within her. And within me. As does Matsubara's.

Ethan May's death is just the beginning.

\#

Chapter Sixty-six

Monday morning and another bench for two. This time it was a warm, sunny May day at Nerima High School. It had rained overnight but they were too preoccupied to notice the damp seat beneath them. Tomoko and Alfie sat eating *onigiri* in the schoolyard at break. Triangular parcels of rice, wrapped in sheets of *nori* seaweed, filled with local staples. Fermented soy beans for her, kelp for him. The rest of the student body gave them a wide berth. Divisions remained around the attitude towards ecomigrants, but fellow students were wary of the raw emotions which were dormant on that bench. The girl who had defied her powerful father and masterminded a fatal demonstration sat in conference with her recently bereaved *gaijin* boyfriend. Did he blame her? No one was prepared to poke the wasps' nest today.

Alfie blinked into the sun and breathed in the aromas of his new home. The familiarity of little more than a month allowed him to identify the soy sauce and miso stock coming from the school kitchen, the incense from the nearby shrine, the pollen thick in the air as spring began to merge into the rainy season.

For once, Tomoko did not break the silence.

"Are you OK?" asked Alfie.

"Sure."

"I don't blame you, you know."

"I blame me. You could have had a chance to get to know your uncle."

"I get the impression that that might not have been a good thing."

"You would have been able to make that judgement for yourself. I played with fire and your family got burned."

"What we did was right. I'd do it again."

Tomoko turned to face him.

"Really?" she asked, her look one of genuine awe.

"Yes, really! Bad things happen when you stand up to inequality, and to bullies. What do the papers say this morning?"

"On the front pages they say that a man was shot dead. That there will be an inquiry, that a rogue extremist acting alone was probably responsible. Between the lines, that Yamada will not be implicated."

"And on the inside pages?"

"That Matsucorp will support the bereaved family, will award a pay-rise to its foreign workers and re-assess their contracts."

"See? You have achieved so much on our behalf. You have enabled us to stay here and live a better life."

She took his hand.

"And that's what I want more than anything. I'd hate it if you left."

"We're going nowhere."

She beamed.

"Let's step back from politics for a while, enjoy each other, keep you safe."

Alfie leaned over, wiped a wisp of *natto* residue from the corner of Tomoko's mouth and kissed her. He felt warmth in body and heart. This beautiful girl had given him a better life than he had thought possible, helped him through the difficult early days, reconciled him with his new life. It was time for a new chapter. It would be much easier from now on.

Acknowledgements

Thank you to Stephanie for reading, for artwork, for advising and for essential moral and emotional support. Thanks also to John McGilley and Richard Brock.

#

If you have enjoyed this story, a **review** would be much appreciated on any of the usual distribution sites.

Contact Maison Urwin at maison@tinygremlin.com

Maison Urwin has been a teacher of French and German for twenty years. He previously taught EFL in Japan. He speaks French, German and Japanese, and is learning Spanish and Hindi. He has two children. He is building an off-grid house with Stephanie somewhere in the Tendring Hundred.

CPSIA information can be obtained
at www.ICGtesting.com
Printed in the USA
LVHW030830140420
653375LV00004B/192